D1521319

REUNION AT THE HAPPY VALLEY
MOTOR INN AND RESORT

by

Leslie Noyes

Published by Scout's Honor, Havana, FL, USA

Copyright 2022, Leslie Noyes

Reunion at the Happy Valley Motor Inn and Resort is a work of fiction. Unless otherwise indicated, all names, characters, businesses, places, events, and incidents in this book are either the product of the author's imagination or used in a fictitious manner. Any resemblance to actual persons, living or dead, or actual events is purely coincidental.

Scout's Honor
PUBLISHING

REUNION AT THE HAPPY VALLEY

MOTOR INN AND RESORT

This book is dedicated to the memory of my beloved mother-in-law, Helen. I really thought she'd outlive us all.

And to the memory of my beautiful sister-in-law, Lyn. I can still hear her voice and see her smile.

Other Books by Leslie Noyes:

Mayhem at the Happy Valley Motor Inn and Resort
[Book 1 of the Happy Valley Series]

Wedding at the Happy Valley Motor Inn and Resort
[Book 2 of the Happy Valley Series]

The Cowboy and the Executive, A West Texas Romance.

PROLOGUE

Paula Jean Arnett clasped her hands over her chest in a feeble attempt to stifle the *thumpity-thump-thump* of her heart. She wondered if the tympanic beats were audible to the man who held the door open for her. *He'd certainly notice if my heart escaped my body and galloped across the floor. I cannot believe I'm about to do this. Maybe it's too soon. Then again, maybe it's not...* She followed the broad-shouldered man down the short hallway and on through the kitchen. *Is his name Chad? Brad? Does it really matter?*

He gestured to the end of the hall. "The bedroom's this way."

She took a deep breath and exhaled in a measured rhythm, just as her yoga instructor taught her to do. *Here goes nothing.*

The man slid open a door and stepped aside. "Make yourself comfortable. Take all the time you need. Just let me know when you're ready."

Paula gulped. "I'll do that. Thank you." She looked the room over. *What an inviting place. It does need a woman's touch, though, and the windows need to be opened. Let some fresh air in.*

She eased down onto the queen-sized bed and kicked off her shoes, reveling in the softness of the carpet. *Feels new*, she thought. *That's because it* is *new, silly.* Falling back onto the mattress, she made an imaginary snow angel on the coverlet. An unexpected giggle escaped her lips.

Her thoughts turned to Cal. *Honey, I'm taking a huge step here. Give me a sign if I shouldn't go through with this.* She counted to sixty without hearing a word from her deceased husband and then, for good measure, counted to sixty again. *No sign—I guess it's all systems go. Let's get this done.* A delicious shiver shot up her spine.

"Brad? I'm ready." Her nerves gave her voice a huskiness that shocked her.

The man's muscular frame filled the doorway. "Ma'am, it's Chad. Now, before we go ahead with this, are you certain you can handle something this size?"

Paula wet her lips. "I'm sure I can. It's absolutely perfect, and I want it more than I've wanted anything in a long time."

Chad cocked an eyebrow and offered his hand. "Why don't we go back to my office to sign the paperwork? Then we'll drink a toast to the purchase of your new motorhome. Welcome to the RV owners' club. The best club in the world."

CHAPTER ONE

Her knuckles white from gripping the steering wheel, Paula blew a stray strand of wheat blonde hair away from her face. *Here's where we find out if I've got what it takes.* "Are you sure there's plenty of room for me to back in here?"

From the passenger seat, Cassie Campbell wrinkled her nose. "You've got this. I think. I can see the hookups from this side. Can you see Melinda on yours?"

Paula glanced at the side view mirror. "Yes. She's waving her hands."

"Waving frantically, as in *stop immediately* or gently, as in *come on back*?"

"Hard to tell. Guess we'll find out soon enough." Paula exhaled and pressed down on the accelerator with a gentle touch. Inch by inch, she guided the motorhome into the designated spot, accompanied by a symphony of dried leaves crunching beneath her tires. She kept one eye on Melinda and the other on the backup camera.

"Stop! You're in," Melinda said.

Paula shifted into park and squealed. "We did it."

"No, you did it, Goldilocks. Now we get to see if you know how to hook this baby up."

Corralling Cassie into a sideways hug, Paula's eyes grew misty at Cassie's use of the nickname Cal had given her. *At least someone still calls me Goldilocks.*

Paula slid out of the motorhome and met Melinda Arnett with a kiss and a hug. "Yay! Thanks for guiding me in."

Melinda squeezed Paula's hand. "I'm so happy you're finally here. The place just isn't the same without you around."

The warmth of Melinda's words kindled a tear in Paula's eyes. "Aw. Don't make me cry. What with selling the house and getting rid of most of my possessions, I'm kind of emotional these days."

"Let's get your camp set up and then we can cry if we need to," Cassie said. "Do you need any help hooking up the utilities?"

Paula pursed her lips. "I don't think so. Hold on a second, though. I need to level this thing first."

Cassie and Melinda exchanged looks. "You know how to do that?" Cassie asked.

"It's mostly automatic; I just have to push a button. Be right back."

Paula scrambled into the driver's seat and started the engine. *Now, where is that panel with the leveling controls? Oh, right there.* She pressed a button and a series of lights blinked on. *Why's nothing happening? Think, Paula. Aha! Forgot to engage the parking brake. Now that's more like it.* Sticking her head out the driver's side window, she asked, "Is it working?"

Melinda walked around the camper and returned to Paula with an approving smile. "Looks perfect. The fluid in the levels is all even."

"Thanks." A flush of pride zapped through Paula's body then disappeared in the space of a heartbeat. *Sheesh. All I did was push a button.* She opened the side door of the motorhome and the automatic steps extended to the ground like a magic carpet. *So glad Chad, or was it Brad, talked me into the premium package. Forget diamonds. Automation is a girl's best friend.*

Paula rejoined Melinda and Cassie near the utility hookups where she was faced with a narrow choice of hoses and cords. She wiped her sweaty palms on her jeans. "This is the part I've been dreading. Just stand by in case I get the hoses mixed up." She closed her eyes, recalling the instructions she'd been given during the new owners' orientation. "Okay. I think I've got it."

Cassie hovered behind Paula. "We're here if you need us."

"Thanks, but I feel like this is something I need to do for myself."

Melinda clasped Cassie's hand, tugging her away from Paula. "She'll be fine."

Beads of perspiration dotted Paula's forehead as she attached the largest hose to the waste depository. She swiped the sweat out of her eyes with her shirt sleeve. *There. The hardest part's done.* After hooking up the drinking water and the electricity, Paula pumped a fist in victory. "How about we go inside and get the air conditioner going? I've got an ice chest full of Dr. Pepper and other beverages since I knew it'd take a while for the fridge to get cold."

Cassie gave the suggestion two thumbs up. "Good thinking. I *need* a Dr. Pepper."

Melinda brandished her phone in the air. "Honey, you always think you need a Dr. Pepper, but we're not going in until I get a picture of Paula standing next to her new home. Here, Paula, stand in front of the door and pose. Arms out. Think Vanna White."

Paula crossed her arms over her chest and pretended to pout. "Do I have to? And since when do you call people *honey*?"

"I think it's a law when you live in Texas for a certain number of years. I've developed a regular drawl. My Indiana friends would be shocked and probably dismayed. And, yes, *honey*, you must pose. Just like that. Hold still, now. There. That's perfect."

Melinda handed her phone to Paula. "Look how cute you are. A certain Dr. Hunky needs to see this."

At the mention of Paula's accidental nickname for Dr. Mark Fields, heat spread through Paula's veins and onto her cheeks, endowing them with a rosy glow.

Cassie elbowed Paula. "Let me look at that. Ooh. Might be too cute for the doc to handle. One look at this and wild horses couldn't keep him away."

With a wave of her hand, Paula said, "Oh, you two. Mark will come home when he gets his parents settled into a suitable assisted living facility and not a second earlier."

Melinda pulled an envelope from her back pocket. "That reminds me. I've got some mail for you already. A lot of it appeared to be junk, but this one looked special so I brought it with me."

Paula's eyes were drawn to the return address. *An actual letter. From Arizona. From Mark.* "Oh, thank you." With trembling hands, she accepted the letter, clutching it to her chest as if it might take flight.

"So, what about that Dr. Pepper?" Cassie asked.

Forcing her attention back to the present, Paula said, "Oh, right, you two come on in and look around. I'll get our drinks." Paula held the envelope as if it were a fine crystal goblet. *Or maybe a crystal ball. What in the world was so important he couldn't put it in an email?*

CHAPTER TWO

Inside the RV, Paula slid the letter from Mark into a cubby beneath the dining table. *Out of sight and hopefully out of mind until I have some privacy.* Her lips twitched in amusement as Melinda and Cassie *ooh-ed* and *aah-ed* over the new motorhome. From inside the bathroom, a mischievous giggle found its way to her ears. Her eyebrows shot up. "Hey, Campbell, you'd better not be messing with my stuff."

Cassie peeked around the door, a hand pressed to her chest. "Who? Moi?"

Paula said, "Yes, you."

Melinda emerged from the bedroom and ran a finger across the shiny new stove. "I love your place. It is so adorable, and you seem to have plenty of storage."

Cassie opened a cabinet door, her eyes sweeping over the empty shelves. "You need some staples, girl. Salt, pepper, flour. The cupboards are bare except for a can of coffee and a box of granola bars. How am I ever going to cook anything out here if you don't even have the basics?"

Paula opened a cooler to retrieve a can of Dr. Pepper for Cassie and bottled teas for Melinda and herself. She scooted onto a bench in the dining nook and gestured for the others to join her. "I know. I haven't had time to go to a proper grocery store. Maybe we can make a trip later."

Melinda sat, pulling Cassie down beside her with a playful tug. "You likely won't need anything this weekend, what with the reunion going on. Just take a few days to get accustomed to living out here."

Paula said, "Good idea. Besides, since I didn't tow my car and I don't want to go through the backing up process again, I'm kind of stuck here until Delbert arrives. He and Melvin picked up my car at the motorhome dealership in Waco. They'll be here soon, I imagine."

"You know you could borrow one of our vehicles if you needed to," Cassie said.

Paula wrapped her hands around the bottle of tea. "Thank you, but I'm good for now." She took a sip, then asked, "So, be honest, what do you two think about my decision to move here full time?"

Cassie popped the top of her drink. "Honestly? I almost fainted when I heard what you'd done. I mean, I never dreamed you'd sell the Dempsey home. And then when you told me you were going to replace it with a motorhome, I thought maybe I'd been transported to an alternate universe. The reality didn't sink in until you pulled up in front of the office in this thing."

"I'm still pinching myself. It feels so unreal—like it must be a dream, or maybe that alternate universe you imagined. But when we were here for Martha and Zeke's wedding, I realized that I'm happier at this resort than I am anywhere else. Life's too short to stay stuck in a rut."

Melinda squeezed Paula's hand. "Absolutely. I've already told you how I feel, and I meant it."

Paula brushed away tears. "I feel like I've come home. Oh--that reminds me. Just a second." She stood and lifted a package from behind the driver's seat. Underneath the wrapping was a vibrant watercolor painting of two men fishing from a boat on Lake Toledo Bend, their expressions rendered in such realistic detail that it might have been a photograph. "I didn't keep many things from the Dempsey house, but this signed original had to come with me."

Melinda's eyes crinkled. "I should hope so. One of my finest works, if I do say so myself. I painted that not far from where we are right now."

"Would you help me find the kind of hardware I need to hang it in here? I'm pretty sure nails aren't the answer in my new digs. I'd hate to hammer a hole through the wall."

"Of course. In fact, I might have just what you need in the office."

Paula sipped on her tea and studied Cassie who sat prim and proper, a hand resting on Melinda's arm. "It just occurred to me. I haven't seen you fidget since I arrived."

Cassie's lips were the picture of serenity as she laid her head on Melinda's shoulder. "I think I finally found my place in the world. I'm happy."

Lifting Cassie's hand, Melinda dropped a kiss onto her knuckles. "Me, too."

"Should we tell Paula?" Cassie asked.

Goosebumps raised on Paula's arms. "Tell me what?"

Melinda glanced at Cassie and nodded. "Of course. I'm surprised you haven't already told Paula, of all people."

"Now you have no choice. Spill it."

Cassie seemed to glow from within. "We're talking about me moving in with Melinda."

Paula whooped. "Really? When? Soon, I hope."

"I still have a semester to go at the culinary institute so, at the soonest, it'll be in late May or early June," Cassie said.

Melinda took a sip of tea and seemed to contemplate her next words. "And I want McKenzie and Jeffries settled first. McKenzie's showing more every day. Like she's smuggling a mini basketball beneath her shirt."

Paula imagined Melinda's slender daughter cradling a rounded belly. "Is she still living here?"

"Some of the time. She's home most weekends to help around the resort, but during the week she's at Jeffries's apartment in Dallas. I was hoping they'd be planning a wedding by now."

"Oh? What's the wait? I thought McKenzie and Jeffries were going to get married as soon as possible. She found out she was pregnant in July, right? And now it's almost November."

A shadow of a frown crossed Melinda's face. "Jeffries hasn't gotten up the courage to tell his folks yet. I think McKenzie is ready to approach Delilah on her own if Jeffries doesn't do something soon."

Cassie raised a manicured hand. "I offered to tell Delilah. You know how charming I can be."

Melinda smirked. "I don't think your feminine wiles will work on Delilah. Besides, if Jeffries and McKenzie are old enough to raise a child, they're old enough to face the music with his parents."

Paula's lips pressed into a thin line. *I'm not getting involved in this. Time to change the subject.* "So, what's the news from Martha and Zeke?"

Melinda's grimace morphed into a grin. "Oh, Paula. They seem so happy. Mama has settled into the life of a rancher's wife. She's even learned to ride a horse, if you can believe that. And I don't think Zeke allows her to lift a finger around the house. Apparently, he employs a full-time cook and housekeeper, so my mom is living a life of leisure. Looking at Zeke Fitzgerald, would you have ever guessed that he had oil money?"

Paula pictured the feisty red-headed man who'd stolen Martha Murray's heart and made her his wife. "Never. He's about the least likely looking millionaire I could imagine. I hope I get to see them before too long."

"You'll get your wish soon. They're planning on popping in tomorrow on their way to a juggling convention in Houston."

"Oh, yay! Can't wait to—Hold on, Martha's going to a Natural Jugglers of America event? She's finally going to watch people juggle naked?" Paula asked.

"She claims she's ready to embrace the whole naked juggling community," Melinda said with a shrug.

Cassie snorted. "Embrace? I hope she doesn't mean that in the literal sense."

"Ew, right?" Paula said.

A questioning meow sounded from the bedroom and Paula clasped her hands. "Ah, there's my girl. Star, come here." A fluffy ball of white fur skittered down the hallway from the bedroom and leapt onto Paula's lap where it began to purr with gusto. "I wondered where you were hiding."

Cassie cooed over the kitten, her voice rising in delight. "Oh, she's grown so much since you found her. Will she let me hold her?"

Paula passed the kitten to Cassie. "She seems to love everyone. Maybe that's why I found her hanging around Martha and Zeke's wedding dance. She just wanted to be part of the party."

Cassie touched her nose to the kitten's. "I'll bet you're right. Cute little girl. Auntie Cassie loves you, yes she does."

Melinda scratched Star behind the ears, eliciting more purrs. "Oh, you like that, don't you? Cass, when you move in, I think we should get a cat of our own."

Cassie's eyes twinkled and she snuggled Star closer. "Absolutely. I could never have one when I was a kid. Court hates cats and he's allergic, as Paula discovered."

Paula accepted Star from Cassie. "Yep. Little Star here ended my first and likely only date with your brother. Court began sneezing from the moment he walked in the door and was still going strong when he left."

"I heard. He joked about buying stock in Benadryl after that encounter. You know you're already half in love with Dr. Hunky, anyway, so I guess it's good that your date with Court didn't go well. Ahh, if not for a cat, though, we could have been sisters."

Paula patted Cassie's hand. "We're practically sisters anyway, *Auntie* Cassie."

"True."

Melinda coughed. "Okay, enough of the mushy stuff, you two. Paula, what did you do with that letter from Mark?"

Paula hugged Star until the kitten squeaked in protest and Paula released her. "Sorry, little girl. It's in a safe place. I haven't lost it, if that's what you mean."

"Are you two staying in touch?" Cassie asked.

"So, Mark and I have been talking almost daily since he's been in Arizona with his parents, and we text all the time. I can't imagine what he'd deem important enough to put into a letter. I'm almost afraid to open the thing. Maybe I've disappointed him in some way."

Cassie popped the top on a second Dr. Pepper and huffed. "You couldn't disappoint that man if you tried. Heck, if nearly drowning him didn't drive him away, I don't know what would."

Paula's mind flashed back to her first meeting with the hunky Dr. Fields. "You're the one who threw the rock that sent him overboard. I was his rescuer, so that's a bad example."

She extracted the missive from beneath her seat. "Part of me wants to read this right now, but the other part wants to be alone when I do. Just in case."

Melinda blinked. "Of course. I didn't mean you should open it now. I just wanted to make sure you hadn't misplaced it."

Cassie pouted. "What if *I* want you to open that thing?"

Paula waggled a finger at her friend and dropped the letter onto the table. "When you start having romantic feelings for Mark, I'll let you read it. How about that?"

"Fair enough, I guess. Although, that would be weird what with me being swept away by this one." She placed a light kiss on Melinda's forehead.

Melinda chuckled as her phone buzzed. "Wow, how'd a call get through out here?"

"Magic," Paula said with a snap of her fingers. "Kind of. Knowing how notoriously bad cell service is at the resort, I had a cell phone booster added to my little house on wheels. How about that? No more running to the Clyde tree when I need to make a call."

"Oh, yes, the good old Clyde tree, where miraculously, great cell service can be found. But remind me why it's called the Clyde tree." Melinda said, her eyebrows knitted together.

Waving in the direction of the tree in question, Paula said, "Because Ellie claims the tree looks like her Uncle Clyde. Even more so since it took that lightning strike last year."

"Oh, yes. I should have remembered that."

Cassie said, "Yeah, but, really, who names trees?"

Melinda looked at her phone and stood. "Apparently, our housekeeper does. And, speaking of our housekeeper, this is Ellie, calling from the front desk. Excuse me while I take this."

Once Melinda stepped outside, Cassie narrowed her eyes. "I can't believe you're not going to let me in on what Mark's letter says."

Paula raised an eyebrow. "You don't include me in everything you and Melinda discuss. Do you?"

"No, but..."

"I rest my case, but if it concerns you in any way..." Paula grinned and waggled the letter. "I'll be sure to let you know."

Cassie sighed. "Okay. Fair enough. I'll drop the subject. So, what's your long-term plan here?"

Paula gestured around the motorhome. "This is it. It'll be a big change for me, but I'm here for as long as Melinda will have me. I don't know how much of the business side of stuff she's shared with you, but the resort is doing well enough that she broached the subject of buying it back from me."

"That's great. I mean, you never had any intention of owning a fishing resort."

"True. When Cal died and you and I came down to discover what he'd been up to, why he'd bought this place, I never dreamed I'd end up falling in love with the resort, or that I'd want to make it my home, but that's exactly what happened. I approached Melinda to see if she'd be interested in forming a partnership. She agreed to the arrangement, so we're having the paperwork drawn up to make it official. Delbert's bringing the contract with him to the reunion."

"So, a fifty-fifty partnership?"

"Close, but since the place is part of Melinda's family history, we agreed on a sixty-forty split. She'll be the primary and I'll do whatever she needs. This way she doesn't have to shoulder the responsibility alone, but she still gets the final say in how we go forward, and we both have funds left over for any unforeseen occurrences."

"Listen to you, sounding all businesslike."

"Right? Wouldn't Cal be proud of me?"

"He was always proud of you, Goldilocks, but he'd get a real kick out of the new Paula. And this partnership between his first wife and his Goldilocks is probably all he can talk about in heaven."

Paula cocked her head and pictured Cal pestering the angels with tales of Melinda and Goldilocks. She chuckled at the image. "I hope so. I think he might have mixed feelings about my new assertiveness. He'd want me to succeed, though, and I can't be successful without taking some chances."

Melinda opened the door and poked her head inside. "Ellie says guests have begun checking in for your class reunion. It seems that some of your old classmates are looking for you two."

"Let the rumpus begin," Cassie said.

Paula looked from Cassie to Melissa and back. "Have you two discussed how you're going to handle your relationship around Cassie's school crowd? We are talking about a group of very conservative folks from Dempsey, Texas, after all."

Cassie blew out a long breath. "We're not going to go around announcing that we're a couple. I do know how to be discreet, you know."

"And I'll somehow refrain from ravishing dear Cassie in public," Melinda said with a dramatic sigh.

"Dahling," Cassie drawled. "However will we manage?"

Paula giggled. "Sorry I asked." She squinted at her reflection. *Ugh.* "Why don't you two go on. I'll be right behind you."

CHAPTER THREE

Waving them out the door, Paula kept an eye on the pair as they walked through the campground, their fingertips brushing as if by accident as their arms swung in an easy rhythm. Once they were out of sight, she opened the letter from Mark, unfolding the paper with care, her fingers trembling as she pressed it against the table. Reading the opening lines, she could imagine Mark's voice in her head.

Dearest Paula,

I'll bet right now you're sitting there looking adorable with a slight frown on your pretty face, wondering why in the world I wrote you an actual letter. You're probably a little concerned. And, yes, I could've called or texted, but something told me to put this down in ink. For posterity, maybe.

Dad's improving a little every day. We've found an assisted living facility for him and Mom. It's really nice. They have all these activities to keep the residents busy and a physical therapist on staff to help with Dad's rehabilitation following his stroke. The apartment they'll be moving into is perfect. They'll have all the autonomy they can handle and then, if they need more help, they'll already be in the right place. Mom's signed up for water aerobics and a ceramics class and they haven't even moved in yet. But it looks like we'll be able to get them into their new place within the next couple of weeks.

I hope you know how much—

Paula groaned when her phone buzzed. "Hello?"

"Hey, Sweetie, it's Sue Ann. We're heading back to the campground to inspect your new home. So, just stay put. Almost there."

Paula forced a welcome into her voice. "Come on back. Mine's the only one out here so far. Can't wait to show it to you." She disconnected the call and stared with longing at the paper in her hand. *Later, Mark. I want to read what you have to say with no disruptions.* She refolded the letter with care and carried it to her bedroom where Star was curled into a tight ball on the bed. Sue Ann's voice rang out from the living area and Paula shoved the letter beneath a pillow. "Be right there."

CHAPTER FOUR

"Girls, welcome to my new abode," Paula said, wrapping her arms around Sue Ann Atkins and Sherry Derryberry in turn. "Where are your ornery husbands?"

Sue Ann slid past Paula into the dining area. "They aren't far behind us. We dropped them off at the motorhome dealership where you left your car, and we didn't wait around for them to follow. I think Delbert and Melvin were going to have your car serviced for you."

"Aw, that's so sweet of them. They didn't have to do that. Y'all look around. The grand tour will take approximately sixty seconds." Paula led them through the galley kitchen and to her bedroom. "About all I've done so far is put sheets and a bedspread on the bed. I still need to decorate so it feels more like home, but it's exactly what I wanted."

"And you drove this thing to Happy Vale by yourself?" Sherry asked, her eyebrows knitted together.

Paula straightened her shoulders. "I got a great deal on this motorhome in Waco and, as a bonus, I didn't have much of a drive from there to here. I know it was a little out of the way for you all. Thanks for taking the time to pick up my car."

"Glad to do it," Sherry said.

Sue Ann peered into the closet. "Hm. You sure don't have room for many clothes."

Tapping the base of the bed, Paula said, "Oh, but there's under bed storage and lots of little nooks and crannies all over the place. Besides, living here I don't really need much more than t-shirts and shorts. Jeans when the weather grows cool and a few sweaters." Her hackles rose at the looks exchanged between the two women. *They don't think I can do this. I'll show them.*

Sue Ann hugged her again. "I'm sure you will be, um, cozy here. You ready to go face the Dempsey High School bunch?"

Paula grabbed a headband from a storage cubby. "Let me do something with my hair and I will be." After fixing her hair, she joined her friends for the walk through the campground over a carpet of crisp autumn leaves. She fought the urge to skip, relishing the crunch underfoot.

Sherry clasped Paula's hand and stopped to face her. "I have to say, you really look good. Healthy. How are you feeling these days?"

Paula was touched by the genuine concern in Sherry's voice. "Thank you for asking. I'm okay. There are still moments when I break down over losing Cal. I still cry myself to sleep some nights, but that doesn't happen as much as it used to. I'm healing."

Sue Ann joined in; her lips molded into a moue of concern. "We've been worried about you, and when Delbert told me your plans, we wondered if it wasn't too soon."

"The house sold way faster than I'd expected. I figured I'd have several months to get my ducks in a row instead of three weeks. Trust me, I've wondered if it was all happening too soon, but it felt right. And with Melinda's mom, Martha, married and living in Oklahoma, and her daughter, McKenzie, about to start a new life, Melinda needed me here. Do you know how wonderful it feels to be needed like that?"

Sherry chuckled. "Oh, I have teenagers. Trust me--I know exactly how it feels to be needed. Sometimes I wish I wasn't needed quite so much."

Sue Ann rolled her eyes. "And remember when they were toddlers, Sherry? There were days I wanted to change my name to anything but Mama. If it hadn't been for you going through the same thing at the same time, I doubt I'd still have my sanity."

Paula blinked away the unexpected tears gathering in the corners of her eyes. *It's not their fault I couldn't have children or that I was left out of that camaraderie.* "Don't ever take those days for granted," she said, with more anguish in her voice than she'd intended. *Sheesh, it's going to be a long weekend if I can't deal with hearing about everyone's kids.*

She pulled away as they neared the office. "Excuse me, why don't y'all go on. I'd better see if Melinda needs any help." Fearing she'd find looks of pity in the eyes of two of her oldest friends, Paula ducked her head and walked headlong into a man's solid chest. "Oh, sorry."

"Paula? Paula Purdy? Remember me?"

She tilted her head and found herself staring up into a pair of denim blue eyes. "Seth? Oh, my goodness, Seth Boone. How are you?"

Seth caught her up in a hug and kissed her cheek. Holding her at arm's length he said, "You're still short and cute."

Paula said, "I seem to have peaked at the epic height of five feet and five inches. It's my burden, you know. I think you might've grown some since I saw you last."

He patted his stomach. "Just around the middle."

"Nonsense. You look good. I'm so glad you could make it." Nodding at the office, she asked, "Have you checked in yet?"

"Nope, I was just about to do that. How about you?"

Paula shrugged. "I'm kind of permanently checked in."

At Seth's baffled look, she took his hand. "As of today, I'm a resident here. I'll tell you the story sometime this weekend if you're interested. For now, come on into the office and we'll get you settled into a room."

As he followed her up the steps, Seth said, "I'm really looking forward to seeing everyone. Especially, um, well…is Cassie going to be here?"

Paula held her breath. *And so, it begins.* "As a matter of fact, she's already here. Let's get your room assignment, then we'll look for her together."

CHAPTER FIVE

Offering a discreet wave to Ellie, the resort's head housekeeper and part-time clerk, Paula entered the office with Seth close on her heels. They stood aside while Ellie assigned rooms to a couple of men Paula didn't recognize. Seth tapped a toe against the hardwood floor in an impatient rhythm while Paula adjusted a painting of a storm brewing over a lake. "Seth, while you're waiting, come look at these paintings. Melinda Arnett, the resort's owner, is the artist. Aren't they wonderful?"

He dismissed them with a glance. "Sure. Great."

Paula tapped a finger against her lower lip. *Not a lover of art, I guess.*

As soon as the men in front of Seth left, Ellie's face lit up. "Ms. Paula, welcome back. Or should I say, welcome home? I can't tell you how excited I've been since Melinda told me you were moving here full time."

Paula rounded the counter and wrapped an arm around Ellie. "It's great to be home. And trust me, I'm so excited I probably won't sleep tonight. Come out to see my house when you have a chance."

Seth bellied up to the counter, towering over the women, and cleared his throat.

"Oh, Ellie, this is my friend Seth Boone. Would it be okay if I checked him in?"

"You sure can. I'm going to take fresh towels out to a couple of rooms if you don't mind manning the desk."

"I'd love to. Take your time."

As Ellie bustled back to the laundry room, Paula typed Seth's name into the computer and bit the inside of her cheek to keep from frowning. "Oh, looks like you're in room number one." *But that's always Mark's room*, she thought. *Of course, it'd be silly for Melinda to keep it open for him when he's been gone for months. But still.*

Seth handed over his credit card, his brows knitted together. "Is there something wrong with Room One?"

Paula scratched her head and rushed to reassure him. "Oh, no, nothing at all. I was, er, looking at something else on the monitor. Sorry. Room One is probably our nicest room, but don't tell anyone else. I'd hate for them to feel like we were playing favorites."

"Can you tell me if it's near Cassie's room? I hear she never married."

Oh dear. Paula nodded at the front door and sidestepped the question. "I'm not sure which room Cassie's in, but here she comes now. You can ask her yourself."

Seth straightened his shoulders and smoothed down an invisible tie. "How do I look?"

Like a man who's in for a heartbreak. Paula feigned a smile. "You look terrific."

CHAPTER SIX

When the door swung open, Paula widened her eyes in dramatic fashion, hoping Cassie would get the message. *Look at me, Cassie. Look at me. Then notice Seth.*

Cassie raised Melinda's hand to her lips and prepared to drop a kiss onto her palm. "I love y—"

Paula coughed. "Hey, Cassie, you remember Seth, don't you?"

With a fluidity of motion that sent Paula's head reeling, Cassie dropped Melinda's hand and took Seth's in its place, planting a kiss there instead. "Seth Boone. My goodness, it's good to see you. What do you think of this place? I was just telling Melinda that I love what she's done with the resort. Don't you just love it?"

Seth bundled Cassie into a hug. His voice grew husky as he whispered, "It's been way too long."

"That's what I was thinking. Exactly what I was about to say. Couldn't have said it better myself," Cassie said, extricating herself from Seth's embrace with a slight frown.

At Melinda's quizzical look, Paula arched an eyebrow and mouthed, "Old boyfriend."

"Oh." Melinda mouthed in return. Her eyes twinkled with mischief.

Paula winked at Melinda and dropped the key to Room One in Cassie's hand. "Cassie, maybe you'd like to show Seth to his room."

"I sure would. C'mon, Seth. We can catch up on the way over to Room…One? Are you sure he's in Room One?"

Melinda shrugged. "We're completely booked this weekend. I needed every room."

Seth's eyes bulged. "Okay. What's up with Room One? Is it the broom closet or something?"

With a pat on the arm, Cassie reassured him. "It's a room reserved for our finest guests. I was just surprised that Melinda here realized that you fit the bill. She's a discerning woman, our Melinda. Yes, she is. Okay. Let's go get you settled in."

Cassie hustled Seth out the door without looking back.

Melinda collapsed in a fit of giggles against the closed door. "Now that's a side of Cassie I hadn't seen before. The fidgets were back with a vengeance. You've got to give me the lowdown here."

Paula put a finger to her lips. "I'll never tell, but I'd sure like to be there when Cassie does."

"Oh, come on. Please? Our Cassie was rattled, and she never gets rattled. Can't you tell me *something*?"

Paula glanced at the door and settled onto a chair. "Just a little, I guess. Cassie and Seth were *the* couple at Dempsey High. The best athletes in the class. Most Beautiful and Most Handsome. The two of them ruled the school like benevolent royalty. Everyone thought they'd marry. In retrospect, everyone but Cassie, that is. They were both offered athletic scholarships to Texas Tech. Seth in football and Cassie in softball. Seth accepted the scholarship, but Cassie declined it and went to the University of Texas at Austin instead, shocking everyone, but most of all Seth. And me."

She grew silent for a moment, recalling how hurt she'd been when Cassie backed out on their childhood plans to share a dorm room at Texas Tech in Lubbock. *All those hours we spent cutting pictures of matching bedspreads and complementary posters out of the Sears catalog and gluing them into scrapbooks. All the hopes we shared.* With a shake of her head, Paula said, "Anyway, Seth tried to keep their relationship going, but Cassie said she needed some space. Finally, he gave up trying. Now, knowing everything I know about Cassie, it all makes sense, but at the time it was confusing and a little hurtful. We'd planned to be Red Raiders together since we were in elementary school."

Melinda sat beside Paula and rubbed her shoulder. "She must've needed the distance from her closest friends to figure out who she was."

"I think so. If only she could've confided in me back then. But then again, maybe it's better that she didn't. I might've freaked out if I'd known she was gay. Maybe I'd have cut her out of my life. I hope that wouldn't have been the case, but I was pretty sheltered back then, and times were different. I can't even imagine how dull my life might have been without her in it."

Melinda clutched Paula's hand. "Thank goodness you don't have to. I'm crazy about her, Paula. If you two hadn't remained best friends, she wouldn't have come with you to the resort after Cal died and I'd never have met her. Do you ever think about stuff like that? All the connections?"

"Oh, all the time. I'd give anything to have Cal back, but if he hadn't died, I might never have discovered this place. I'd never have met you and your family. You and Cassie wouldn't be together. I'd likely still be clueless about Cassie's sexuality, and she'd be miserable hiding herself away in Dempsey."

Melinda's eyes sparkled with unshed tears. "What's that old saying about God never closing a door without opening another? We're living proof of that, aren't we? And I guess Cassie has a right to be a little jittery around her old flame. Just curious, though...did they ever..."

Paula held up a hand. "Now *that* is a question you'll have to ask Cassie."

The bell above the door jangled and Melinda stood to greet their incoming guests. "Welcome to the Happy Valley Motor Inn and Resort. We're so glad you're here."

CHAPTER SEVEN

Paula's pre-reunion jitters melted away as she assisted Melinda in the office, welcoming old friends, and old antagonists alike. She hugged Neil Dunn whose teasing during fifth grade still rankled a bit. *Why'd he always have to call me Birdy Legs Purdy?*

She bestowed her sunniest smile on him. "Neil, it's so wonderful to see you." *Hm. I think I actually meant that. Funny how time erases most hurts.*

As the line of arriving guests dwindled to a few stragglers, Melinda jostled Paula's shoulder and nodded toward the door. "Go mingle," she said. "Oh, and why don't you check on how Cassie is faring with her old beau."

Paula flipped her hair out of her eyes. "Are you sure? I can hang around for as long as you need me."

"I'm fine. And curious. About old whatshisname."

"Seth. His name is Seth, and don't worry about him even a little bit. I know Cassie and how she feels about you."

"He is a handsome fellow, though."

"Emphasis on *fellow*, so not Cassie's type. Right?"

"Point taken. Still..." Melinda said, a note of concern in her voice.

Paula sighed. "For you, I'll go do some reconnoitering. Got any boyfriend-be-gone I could sprinkle around?"

Melinda laughed and waved Paula out the door. "Report back."

Paula snorted and skipped down the steps of the cabin. Surveying the parking lot, where people she'd known since kindergarten gathered in clusters, she took a deep breath. *These are my people. Which group do I join first? Am I ready to face the questions and sympathetic looks?* She exhaled and fastened a smile on her face.

"Paula, over here."

Paula waved and approached a woman whose highlighted blonde curls fell about her shoulders in carefully tousled waves. *Who is this woman who appears to have stepped from the pages of a fashion magazine?* She squinted at the name tag attached to the woman's blouse. "Arlene Baxter? Oh, my goodness. How long has it been?"

Arlene pecked the air on either side of Paula's face. "Since graduation day, I'm certain. I moved away the day after. But it's Arlene Davis, now. I just learned about your husband's death, hon. So sorry. I would've sent flowers if I'd known when it happened. Guess I just lost touch. Can you forgive me?"

Paula patted Arlene's arm. "There's nothing to forgive."

"At least your children can keep you busy. You do have children, don't you?"

Hoping Arlene didn't notice the quaver in her voice, Paula swallowed the oversized lump clogging her throat. "No. Cal and I didn't have any children."

Arlene knitted her brows together. "Oh, but we're still young." She poked an elbow into Paula's side and winked. "Find you a guy right here this weekend. There's more than one who had the hots for you in high school, and some of these men would do just fine."

Oh. My. God. "Really, I'm good all by myself. Now, what have *you* been up to?"

Arlene took over the conversation while Paula forced herself to pay attention. *I'll smile in all the right places. Frown*

*in others. Nod a lot. That should keep me from needing to field
questions about Cal's death and my fertility issues.*

Arlene said, "You know, I'm on husband number three."

Paula blinked. *Should I smile or frown. I'll just nod.* "Oh,
is he with you?"

"Are you kidding? He's a nice guy, but just between you
and me, a little on the boring side. I'm looking forward to a
husband-free weekend. After all, you just never know…"

Paula's eyes widened. She scanned the crowd hoping for
someone to rescue her as Arlene prattled on. *Where are the
knights on white horses when a girl needs one?*

During a lull in her monologue, Arlene scribbled
something onto a business card and pressed it into Paula's hand.
"Here's my address and personal cell phone number. Any time
you're in Dallas, give me a call and we'll do something fun. I'm
acquainted with lots of single men, you know."

Paula mumbled her thanks as Arlene carried on the
lopsided conversation.   When a new arrival caught Arlene's
attention, her eyes lit up, and without even a goodbye to Paula,
she called out, "Vanessa, thank goodness. There you are. Finally.
I've been looking all over for you."

Thank goodness for Vanessa, indeed. Paula pivoted and
scanned the parking area for Cassie. *Surely, Cassie's not still
hanging out with Seth.* On her way to Seth's room, she stopped
every few yards to greet former classmates, exchanging hugs and
handshakes. Throughout her encounters with old friends, her
mind remained occupied with thoughts of Mark and the letter
waiting for her. *What if he's decided we aren't compatible? We
have had some pretty steamy conversations, though. And he's
certainly not shy about telling me how much he enjoyed those
kisses we shared in July. But maybe he's found someone in
Arizona. Probably one of his dad's nurses. It could have
happened. But he started the message with 'Dearest Paula,' —
Surely that means he's still into me. Or maybe he's trying to let
me down easy. Mark's the kind of guy who would do that.*

Around and around her thoughts flew, like so many fireflies trapped in a Mason jar, their lights blinking on and off trying to capture her attention.

Paula jolted to a stop when a hand latched onto her arm. Her eyes narrowed as she faced the person who accosted her. "Hey."

"I wasn't sure it was you, but it is. Paula Purdy."

Looking up, Paula squinted. The name of the rugged, yet handsome man, teetered on the tip of her tongue. She cocked her head and searched his Lynyrd Skynyrd t-shirt for a name tag to no avail. "Give me a clue…"

"Senior year? Yearbook staff? Notorious writer of dirty limericks?"

Paula did a doubletake. *This tall, good-looking guy?* "No way. Jake Martinez. You scoundrel, you. I'd say you hadn't changed a bit, but look at you."

Jake laughed and bowed from the waist. "At your service. I'm not quite the scrawny guy I was in high school. And I have to say, you're just as cute as you always were. I thought that was you talking to Obnoxious Arlene, but I needed to get up close to make sure."

Clapping a hand over her mouth, Paula captured a guffaw. "I'd forgotten your nickname for her. Oh, by the way, it still fits."

"I should've rescued you, but you looked so absorbed in her diatribe I couldn't bear to interrupt. And, honestly, she used to scare me a little. Remember, her other nickname was Amorous Arlene."

Paula shook a finger at Jake. "Oh, dear. I don't even want to know why. Just between you and me, though, the whole time she talked, I was mentally working on a list of things I need to do this afternoon."

"You always were good at multitasking."

"I've still got it." Paula said, sketching a circle in the grass with the toe of her shoe.

"Too bad you can't use that in the class talent show. Multitasking, that is."

Paula scrunched up her nose. "Talent show? What talent show?"

CHAPTER EIGHT

As Paula followed Jake across the parking area to a picnic table beneath one of the massive oak trees that circled the property, she realized he had a slight limp and slowed her steps to keep from bumping into him. *After all these years, we've all probably developed a few scars. Some are just more visible than others.* Paula jostled his shoulder. "I see the Rootin' Tootin' Hifalutin' Sinclair twins are manning the registration table."

Jake snorted. "Always in charge, those two."

Rudy and Judy Sinclair, class co-presidents and the class's only set of twins, sat behind the table, distributing packets and name tags to their classmates. When Paula reached the front of the line, Judy rose to embrace her.

Judy said, "Finally. We thought maybe you'd invited us all here and then escaped before the event."

"Never. It's so good to see you two. I'm glad you decided to hold the reunion at our resort."

Rudy shook Paula's hand. "I was worried we wouldn't have a great turnout, but most of our classmates live either in Dallas or Austin these days. Happy Vale was much easier to get to than Dempsey would've been. It's perfect. Besides, the deal Melinda gave us on rates was hard to pass up."

"Well, thank goodness it all worked out," Paula said.

Jake threw an arm around Paula's shoulder. "Hey, you two, Paula doesn't know about the talent show."

Judy performed a double-take. "Oh, didn't you get your information packet in the mail?"

"No, but then, I recently sold my home in Dempsey and moved here full time. I haven't had an opportunity to go through all my mail yet."

"Aha." Rudy wagged a finger. "Then you're excused. But not from the talent show. Or should I say the Anything But Talent Show?"

"But I have no talent. Unless you consider doing laundry a talent. I excel at laundry."

Judy dug through a stack of papers on the table until she found the right one. "Then you're our target participant. Here it is. Third paragraph."

Paula scanned down the page, her eyes lighting on the words 'ANYTHING BUT TALENT SHOW FUNDRAISER'. "It says here that class members are encouraged to perform some talent other than what they were known for in high school. So, for example, Cassie won't be allowed to sing, right?"

"Exactly," Rudy said. "So, nobody's going to be a shoo-in to win this thing."

Paula studied her fingernails. "But it doesn't seem to be mandatory either, so..."

"We couldn't very well insist that everyone perform," Rudy said with a shrug.

Judy tapped on the stack of papers with a red-lacquered fingernail. "But folks will vote for their favorite act by putting money in the jar with the performer's picture on it. All the proceeds will go into the class fund for our next reunion, and the person whose act garners the most money will win a weekend stay at this resort and dinner at a local cafe."

"Oh? Is that so?" Paula asked, squinting to read the fine print.

Rudy said, "Yeah. Melinda offered the prize when we approached her with the idea. She's a very nice lady."

With a nod, Paula said, "Yes, she is. Anyway, I hope you have a whole bunch of entrants."

Jake jiggled Paula's shoulder.   "You're entering of course."

At Paula's strangled protest, he persisted.   "Look, I remember how much you hated being in the spotlight, but we'll come up with an act that will raise money for the class without making you uncomfortable. I'll join you on stage if you'd like, and it'll be fun."

"Okay. The fun part sounds impossible, but I guess it won't hurt to at least consider doing something. It is for the good of the class, after all, and, if by some miracle I happen to win, I'll just donate my prize to the runner-up."

"That's the spirit." Rudy glanced at his watch. "Oh, we have a class meeting at the campground in about an hour. Don't be late."

With a sigh of resignation, Paula accepted the registration packet from Judy. She fastened her name tag onto her shirt and fell into step beside Jake.

"What next?" He asked.

"Have you checked into your room yet?"

Jake shoved his hands into his pockets and scuffed a mark in the dirt. "About that. I don't *exactly* have a room."

"What? Don't tell me you forgot to make a reservation."

"Look, this is embarrassing. I didn't forget. I'm a musician and between bands at the moment, so money's been a little tight, and by the time I had sufficient funds, the place was booked solid. I was hoping I could bunk in with a friend. Any suggestions?"

Paula slipped her arm through his. "Me. You could bunk in with me."

Jake stopped in his tracks. "Paula, no. Don't get me wrong. I appreciate the offer, but that would be a little awkward, wouldn't it?"

"It'd all be above board. I have a motorhome with plenty of space for a guest. I guess I should warn you that I also have a kitten, so if you're allergic to cats, you might want to look elsewhere. But you're totally welcome to—"

Jake threw his arms around her. "Thank you. I adore cats."

Paula patted Jake's back. "Um, help. You're cutting off my air supply."

"Oops. Sorry. I was afraid I'd end up sleeping in my van curled up around my drum set using my guitar for a pillow, and that would've been embarrassing. I've done it before but, with my bum knee, it's not all that comfortable."

Paula nodded toward the parking area where new arrivals were greeted with hugs and cries of endearment. "To tell the truth, I doubt anyone would notice where you're sleeping. Everyone's just happy to be together again. Still, my camper will be more comfortable than your van. If you'll help craft a performance that won't result in me developing a case of the hives, it'll be worth it to share my home with you."

Jake crossed his heart. "I promise to help you. You just wait—you'll be a huge hit."

"I'm not making any bets on that. Let's go move your van to the campground. Then I need to find Cassie."

CHAPTER NINE

Leaving Jake to settle his belongings in the motorhome, Paula went in search of Cassie. She rounded the corner of her home to find Ray Landry, once known by the affectionate nickname, King of the Band Geeks, setting up his trailer in the spot next to hers.

Paula greeted him with a kiss on the cheek. "Ray! So good to see you. You haven't changed a bit since high school."

Ray grinned and held in his stomach. "Aw shucks. I might've gained a few pounds, but it doesn't look like you have. Cute as ever."

"And you're still full of it."

He laughed. "I'll have you know, I'm serious as a heart attack. You know, I've been looking forward to this weekend for months. So, is that your motorhome?"

Paula said, "It sure is. I guess that makes us neighbors."

"In that case, neighbor, can I offer you a beer while I hook everything up?"

"I'm on a mission to find Cassie but save me one for later?"

"That I can do. We are in for a good time, aren't we?" He waved her on and the warmth of his words stayed with her as she trod the path to Seth's room. *Ray always was the eternal optimist.*

She patted the Clyde tree for good luck as she left the campground area and ventured into the motor inn section of the resort, headed for Room One. *Room One. Mark's room--only without Mark. That just feels wrong.* Cassie's laugh floated like a falling leaf in the light autumn breeze, leading Paula to her destination. Rounding a corner, Paula spotted Cassie and Seth sitting side by side on a pair of vintage metal chairs in front of Seth's room.

"Hey, you two. Mind if I join you?"

Cassie startled as if her hand had been caught in the proverbial cookie jar. "Of course, we don't mind."

Seth scowled.

Paula glanced his way and pulled up a chair. *Good thing his good manners prevailed.* "You'll never guess who I ran into as I came looking for you two. Jake Martinez, for one, and then I came across Ray Landry."

Cassie's brown eyes sparkled. "Oh, they were both so much fun that year we were all on yearbook staff together."

"Weren't they, though? Jake's parked out by my motorhome, and Ray's camper is next door. Why don't y'all come hang out with us. The class meeting's set to begin in a half hour or so."

"Well, um..." Seth said.

Paula winked. "I have beer."

Seth offered a grudging smile. "In that case, how could I resist?"

"Cassie, Melinda has a question for you. How about if Seth and I head on back and you can join us after touching base with her?"

"She does? Cool. Sounds like a great idea. I'll see y'all back there. Yeah. That's just what I'm going to do."

Paula stifled a giggle as an array of emotions washed over Cassie's face. *I'll have to remember to ask what she was thinking. No, I'll have to remember to ask* if *she was thinking.*

Seth's eyes misted over as Cassie jogged away. "She's still as perfect as ever."

Paula linked arms with Seth, steering him in the direction of her camper. "So, Seth, what have you been up to since graduation?"

His face lit up. "Oh, I guess you know I played pro-ball for a few years. Quarterbacked for Tennessee. Blew out a knee and took an early retirement even though the Titans practically begged me to stay on. I've coached here and there. Hoping to make it into broadcasting."

"Interesting. Tell me more. Have you been married?"

Sighing, Seth said, "I was married for a few years but, and I wouldn't be saying this to anyone other than you, she wasn't... Well, to be honest, she wasn't Cassie."

Oh, mercy. Paula jolted to a stop. "Seth, I hate to break this to you, but Cassie isn't perfect."

"Shucks, I realize that, but she was... No, she *is* perfect for me. I realized early on in my marriage that I'd made a huge mistake. And now I have a chance to rectify that. I'm not going to let her out of my life again."

Shucks? Who even says shucks these days? And how do I soften the upcoming blow without giving Cassie's secret away? "Just don't get your hopes up, okay? I'm pretty sure Cassie is dating someone. And it seems to be serious. They're thinking about moving in together."

Seth's chiseled chin jutted forward. "No. I won't give up that easily. All she needs is a big ol' dose of Seth and she'll change her mind."

Ew! "Okay, but don't say I didn't warn you. Now, how about that beer?" *Or maybe three...*

CHAPTER TEN

Paula parried Seth's questions about Cassie throughout the trek to her campsite. *Will the man ever stop talking? It's not like I'm the official encyclopedia of everything Cassie-related, after all.* She sighed with relief when they reached their destination. Jake stood to greet them, a Dr. Pepper in hand. *Ah, reinforcements.* "I'm glad you found the drinks, Jake. You remember Seth Boone, don't you?"

When Jake stood to shake Seth's hand, Paula realized that Jake was now the same height as Seth. *And better looking to boot. The once skinny geek now might be mistaken for a former high school jock.*

Jake asked, "How could I forget? Man, you set all kinds of records on the football field. You probably don't remember, but I covered sports for the school newspaper."

Seth slapped Jake's back. "That was you, eh? Heckuva reporter, even in high school. I guess you went into journalism?"

"Not exactly—"

Paula cleared her throat. "Excuse me for a minute, gentlemen. What kind of beer can I get you, Seth? I've got Shiner and Coors Light. There might even be a Guinness in there."

"A Shiner sounds good."

Paula paused, her hand on the doorknob. "And Jake? Want something stronger than that Dr. Pepper."

"I'm good. This is my drink of choice these days."

"If you change your mind, most of the beer is in the cooler."

Inside the motorhome, Paula's eyes took a moment to adjust to the change in lighting. The buzz of the men's banter about their high school glory days played in the background as Paula scanned the living area for signs Jake had moved in. A glimpse of army green beneath the dining table caught her attention. *Ah, there's a duffel bag. If not for that, I wouldn't even know he was planning on staying here. Bless his heart.*

She grabbed Shiners for herself and Seth, then dug into the cooler for Cassie's Dr. Pepper.

Star joined her, looking into the cooler. She nosed at a piece of ice and drew back in confusion.

"The ice is not for you, silly kitty."

The kitten rolled onto her back and ventured an inquisitive meow. Paula scratched Star's belly. "I can't stay right now, and you need to stay inside. Too many people out there. I wouldn't want to lose you. Guard Mark's letter, okay?" Star clamped her claws around Paula's hand. "Ow! No claws, sweetie." The kitten trotted off to the bedroom while Paula examined the red gouges on her arm as she stepped out of the camper. *Those are gonna need antibiotic cream. I really should know better by now than to mess with that girl's tummy.*

"What happened to your hand?" Seth asked as she handed him a beer.

"The cat happened, that's what. She's my first kitten, and sometimes I forget that she is, in truth, a little assassin camouflaged in soft white fur."

Jake said, "Let me look at that. Ouch. I've got a first aid kit in the van. There might be some antibiotic cream in there. Hold on." He climbed into the back of his van and emerged with a tube of Neosporin. "Here, keep this. I'll pick up some next time I'm at Walmart."

"You don't have to do that. Honestly, I can get my own."

With a shake of his head, Jake said, "You need to keep doctoring the scratches. And keep an eye on them. Cat scratches are notorious for causing infections. Besides, I owe you."

"If you're sure. Thank you." Paula dabbed the scratches with a generous dose of the cream as the men visited.

Seth downed a hefty swig of his Shiner and belched. "Jake, remember when we beat Friona for the district championship?"

"I wouldn't have been much of a sports reporter if I didn't. You faked a pass to Garrett Fisher from the twenty-yard line, and the defense fell for it hook, line, and sinker, while you trotted into the end zone untouched. It was a thing of beauty."

"We should have won state that year. Those incompetent refs had it in for me from the very beginning of that game. Couldn't get a break."

Jake's brows knitted together. He raised a hand. "Now, that's not how I—"

Paula rushed to change the subject. "Um, so, Jake, you were saying that you're a professional musician?"

Jake beamed at Paula. "Yep. I got the bug early on. You remember I played drums in high school band?"

"Of course, I do. You were a natural, and I was so jealous of you. Mr. Weber wouldn't even think about letting me play drums, even though I begged. I still remember how patronizing he sounded. 'Girls like you should stick to feminine instruments like the flute and clarinet.' Girls like *me*? What did that even mean?" Paula snorted.

Seth patted Paula's hand. "I should think you'd take that as a compliment. He thought of you as sweet and dainty."

Paula took a deep breath and counted to five. "Maybe he did, but did that give him the right to keep me from doing something I really wanted to do?"

Jake cleared his throat. "Um, anyway, I tried out for the college marching band and made it. Then several of us formed a country band. Maybe you've heard of them—Fair to Middlin'?"

Paula's jaw dropped. "No way. I attended one of your concerts in Lubbock several years back. You were their drummer? Wish I'd known."

Ducking his head, Jake said, "Chances are I'd already left the band by then. We, uh, had a falling out, and I took kind of a break before moving on to Nashville. Since then, I've been picking up gigs here and there. Sometimes I work as a studio musician. I just auditioned to replace a drummer for a band out of Amarillo. Hoping to hear something soon."

Paula said, "That sounds exciting. Be sure to let me know. Maybe I'll be able to catch a concert."

Cassie sauntered over. "I sure hope that's not one of my Dr. Peppers, Mr. Martinez. I'd hate to have to arm wrestle you for it." Cassie embraced Jake when he stood. "I wouldn't have recognized you if Paula hadn't prepared me. You grew up nicely."

Jake winked. "Mm. So did you. Good job."

Cassie laughed and kissed his cheek.

Paula held her breath as Seth bristled, his eyes darting from Cassie's face to Jake's. He patted his knee. "Cassie, here. I saved you a spot."

Cassie blinked even as her smile stayed fixed. She accepted a Dr. Pepper from Paula. "Um, no thanks. Besides, it's time for the class meeting. I've already secured a place closer to the action. C'mon over and bring your chairs."

CHAPTER ELEVEN

After dodging clusters of class members in chairs scattered near the concrete slab stage, Paula unfolded her chair next to Cassie's. She pointed at her own name tag. "Did you register yet?"

Cassie nodded as the crowd settled down for the meeting. "I forgot to pin my name tag on, though."

Judy stepped onto the makeshift stage and took the microphone, calling for order. "Welcome to my fellow Dempsey Diamondbacks. Good to see so many of you wearing the emerald and ebony tonight."

Looking down at her own blue jeans and pink t-shirt, Paula leaned into Cassie, whispering, "I didn't get that memo."

Judy cleared her throat. "As co-presidents of the Dempsey High School graduating class of way too many years ago to admit to, my brother, Rudy, and I would like to say it's great to see everyone again. Seriously, when our ten-year reunion was canceled due to that nasty airline strike and our fifteen-year get-together was scrapped thanks to an outbreak of the flu, I was beginning to wonder if we'd ever be together in one place again."

She made a show of brushing an imaginary tear from her eye. "Yet here we are. We might be between landmark years, but something just told us that we needed to be together as a class this year. Maybe it's to celebrate the success of our very own celebrity triathlete, Vanessa Allen, who has completed the Ironman in Hawaii three years in a row and was featured on the cover of *Texas Triathletes* last year. Vanessa, stand and take a bow."

Rudy displayed an oversized copy of the magazine cover featuring their classmate, and Judy paused as an enthusiastic round of applause erupted from the crowd.

"Maybe it was the loss of one of our dear classmates to cancer."

Holding a photo of Rose Ellen Menard, Rudy said, "Rose Ellen, we remember your laugh."

Paula sniffled and rested her head on Cassie's shoulder. "I didn't know she'd been sick. She was always the sweetest thing."

Judy scanned the audience. "Maybe it's because the husband of one of our classmates passed away without us ever even getting to know him."

Rudy displayed a photo of Cal and Paula on their wedding day, and Paula gasped.

Cassie squeezed her shoulder and said, "I have no idea how they got ahold of that picture, Goldilocks, but I will find out, and they will pay for it."

Under her breath, Paula said, "It's okay. I promise. Just took me by surprise."

Rudy said, "Cal Arnett, we hear you were a wonderful husband to our Paula Purdy."

After a moment of silence, Judy raised her head and straightened the glasses on her nose. "Or maybe we all just needed to touch base with the people we can trade 'remember whens' with. I imagine there's a great deal of that taking place already, and a great deal more to come."

A voice called out from the crowd, "Remember when you and I were boyfriend and girlfriend in sixth grade?"

Everyone laughed as Judy peered in the direction of the speaker. "Is that you, Sidney Floyd? What I remember is that you tried to French kiss me in the lunch line and I kicked you in the groin. The detention I served was worth it."

The men in the audience groaned as the women cheered. Jake tapped Paula's shoulder and said, "Sidney couldn't walk for a week."

Paula's cheeks hurt from laughing. "Served him right."

Judy tapped on the microphone to restore order. "It really is good to have almost every member of our class present. I hope everyone has checked in and that you are wearing your official name tags. Otherwise, you might just be known as Hey You all weekend."

Paula pointed a finger at Cassie, "That's you they're talking about."

An unexpected hand landed on Paula's shoulder, startling her. She looked up into Melvin Atkins's bright eyes, then nodded to him and Delbert Derryberry. "Hey, guys. Thank you for bringing my car down. I guess it made the trip okay."

Melvin winked at her. "Yep. It's fully serviced and parked by your motorhome. Do you happen to know where our wives are?"

Paula shrugged. "They're bound to be close by. I talked to them earlier but haven't seen them since. My home's unlocked. Help yourselves to a beer and don't let the cat out."

Delbert tipped his hat. "Beer is good. But about that cat..."

"Be nice," Paula said with a wag of a finger.

Rudy called for quiet, and Paula returned her attention to the stage. "Okay, we have a few things to discuss before we let everyone loose on the communities of Happy Vale and Hemphill. There are a few planned activities for the weekend. There's a printed schedule in your registration packets, but just in case you don't have those with you, I'll give you a quick rundown. This evening, we're having a meal catered by a local restaurant, Oaks on Main. They're setting up in front of the office right now. I've got it on authority that the food is excellent, and the price was included in your registration. There'll be a continental breakfast in the morning out here in the campground. Lunch is on your own tomorrow, but dinner tomorrow night will be catered by a local barbecue place."

He looked down at his notes. "For those interested, there's a cornhole tournament starting at 10 a.m. tomorrow, and the horseshoe tournament starts at noon. You can register for either or both at the table set up behind me. There are trophies for the winners. They might be some of my old speech trophies, but they're still trophies. And anyone who's interested in a trip to a local plant nursery should sign up. The group heading that way is leaving at 11:30 tomorrow for lunch and a tour of the nursery. I understand there's wine involved, so it's going to be a lot of fun. There's also world class fishing on Toledo Bend Reservoir. That's on an individual basis, but I'm sure you'll have plenty of company if you decide to do some angling. The lake's just through those trees, past the campground area." He gestured to an opening before continuing.

"And I'm playing golf tomorrow at Cypress Bend just across the state line in Louisiana. We've booked three tee times starting at ten tomorrow morning, and I think we have enough golfers to do a two-person scramble. Winners get bragging rights and, you guessed it, my old speech trophies. Check with Travis Moody or me for more on that tonight so we can get you on the list. Anything else?"

A female voice called out from the audience. "Shopping?"

Rudy offered a broad wink. "Yes, my lovely wife. I understand there are a few boutiques nearby. Check with the front desk for more information, and good luck finding my credit card."

Someone called out, "You old cheapskate!"

He waited until the good-natured ribbing died down. "The main event, though, will be the Anything But Talent Show to be held tomorrow night right here starting at seven-thirty or thereabouts. Remember, no one can perform a talent they were known for in high school. That means Judy and I can't do any acting or public speaking, and Seth Boone, no football heroics. Dollars count as votes with the highest earning act winning another of my old speech trophies. Seriously, my wife wants me to give them all away, so second and third places will get trophies, as well. All the proceeds, though, go to funding our next reunion."

Judy whispered in her brother's ear. "Oh, right. As if one of my trophies wasn't reward enough, the grand prize is a weekend's stay here at the Happy Valley Motor Inn and Resort. For that, we'd like to thank Melinda Arnett, owner of the resort."

Cassie clutched Paula's hand as Melinda stepped to the microphone to enthusiastic applause. "Hello everyone. We're so happy to host this reunion. Two of your classmates, Paula Arnett and Cassie Campbell, are very special to me and it's an honor to meet those they attended school with. If there's anything we can do to make your stay here more comfortable, or if you need information on local attractions, please let me or whoever is working the office know."

Rudy reclaimed the microphone. "Thanks, Melinda. One other thing, breakfast on Sunday will be catered and, after that, we can begin saying our goodbyes and heading back to our homes. I think that's it unless someone has a question."

Seth's hand shot into the air. "Where's the beer?"

"Ah, good question. Beer and mixers are set up in room twenty-three. Boley Jackson donated a whole bunch of the good stuff, so make sure you thank him for that by dropping a few dollars in the bucket to reimburse him. Some of you will need to do more reimbursing than others, I imagine. Late arrivals can pick up their registration packets there, too. Any other questions? No? Okay, I think that's it. Let's get this party started, y'all!"

CHAPTER TWELVE

Paula stood. Her attempt to stretch was hindered by Cassie who was attached to her arm like a cocklebur. "You're clinging. Why are you clinging?"

Cassie clamped down tighter. "Please don't leave me alone with Seth again. He's a little, um—"

"Intense?"

"You feel it, too, then? Goldilocks, he's giving me weird vibes. How did I date him for three and a half years?"

"If it makes you feel better, I think he's changed drastically since high school. I'm certain we'd have noticed if he'd been so ardent in his affections back then."

Cassie nodded at a knot of men gathered nearby. "Look, he's engaged with a group of his old football buddies. Here's our chance to slip away while they're occupied with remembering what happened in the final seconds of the fourth quarter in the last game of October our junior year when someone went right instead of left and all hell broke loose."

Cassie's rendition of the long-ago football game made Paula laugh as they scurried to the resort's main cabin. "Why don't we cut through the office and get in line for Delilah's food. That should throw him off for a while."

"Good idea. Try to keep up." Cassie pushed through the back door with Paula close on her heels.

Paula leaned against the door and blew out a breath. She peered through the window and spotted Seth holding the attention of his peers. His right arm was pulled back as if to throw a football and his animated expression hinted that he was regaling his audience with some gridiron escapade. "Huh. That dramatic move was for naught. He has no idea you've left the area."

Cassie gestured for Paula to follow her through the living room. "His ego is humongous. Honestly, I think he believes we're all here for his benefit. Did you see him pat his knee for me to sit on? What was up with that?"

"That was pretty weird but wait 'til I tell you what he said about giving you a big dose of Seth."

"No. Please tell me he didn't say that. Ew."

Paula chuckled as Cassie pretended to gag. "My reaction, too."

As they headed toward the office, Cassie said, "I'm ready to come clean and let everyone know about Melinda and me. What could it possibly hurt? I'm certainly not embarrassed about my relationship with her. In fact, I couldn't be more proud. They're all just going to have to deal with it."

"Listen, I get it. I'm a big believer in honesty but, if you do that, you have to be prepared to be *the* topic of conversation all weekend long. Is that really what you want?"

Cassie huffed out a breath. "Damn. You're right. The last thing I want is to put the focus on me. But I can't pretend to be attracted to Seth."

Paula said, "Then don't. I already let him know you were seeing someone. Just confirm that and move on. He's a big boy. He'll move on, too." *Eventually. Maybe.*

They entered the office to find Ellie engaged in conversation with the local deputy sheriff. A pretty blush bloomed across the petite woman's cheeks when Paula and Cassie came into sight.

Paula shook the deputy's hand. "How are you? I sure hope this isn't a professional call."

The deputy's blush matched Ellie's. "Yes, ma'am. I mean, no ma'am. I mean, it is but it isn't. I'm just stopping in to make sure everything's okay. Miss Ellie tells me you're having your big high school reunion this weekend. You just let me know if you need anything."

"We'll do that. Thank you. Say, we're just passing through on our way to get a plate of Delilah's cooking. Want me to ask if she brought extra?"

Ellie busied herself with paperwork. "That's mighty nice of you, Ms. Paula, but Eugene and I have plans for this evening."

On the inside, Paula jumped up and down while, on the outside, she tossed them a casual nod. "I hope you two have a great time. Cassie, let's go see what Delilah's cooked up."

CHAPTER THIRTEEN

A handful of people stood in the buffet line as Paula and Cassie joined the queue. Paula accepted a plate from a young woman. She waited for Delilah Oaks to look up from serving fried chicken to Judy, then said, "Hey, Delilah."

Delilah's eyes sparkled with delight. "Oh, Paula, I've been wondering where you were. I'm so happy to see you again." She bustled around the table and smothered Paula against her ample bosom. "What's this I hear about you becoming the newest resident of Big Lake County?"

"You heard right. I felt a real need to be closer to your cooking."

Delilah laughed. "I'm sure there's more to it than that, but whatever the reason, we're glad to have you."

"As soon as I have a chance to settle in, I'll have a girls' night out at my motorhome, and you'll be invited. Oaks on Main is closed on Mondays, isn't it? So maybe you could spend an evening with us."

"It sure is, and I'd love that. What a great idea. Just let me know a few days in advance, and I'll make some hors d'oeuvres for the night."

"You don't have to do that. I just want you there."

Delilah waved her off and kissed Cassie's cheek. "You know it makes me happy to cook for others. Speaking of which, I'd better get back to work."

Delilah's son, Jeffries, offered Paula a helping of fried okra. "Ms. Paula. It's good to see you again. Let me know if you need any help setting up your new place."

Paula peered up at him. "That's so sweet. Thank you. So, where's McKenzie this evening?"

He slid a hot roll onto her plate. "Getting in her hours at the student salon tonight. She'll be here tomorrow."

Paula narrowed her eyes. "Good. I can't wait to see her. Um, how's she doing?"

Jeffries glanced at his mom and nodded. Lowering his voice, he said, "McKenzie is beautiful. So beautiful. She's ready to see you, too. And everything's going to be fine. I promise."

The tightness in Paula's chest eased. *Jeffries might be young, but he's a good guy. He'll do the right thing.* "I believe you."

She grabbed an iced tea and a dessert at the end of the buffet and looked around for a place with room enough for Cassie and her. She spotted Jake and Ray, sitting at a picnic table along with several others she'd become friends with during her stint on the yearbook staff senior year. Nodding in Jake's direction she said, "Cassie, let's head over there. There isn't room for Seth at that table."

"I like the way you think, you devious wench."

"May we join you?" Paula asked.

"Of course," Jake said, edging over to make room. "Y'all remember Cassie and Paula, don't you?"

Paula nodded at everyone seated around the table, including the one person she didn't recognize. *Who is this man?* She exchanged smiles with him. "I'm so sorry, but I can't recall your name. Are you here with someone?"

Jake elbowed her. "Surely you haven't forgotten Mr. Lewis. Senior English? Yearbook and senior sponsor?"

Her eyes widened. *Andrew Lewis. How many times did I scribble I love Andy on my notebook? A thousand at least.* A slow surge of heat crept up her neck. "Mr. Lewis. I knew they'd sent invitations to our class sponsors, but I had no idea anyone would actually attend. So glad you could make it."

"Paula Purdy, I'm shocked and disappointed that you didn't remember me." The obvious amusement in his eyes belied the severity of his words.

Cassie slathered butter onto a hot roll. "You were absolutely our favorite teacher. Partly because you weren't that much older than we were and partly because you were so good at your job. I hated poetry until your class. Now I can tolerate it. Occasionally."

He laughed and patted his lips with a napkin. "First of all, I think you can all call me Andy now. And, after all this time, I can finally confess how scared I was that year. My first teaching assignment and they dumped yearbook and senior sponsor in my lap. But I must say, this group, those of you gathered right here at this table, made me realize I'd gone into the right profession."

Paula watched Andy as he interacted with the others. *He's gained a little weight, and there's not as much of his curly dark hair as there once was, but with those black rimmed glasses he's still handsome in a bookish sort of way.*

"Remember Senior Skip Day, Mr. Lewis? Sorry, *Andy.*" Jake said.

"Remember it? I thought it was going to get me fired."

Paula dipped a piece of fried okra in ranch dressing. "Why? It was an annual event. Everyone expected the seniors to skip school on Senior Skip Day. Parents wrote goofy excuses, and the administration turned a blind eye."

"Even Perfect Little Paula Purdy skipped that day," Ray said, adding air quotes around the nickname.

Paula shot him a mock dirty look. "Gee, thanks for the reminder, *neighbor.*"

Ray snorted and hoisted a beer in salute.

Their former teacher grimaced. "But I didn't know that. All I knew was that one day in the second semester of your senior year, I mentioned to the students in my advanced English class that I had skipped a day of school during my senior year to attend a Cleveland Indians game, and the very next day, all of you were absent. I thought I planted the seed. I had no idea the date had been planned since the beginning of the year."

"Oh, no. You must've been a nervous wreck all day," Cassie said.

"Even worse, I went to Mr. Landers and confessed."

Laughter rippled around the table.

"What happened?" Paula asked.

Andy pulled his spine into a rigid position and placed his palms on the table. "He sat like this the whole time I apologized. His eyes never wavered from mine. I told him I took full responsibility and hoped I could retain my position. He let me ramble on for a good five minutes then said, and I quote, 'Young man, don't let it happen again. Until next year.'"

"Didn't know Mr. Landers had it in him. That's brilliant," Jake said.

"It was. And we made it a tradition. I'd go in and apologize and he'd offer the same words. I taught there for several more years while most of you were away at college. I understand Mr. Landers passed on about a decade ago. He was a good man."

"To Mr. Landers," Jake said as he raised a glass of tea.

"Absolutely," Andy said, clinking his glass with Paula's.

"So, are you still teaching?" Ray asked.

"I teach part time at a community college in Tallahassee, Florida, and I'm in the process of writing my third novel."

Paula's ears perked up. "Oh? Do tell."

"You always were an avid reader. I wonder if any of you have read my—"

Seth bellied up to the table. His voice cut through the conversation. "Cassie! I've been looking all over for you. Thought you were going to wait on me."

Cassie sketched a curt nod in Paula's direction. "Seth, we need to talk. Y'all, please excuse me for a minute."

CHAPTER FOURTEEN

Paula craned her neck to watch as Seth steered Cassie to an empty picnic table. She twisted her hands together in her lap. *Is Seth angry? Maybe I should join them and diffuse the situation. But Cassie seems to be doing okay. She is a big girl after all. Probably wouldn't appreciate me butting in. I'll just stay out of this. Or will I?* She kicked Jake under the table and whispered, "Does Cassie look like she's in distress?"

"What? Why? Do you want me to go over there?"

"No. I don't think so. I just want to keep a close eye on them."

Andy cleared his throat. "Paula, I was about to tell you about my novels."

"Oh, yes. Please."

Andy's face grew animated. "As I've said before, I'm on book three. It's the final installment in a trilogy I've titled, *Echoes of the Plains.*

"A western?" Jake asked.

"One would think so, but it's a post-apocalyptic tale set in the Great Plains—Texas, Oklahoma, Kansas, up into the Dakotas, which comprise the new Garden of Eden. In the first book..."

As Andy continued to wax eloquent about his novels, Paula's attention wandered to where Cassie sat, her hands encased in Seth's.   Cassie shook her head in response to something he said, and Seth stood, his hands balled into fists at his sides as he towered above her, glaring.

When he raised a hand, Paula gasped. "Oh, no you don't!" She slid off the bench and rushed to Cassie, inserting herself between her friend and the former quarterback. "Back off, Seth Boone. What's wrong with you?"

Seth's breaths came in staccato gusts, his chest heaving as he hovered over the two women.

Tugging on Paula's arm, Jake said, "Let me handle this."

She shook him off. "No. I don't want a fight here. Seth, get ahold of yourself. Now."

Seth shivered. His eyes shifted from Cassie to Paula, and then to Jake. His mouth hardened. "I—I don't understand. But when you change your mind, Cassie, and you will, I'll be here."

Jake wrapped protective arms around Cassie and Paula as Seth strode away. "Okay, that was heavy. You two all right?"

"I'm guessing that was Seth's response to the news that you're in a relationship," Paula said.

Cassie held out a shaky hand. "Yep. Never imagined he'd react like that."

"Too bad your guy couldn't be here this weekend. Seth might be one of those men who needs proof. And by that, I mean a dude who'd go toe to toe with him."

Exchanging looks with Paula, Cassie said, "Jake, there is no guy. No dude."

Paula cocked an eyebrow. "Cassie..."

Cassie backed away from Jake's embrace. "It's fine, Paula. We can tell him. So, here's the deal. Melinda? The resort's owner? She and I, um, we're a couple. Whew. It felt good to say that."

A series of emotions flashed across Jake's face, and Paula held her breath. *I wonder which one will win out. Doubt? Judgment? Acceptance?* When he caught Cassie up in a hug,

Paula's shoulders relaxed. She lifted a finger to her lips. "She hasn't told anyone else, so…"

Jake mimed zipping his lips. "Cassie, your secret is safe with me. A lot of these folks just wouldn't get it, even though I can almost guarantee that every one of them has a secret of their own."

"Even you?" Cassie said.

Jake's smile dimmed. "Yeah. Even me."

Paula sensed the sadness that gathered in Jake's eyes. "Whatever it is, you don't have to share it with anyone unless you want to. Let's go finish our meal."

CHAPTER FIFTEEN

Keeping an eye out for Seth, Paula linked arms with Cassie as they returned to the table where Andy held court. She slid onto the bench, leaving room for Cassie and Jake, and focused all her attention on Andy's stories as words spilled from his animated mouth, the volume falling and rising, as he punctuated the tale with vigorous gestures. The tension Paula held in her shoulders melted away as she lost herself in his imaginary world. *Thank goodness Seth's outburst went unnoticed, thanks to Andy.*

"Sorry," she mouthed when Andy paused to acknowledge their presence.

"I was finishing up, anyway. If I talked any longer, everyone would know the ending. Can't have that now, can we?"

"I'll just have to buy your books. I don't suppose you brought any with you?" Paula asked.

Andy shook his head. "I intended to. I can picture them stacked on the table looking all forlorn at having been forgotten. Hope they can forgive me."

Cassie raised a finger. "Ah, personification. Giving inanimate objects human characteristics. You taught me that."

Their former teacher stood and pushed a lock of hair from his forehead. "Oh, yes. Personification. I'm glad you were paying attention that day. I think I'll go mingle now."

Jake's fingers drummed on the tabletop as Andy strode away. "Hm. That was sudden. But look, he must have wanted to touch base with Arlene."

Following Jake's gaze, Paula said, "That's Vanessa with her, right? The triathlete?"

"Yeah," Ray said. "Haven't seen either of those girls in ages."

Jake elbowed him and winked. "That's probably a good thing, isn't it old pal?"

Ray mumbled something under his breath. "Hey, remember when Jimmy Randall rode his motorcycle down the freshman hall?"

"Oh, my gosh, I'd forgotten all about that," Paula said. "Last day of school senior year. They almost didn't let him walk the stage with the class."

"Is he here for the reunion?" Cassie asked.

Ray swiped at his mouth with a napkin. "I haven't seen him. He's got some high-powered job in Tennessee. Probably couldn't get the time off, but I hear he still rides."

With a wistful smile, Paula said, "He was an ornery one. Sure wish he could be here with us this weekend."

Jake looked around the table. "So, I'm going to do some mingling of my own. Anyone else?"

Paula said, "Sounds like a plan. I'm just going to finish off this cobbler."

Ray gathered the remains of his meal. "Hey, I'll come mingle with you. And in case you're interested, Jake, what do you think about making a little music out in the campground this evening? You bring an instrument?"

"As a matter of fact, I did. Let me grab it out of my van. Cassie, will you come sing with us?"

"Love to as soon as I've finished eating. Easy songs, though. Nothing I have to work too hard at."

The two men sauntered away, and Paula dabbed at the corner of her mouth. "I'm going to check on Star and grab a jacket. Want to walk back there with me?"

"Sure. Two more bites and I'm done."

Paula's brow creased. "You okay?"

Cassie sat staring at her plate for a moment. When she faced Paula again, she said, "Yeah. Seth's reaction spooked me a little. I don't think he was going to hit me, but he sure was angry. Thanks for coming to my rescue, though. Paula the Fierce."

"From where I sat, it certainly looked like he was about to strike. Scared me silly."

Wrinkling her nose, Cassie said, "I don't think he gets told no very often. If ever. He'll get over it. Want the last bite of my cobbler?"

Paula shook her head. "Did you know he played pro ball?"

Cassie snorted. "He was backup to the backup quarterback at Jacksonville. I don't think he played more than two quarters the whole time he was there. Blew out a knee in pre-season his second year, and that was that."

"Really? Seth made it sound like he'd practically been the MVP. You've kept up with him, though."

Cassie pushed a stray peach from her cobbler around her plate with a fork. "I liked Seth a lot. The old Seth, though, not this new hyper intense Seth. When you married Cal, I considered rekindling my relationship with him just to feel like I fit in—to get on with my life. How pitiful is that? I knew I didn't love him, but he loved me and maybe that would've been enough."

Paula wrapped an arm around Cassie and squeezed. "Oh, sweetie. I'm so sorry. I wish I'd known. Wish I'd been the kind of friend you could've trusted with your secret."

Cassie waved her off. "Oh, hell, at that time in my life, *I* couldn't even be trusted with my secret. And, I couldn't have asked for a better friend. Besides, you brought me here. To Melinda."

After a second squeeze, Paula released her friend. "Still... You ready?"

"Yep. Let's go. Just steer clear of you know who."

CHAPTER SIXTEEN

Paula skirted the office with Cassie by her side. Taking a meandering route through the campground, Paula kept a wary eye out for Seth. She nodded to where he sat amid a group of men gathered near a campfire, gripping a bottle of beer. His head hung low, and his shoulders slumped. "Looks like he's more subdued now."

Cassie ducked her head and quickened her pace. "Good. Let's hope he stays that way."

"So, are you staying in the cabin with Melinda this weekend?"

"No, I went ahead and got a room. Martha and Zeke are coming tomorrow night and McKenzie will be here all weekend. I didn't want to make things awkward."

Paula poked Cassie in the ribs. "Seriously, I hope Melinda gave you a nice discount."

"I had to make Ellie take my money behind Melinda's back. I'm in room twelve, by the way, if you need me."

"You could've stayed in the camper with me, you know. I had an extra bed."

"Had?"

Paula said, "Don't say anything, but Jake didn't remember to make a reservation, so I offered to let him stay there."

Cassie's hands shot to her chest. "So, that's his secret? Oh my goodness, Goldilocks, whatever will people say?"

"Nothing if you don't tell them about it. Besides, it's no one's business, now, is it? I mean, he's a friend. An old friend, and..."

Cassie jostled Paula's shoulder. "Just giving you a hard time, but he is so blooming handsome now. And single."

"I noticed the lack of a ring but, honestly, Jake just doesn't make my heart tingle in anticipation."

"Because he's not Dr. Hunky?"

Paula's lips curved into a Mona Lisa smile. "No, he's definitely not Mark."

Star met them at the door with a plaintive meow. She nudged Paula's leg with a head bump, lighting up Paula's eyes. "You missed me? Aw, I missed you, too. Cassie, would you get us some drinks to take to the campground while I feed Miss Star?"

"Will do. Shiner for you?"

Paula ran fresh water into the cat's bowl. "Yep, thanks. I'm going to grab a light sweater. Do you need one?"

Cassie took a swig of beer. "No, I'm good. The guys are tuning up out there."

Paula cradled Star in her arms and breathed in her sweet kitty scent. "I'll be right back." From the bedroom, she grabbed a sweater and gazed with longing at the place where Mark's letter lay hidden. Her fingers itched to hold it again. *Soon*, she thought.

CHAPTER SEVENTEEN

The late October sun slid behind the resort's massive oak trees, casting an orange hue over the campground as Paula and Cassie walked arm in arm to the campfire. *Perfect weather. Perfect setting.* "Could this get any better?" Paula asked.

"Needs a little music, is all," Cassie said with a wink.

Jake and Ray sat on the other side of the small blaze, strumming their guitars, and requesting song suggestions.

Paula said, "How about some Eagles?"

Jake nodded at Cassie. "Depends on what our chanteuse wants."

"Let's try "Peaceful Easy Feeling," Cassie said.

"I can do that one. Jake?" Jake nodded and Ray counted off the beat as Cassie joined them.

Paula closed her eyes and sank into her chair as Cassie melded her sweet voice to the sounds emanating from the men's guitars. Cassie's beautiful voice sent shivers up and down Paula's spine. *To think she might've settled for Seth Boone. Thank goodness she resisted that urge.*

Her eyes fluttered open as Delbert and Sherry Derryberry and Melvin and Sue Ann Atkins joined her. Paula held out a hand as they pulled their chairs up close on either side of hers.

Clutching Paula's hand, Sherry said, "Even after all these years they sound so good.   Especially Cassie.   Isn't she wonderful?"

"Oh yes," Paula said, relaxing into the music again.   "I could listen to Cassie sing all night long."

As the song ended, Paula felt a hand on her shoulder.   She blinked and found Seth standing beside her.

"Hey, Paula.   Could we go somewhere and talk for a minute?"

Paula looked him over with narrowed eyes.   "Sure.   How about we stay right here, though?"

His shoulders slumped.   "I really would prefer to speak privately.   I promise I'll behave."

Delbert wrapped a strong arm around Paula.   "Is there a reason she might think you're unable to behave?"

Paula studied Seth's face, then patted Delbert's arm.   "I think it'll be fine.   We won't go far.   This way."

"Okay, but we're here if you need us," Melvin said.

She led Seth to the Clyde tree and perched atop the picnic table. *Odd that this old tree feels like a trusted friend while an old friend feels like a complete stranger.*   She straightened her spine and spun to face him.   "What you did earlier was not okay. If you'd hit Cassie, I'd have had a sheriff out here before you could say Tennessee Titans."

Seth's chin dropped to his chest as he sat beside her on the table.   "About that.   I might've exaggerated a little."

Paula waved him off.   "That's not the issue here.   You looked like a wild man back there.   I thought you were about to hit my best friend.   I'm not sure any explanation you have is going to be excuse enough to make me forget that."

He sighed.   "Probably not, but just hear me out.   The past few years have been tough.   My football career went down the drain without ever really getting started.   My wife left me because I wasn't the big time, big money quarterback she thought she was marrying.   I pinned all my hopes on reconnecting with Cassie. I promise, though, I wasn't raising my hand to hit her. I'd never hurt a hair on Cassie's head. On any woman's head. I'm sorry that's what you thought. I was just railing at the heavens. Can we start fresh here?"

Paula pinched the bridge of her nose and shook her head. "In your favor, Cassie said she didn't believe you were going to hit her either and she wouldn't lie to me. Okay. Fresh start. No more lying, though. But if you do one thing that makes me regret giving you another chance..."

Seth's eyes remained fixed on Paula's. "I promise I won't give you any reason to doubt me. Scout's honor."

She nodded toward the trio of musicians. "You know this is all up to Cassie anyway. She's the one you need to apologize to."

"And I will. You can be my witness."

With some hesitation, Paula shook Seth's hand. "Okay. Now, let's go back and enjoy the music. Just remember your promise."

CHAPTER EIGHTEEN

Leaving Seth with one of his football buddies at the edge of the campground, Paula hurried back to her place between Sherry and Sue Ann. The trio of musicians had grown to a quartet in her absence, and Cassie was trading harmonies with Jake on "I Can't Tell You Why." Paula sipped on her beer and hummed along. "Thanks for saving my spot," she whispered to Sherry.

"Of course," Sherry said. She nodded to where Arlene stood with a man. "Who's that handsome guy over there? The one Arlene's practically draped over. That's not husband number three, is it?"

"No, she left number three at home. That's Andrew Lewis. Mr. Lewis from our senior year."

Sherry's mouth dropped open. "Oh, wow. I had a huge crush on him back in the day."

Paula smirked. "You and every other girl in school."

Sherry leaned across Paula and tapped Sue Ann's arm. "Sue Ann, look. Over there. Remember Mr. Lewis?"

Sue Ann fell into a mock swoon. "Ohhh, Mr. Lewis!" The song ended as Sue Ann's exclamation rang out across the campground.

Andy pivoted. "Yes? Did someone call my name?"

Sue Ann ducked behind Paula who swatted her.

"Sit up, Sue Ann. He's gonna think it was me."

"Better you than me. At least you're single."

Paula laughed. "Melvin, your wife's a mess."

Melvin flashed a grin. "Tell me something I don't know. Y'all want something else to drink? Delbert and I are gonna make a run to the hospitality room."

As the men left, Sherry asked, "Have you talked to Mr. Lewis yet?"

Paula batted her eyelashes and pressed a hand against her chest. "Oh, I did more than talk to him. I'll have you know that *I* dined with *Andy*."

Sue Ann's shoulders slouched as she sighed. "Lucky. He seems as adorable as he did senior year. I swear I used to dream about him. He was so romantic. Thanks to him, I still love Shakespeare. I always substituted his name for Romeo's when reading *Romeo and Juliet*."

Sherry giggled. "Sue Ann had it bad. 'Andy, oh Andy. Wherefore art thou, Andy?'"

Paula's eyes widened. She poked Sherry and pointed her chin to where Andy and Arlene stood nose to nose. "Is Arlene about to kiss him or slug him?"

Sherry said, "Looks like it could go either way. Should we intervene?"

"Maybe, but on whose behalf?" Sue Ann asked.

Paula gasped. "Looks like Andy is making a move."

The wide-eyed women goggled as Andy cupped Arlene's chin and leaned in for a kiss. The couple faded into the privacy of the trees as night settled on the campground.

Sherry shook her head. "Mercy me. Tell me I didn't just see what I think I saw."

"I sure wish I could, but Arlene always did push the boundaries. Remember senior trip? She smuggled in a bottle of Jack Daniels and threw a party in her room. Not that any in our little circle of friends were invited," Paula said.

Sue Ann twisted in her seat and clasped Paula's hands. "I'd forgotten about that. But this is different. Mr. Lewis was our *teacher*."

Paula returned the squeeze. "But just a few years older than us. I remember that some of the boys in our class looked older than he did."

"True, but still," Sue Ann said. "It just doesn't feel right."

With narrowed eyes, Paula said, "I imagine her husband would agree. Let's enjoy the music and not worry too much about what's going on in the dark."

The strains of "Lyin' Eyes" floated on the breeze. Paula did her best to follow her own advice as her thoughts continued to wander back to Mr. Lewis and Arlene. *Sue Ann nailed it--this just doesn't feel right. Okay, Paula, stop being so judgmental.* Still, she couldn't help but keep one eye on the musicians and the other on the place where Arlene and Andy had disappeared.

CHAPTER NINETEEN

Paula bid goodnight to her friends as the impromptu band exhausted the repertoire of songs to which they knew all the words.   Paula stayed around to giggle at the group's improvised lyrics for "Hotel California."

"I'm pretty sure they meant the warm smell of colitas instead of the smooth taste of mojitos," she said to no one in particular.   "But then again, I might've had one too many Shiners."

She helped the musicians extinguish the campfire while telling Cassie and Jake the details of her conversation with Seth. "He promised he'd apologize to you, Cassie. Of course, that doesn't mean you have to accept it."

Cassie sloshed a bucket of water on the fire.   "I'd appreciate an apology, but I have no desire to hang around with him for the remainder of the reunion. I hope he understands that."

Jake's lips drew into a frown. "If he bothers you just let me know."

"Oh, don't you worry. Everyone within ten miles of this place will know if he steps across the line."

"Sorry I wasn't paying attention when all that went down, but I'm here if you need me," Ray said. "Hey, Jake, I don't guess you brought any tools with you? I need to fix some things in my trailer. I don't go camping all that often, and the trailer's got some issues that are driving me crazy."

Jake dug his keys out of his pocket and tossed them to Ray. "Sure. You're welcome to borrow anything you need. There's a box with duct tape, and some tools, even some silicone and hose in the very back of my van. I'm parked on the other side of Paula's motorhome. Just leave the keys in the driver's seat when you're through."

"Thanks, man," Ray said as he sauntered off toward the woods.

Paula stirred a few glowing embers that refused to burn out. "Jake, I think we need more water. Would you mind getting some? The faucet's right over there." She waited until he was out of earshot. "Does Seth know which room you're in?"

Cassie's face blanched. "I might've told him when I showed him to his room. I think I might've been flustered enough that I'd have given him my social security number and my ATM PIN if he'd asked for them. You don't think he'd confront me again tonight, do you?"

Paula's eyes scoured the campground where people were gathered in small groups. "I don't see him here. If you're worried, sleep in the cabin with Melinda tonight, or better yet, come stay with me. My bed's easily big enough for two."

Cassie puffed out a breath. "Oh, I'll be fine. I'll lock the door and put the chain on. Besides, Melinda tells me I snore."

Paula shrugged. "I could've told you that. Why do you think I always ended up on the couch during sleepovers?"

"Oh. Ha. I guess I owe *you* an apology."

Paula hugged Cassie close. "Just don't let Seth in if he comes knocking."

"Do I look stupid to you? Don't answer that. Besides, I'm worn out from hugging everyone in sight. I'm going to wash the stink of smoke from my hair and go to bed. I'll be snoring ten minutes from now."

Jake returned, splashing water across the fire. "That should do it. I'm going to head back to Pau--, um, my campsite. Unless you want me to walk you to your room, Cassie."

"I'll walk with her," Paula said.

"Y'all, I'll be fine. I'm going to say goodnight to Melinda, so go on."

Paula pecked Cassie's cheek. "If you're sure. See you in the morning." She kept an eye on Cassie until she rounded the corner toward her room. "She'll be okay," Paula said, as much to herself as to Jake, as they wandered in the direction of her camper.

Jake shoved his hands into his pockets. "I almost blew my secret about where I'm staying this weekend."

"Oh, Cassie knows. Of course, she had to tease me a bit."

Jake came to a limping halt in the middle of the path. "You told her? You said no one would know."

Paula gazed up into Jake's eyes, recognizing the sorrow there that she'd glimpsed earlier. *What is it that haunts him so?* She placed a hand on his arm. "Jake, all Cassie knows is that you forgot to make a reservation. The resort doesn't have any vacancies. You're staying with me because there wasn't another option. Right?"

He relaxed and a smile twitched at his lips. "I guess that's okay then. And I do know Cassie's secret, after all. C'mon, last one to your place is a rotten egg."

Paula picked up her pace as Jake headed in the direction of her camper, then came to an abrupt halt. "Wait. No fair! I just remembered--Melvin has my car keys and I need them first thing in the morning."

Jake glanced over his shoulder. "Guess we know who the rotten egg will be then."

CHAPTER TWENTY

Paula pocketed her car keys as she approached her motorhome and glanced up at the light shining out of the window. *Maybe asking Jake to share my space wasn't such a great idea. I mean, how well do we know each other after all these years?* Her worries evaporated as she stepped inside. Jake had fashioned a privacy curtain from a plaid flannel sheet and duct tape. "Would you look at this? How'd you create this space so quickly?" she asked.

Jake poked his head around the sheet. "Hey, there, rotten egg. Duct tape solves everything. A real man always has a roll or two handy."

Paula's hand paused on her bedroom door. "Then I guess that qualifies you as a real man."

Jake fully emerged from his makeshift room. "Hey, I just wanted to thank you again. You didn't have to do this."

She leaned against the door, a smile playing on her lips. "You're welcome. This is my first night in my new home. And, honestly, I'm glad to have some company. If anything goes bump in the night, I'll know it's you."

He grinned. "I'll do my best to keep things down."

"I haven't stocked up on groceries, yet, but you know where the drinks are and there's coffee if you want to make a pot. Just make yourself at home."

Jake said, "I sure appreciate it. And, Paula, I was sorry to learn about your husband. How long's he been gone?"

An old familiar pain filled her chest, stealing her breath. "Fifteen months now. A month for every year we were married."

Fresh tears glimmered in Jake's eyes. "I know how hard it is to lose someone you love. But look at you. Maybe you'll tell me *your* secret one day."

"Who? Me? I don't really have any secrets," Paula said with a shrug.

"Oh, I think you do. Your secret is knowing how to do more than just survive when the one you love dies. That's pretty powerful. 'Night, friend."

He slipped behind the curtain leaving Paula with a Texas sized lump in her throat. She ached to tell him that sometimes she was hanging on by the thinnest of threads--that there were still days when she struggled to get out of bed. That she'd grabbed this opportunity to move forward as a lifeline and was still overcome with doubt. *Oh, Jake. We both need to heal.* She closed her eyes and prayed for him. Then she said a prayer for herself.

CHAPTER TWENTY-ONE

Inside the bedroom, Paula slid the pocket door closed and found Star curled into a tight ball, lounging on the pillow that guarded Mark's letter. The kitten blinked and yawned, her paws reaching to pat Paula's face as Paula moved Star to the spare pillow. "Looks like you took your guard duties seriously. Thank you, little girl. Now, let's read what Mark has to say."

Paula changed into her pajamas and reclined on top of the covers. The faint scent of campfire clung to her hair as she examined the envelope. *If this says he's not coming back, am I going to lose it? Did I move here thinking he was my future? No. I moved here for me and to help Melinda out. Still, it would be nice if Mark was in the picture.*

Paula skimmed over the part she'd already read, slowing down when she arrived at the words:

I hope you know how much...I miss you. My sisters tease me about being a space cowboy. My mind's on you, and I guess I'm not very good at hiding that.

She clasped the letter to her chest as a frisson of happiness pulsed through her. Taking a cleansing breath, Paula read on.

> *One thing you should know is that I've never been good at dating. In my mind, I'm still the awkward kid with big ears. Dumbo, you know. And every time I think of your nickname for me, I blush. Then I laugh. Dr. Hunky, indeed. I still think our first planned outing should be to an eye doctor. I know a good one in the area...*

> *And then there's you. I'm not going to lie—I've been hooked on you since the first moment I saw you attempting to save that fish at the lake. Since then, I've been doing my best to reel you in. I think you're fintastic. Stop laughing. These are terrible puns.*

Paula giggled.

> *You're the most beautiful woman I've ever known. Inside and out. And I want to be wherever you are. For as long as you want. Even if your eyesight isn't all that great. Nobody's perfect, after all.*

> *So, is it wrong for me to say that I think I'm falling in love with you when we haven't even had a real date? I'm willing to risk it and ask forgiveness if it is. I love you, Paula Arnett. And, as soon as possible, I'm going to say those words in person—unless you'd rather I didn't. If it'd be awkward for*

you, then next time we're together, just blink twice, and I'll know to keep my mouth shut. But if you're ready to hear me say the words out loud, blink at least a dozen times. Really fast, so I don't have to actually count.

I should tell you that I've only ever said I love you to one other girl—Emily James. We were in fourth grade, and she threw her lunch tray at me as soon as the words were out of my mouth. I wish I'd come up with the blinking thing back then. She ruined my new yellow Converse sneakers. I think she had a ketchup fetish. Live some and learn some.

I'm hoping for dozens of blinks, but preparing for two, because really, I should ask you for a date first. And saying I love you doesn't commit us to anything past that moment. I figure we need to be together at least for another ten, maybe fifteen minutes, before declaring lifelong intentions. Still, I went ahead and wrote these words down. Now, no matter what, you'll always know how I feel.

Yours,

Dr. Dumbo

Holding onto the letter like a life preserver, Paula considered Mark's words. *It really is too soon for declarations of love. But then why does it feel so right?* She reread the letter again. Then a third time, laughing in all the same places. Growing warm from her head to her toes in others. Then her rational mind took over. *Am I ready to go where I think this is going? Cal was my first and my only. What if I get it all wrong? What if he doesn't like what he sees? I'm not twenty-something anymore. He's already declared his love, but what does he really know about me? What do I really know about him? I know he's kind and smart. And patient. Insanely patient. And, then there's the hunky part.*

"Well," she said to Star who, in response, opened one crystal blue eye. "At least I have a little time to think about my reaction and where this relationship is going. Am I going to blink twice or until he thinks I've lost my mind?"

Paula tried out two slow blinks, then a flurry of flutters while Star looked on in feline concern. Laughing, Paula said, "I promise you this feels as ridiculous as it looks, girl."

She replaced the letter inside the envelope and slipped it beneath her pillow, then crawled underneath the coverlet and turned off the lamp beside her bed. Star snuggled beneath Paula's chin, purring against her skin, and lulling her to sleep and into dreams of Mark's arms holding her close.

CHAPTER TWENTY-TWO

A crash startled Paula from a dream involving her rowing a boat across a deep blue lake as Mark sat reading a book in the stern. A giant fish rose between their boat and the shore and fell into the water with a resounding splash. She shook the cobwebs out of her head, wondering if the sound had been from the real world or the one in her dream. Beside her, Star hissed; her white fur splayed across her arched back as if she'd stuck a paw into an electrical outlet. Paula rubbed her eyes and squinted at her watch where it lay charging on the bedside table. "Two-fifteen. It's okay. Probably just a raccoon knocking over a trash can."

At the cat's insistence, Paula rose. She pulled on a robe. "Okay, okay. I'll go check." The sound of a woman screaming sent a chill down her spine, stopping Paula in her tracks. She grabbed her phone and ventured outside of her bedroom to find Jake standing at the main door. *At least I wasn't dreaming.* "Did you hear what I did?" she asked.

He removed an earbud from his ear. "What? Yes. The crash. Woke me up."

"And the scream? Did you hear that?"

His eyes narrowed. "A scream? I don't think so. Are you sure?"

Paula nodded and peeked through the curtains just as lights blazed on in the camper next to hers. The door to the neighboring camper opened and Ray emerged, his phone to his ear. Paula said, "Ray's outside. Stay here." She ventured into the night, joining Ray in the space between their campsites. "Did you hear—"

Ray held up a finger and responded to whoever was on the other end. "Yes. It sounded like a scream. First a crash, then about a minute later, maybe less, a scream. Just a moment." Putting a hand over the phone, he asked Paula, "Did you hear that, too?"

"I did. Is that 9-1-1 you're talking to?"

He handed Paula the phone. "Can you give the operator the address?"

Paula relayed the information and disconnected. She said, "They're sending an officer out to check. I thought I'd imagined the noises. I'm glad that someone else heard the scream. Especially since, Ja-, um nobody else seemed to." *Almost said Jake. That wouldn't do.*

"Kind of thought I might've imagined it, too."

"The sheriff's office is pretty quick to respond out here. I'm going to throw on some jeans and walk over to the office cabin to be there when they arrive. That is, if you'll come with me. I'm a little creeped out right now."

"Of course. I wouldn't want you to go alone. Not after that commotion. Hang on and I'll meet you back here in a few minutes."

Paula hurried into her camper where Jake sat nursing a Dr. Pepper. "I'm going to the office to wait on the sheriff. Ray's going with me. That'll give you an opportunity to dress and join us when the sheriff comes so nobody suspects you're staying here. Honestly, what would it hurt if they did, though?"

Jake ran a hand through his hair. "I just don't want everyone to know what a loser I am. It's bad enough to be one."

Paula sighed. "You're no loser. But the sheriff might want to know where your camper is and where you were when you heard the crash. Wouldn't it be easier to tell the truth?"

"Maybe... But maybe I'll just stay inside. I'll keep an eye on your place."

Paula shook her head and stepped inside her bedroom. As she dressed, she called through the bedroom door. "Okay. Do what you think is best. But if the sheriff asks if I was alone, I'll tell the truth."

When she left the motorhome, Ray was waiting at the end of her camper with a flashlight. "Were you talking to someone?" he asked.

"The cat. She worries." *Some truth teller I am.* She cast a look back at the camper where the curtains parted and closed again within seconds. *Maybe inviting Jake to stay with me wasn't such a great idea...*

CHAPTER TWENTY-THREE

Paula and Ray rounded the corner of the office and found a cruiser from the Big Lake County Sheriff's department idling in the parking lot. Paula hurried to intercept the officer. *I don't want him to wake up Melinda.* He exited the car and she approached him with her hand extended. "Sheriff Hill. I'm surprised that you answered the call instead of a deputy at this time of night."

The sheriff accepted her hand with a firm grasp. "Ms. Paula, good to see you; although, not necessarily at this time of the morning. My deputy had the night off and my other on-duty officer is tending to another call. So, you got me. Hope that's okay."

Paula said, "It's always good to have you pay us a visit. Thanks for the quick response."

The sheriff took a notebook from his pocket and flipped to a blank page. "Whatcha got going on out here?"

Paula introduced Ray, then they explained what they'd heard as the sheriff scribbled the details.

"A crash, followed by a scream. You said it sounded like a woman." At Paula's nod, he said, "And it woke you two up. Okay, let's go take a look." Sheriff Hill hoisted a flashlight to his shoulder and accompanied Paula and Ray through the campground.

Ray paused next to his camper. "I was in here. Paula was in the motorhome there."

"And where did the sounds seem to come from?"

Paula and Ray exchanged looks. She pointed into the darkness beyond the trees. "Hard to tell, but I'd say from the direction of the lake. Ray?"

"Maybe. I was thinking it was closer. Like between our campers."

"How would you describe the crash?" the sheriff asked.

"Like someone knocking over a trash can," Ray said.

Paula nodded. "That's what I thought, too. I told the cat not to worry, that it was just a raccoon looking for a meal. But then, the scream..." She hugged herself and shuddered.

"Stay here," Sheriff Hill said. He wandered into the brush behind Paula's camper and circled around Ray's. He kicked through fallen leaves as he made his way back to them. "Looks like some animal tracks, but hard to tell when they were made. Where are the nearest trash cans?"

Paula surveyed the area. "Each site has its own. Ours didn't look disturbed and I didn't notice any on the way to or from the office that looked like they'd been rattled around, but there are some nearer the lake." *Where I thought the sounds came from in the first place.*

"Can you show me?"

As Paula led the men to the small beach bordering Lake Toledo Bend, she said, "Look, that trash can is missing its lid, and there's garbage all around it."

"Ah, it does appear that an animal got into the trash. I'm surprised Ms. Arnett doesn't put chains on the lids."

Paula frowned and pointed to the other trash receptacle on the beach. "All the cans in the campground have lids chained on. Except this one. Maybe someone cut it off?"

Ray asked, "Why would anyone do that?"

"Weird. Maybe someone wanted us to think raccoons were to blame." Paula said.

The sheriff coughed. "I'm inclined to believe that this one didn't have a chain for some reason and that an animal took advantage of the opportunity."

Paula folded her arms across her chest. "But what about the scream?"

"Look at these tracks," the sheriff said, kneeling beside the trash can. "See these little tracks? Those are raccoon. But look here."

Paula and Ray knelt beside him. She looked to where the sheriff shined his flashlight and gasped. "That's a cat print. A big one."

"Probably a bobcat. Here's what I think happened. The raccoons were involved in raiding the garbage when along came a bobcat who took off after them."

"Still, the scream--" Paula said.

The sheriff removed his hat and offered Paula a smug grin. "Ms. Paula, a bobcat sounds a whole lot like a woman screaming."

"Oh? Huh."

Ray shook his head. "I should've known that. Now I feel silly for calling you out."

The sheriff waved him off and stood with a stretch. "You did the right thing. Y'all got something big happening out here this weekend?"

"Our class reunion," Paula said.

"Let's hope this is the only time you need my services. Glad it was easy to solve. If you need anything else, you know where to find me." The sheriff tipped his hat then left them outside their campers, his flashlight bobbing ahead of him through the early morning darkness.

"So," Ray said.

"So." Paula peered at her watch and yawned. "I'm going back to bed. Not sure I'll be able to sleep, but I'm going to give it a try."

"Goodnight, then."

"Or morning."

Paula tiptoed into her darkened trailer. She locked the door then looked for Jake. The curtain was gone, as were all his belongings. "Jake?" *It's as if he was never here.*

Star wound between her ankles until Paula took the hint and gathered her close for a hug. "Where'd he go, girl?"

Paula knocked on the bathroom door, opening it when there was no answer, then peeked inside her bedroom. "Wonder where he disappeared to?"

Star mewed and Paula snuggled her closer. "I'm just not going to worry over him. I'm sure he went to sleep in his van."

Paula parted the curtains and squinted across the space at Jake's vehicle. *No lights on. But then he wouldn't want anyone to know he was in there. I guess we'll find out in the morning.* She undressed and slipped beneath the covers, clutching Mark's letter for comfort. But it was the image of Jake's somber eyes that followed her into sleep.

CHAPTER TWENTY-FOUR

A strident meow woke Paula from troubled dreams of giant racoons chasing her through the campground. *It's hard to hide from a twelve-foot tall, four-legged creature with excellent night vision.*   Exhausted from running for her life in the nightmare, Paula rolled over, burying her face in the pillow. "Not yet, cat. Let me be. You're not going to starve."

Star took a strand of Paula's hair into her mouth and tugged. Paula winced. "Ow! Okay. Okay. I'm getting up. Sheesh."

The kitten adopted a ladylike pose, her bright blue eyes following Paula as she dumped a can of food into a bowl and refilled the cat's water dish. The cat sniffed and ignored the food, disappearing into the bedroom.

"Little stinker. You just wanted me to get up."

Paula washed the campfire smoke from her hair, dressed, and changed the sheets on her bed, careful to place Mark's letter in the top drawer of the nightstand. She half remembered seeing him in a dream—*the one bright spot from my restless night*.

Glancing at the messages on her phone, she pressed her lips together. *Nothing from Dr. Hunky*. She tapped a quick text message to him: *"Practiced my blinking skills."* Almost of their own volition, her fingers added a kiss emoji and she pressed enter. *Let him think about that one.* She tucked the phone into a pocket of her jeans and headed out in search of breakfast.

Classmates milled about the campground, chatting, and sampling the variety of pastries from a buffet table near the Clyde tree. Paula followed her nose to the coffee maker and helped herself to a cup. She took a sip and made her way to where Delbert and Melvin sat at a table on the other side of the campground.

"Morning, Goldilocks," Delbert said, raising his cup in a salute.

Paula kissed his cheek and joined the two men. "Morning, friends. How was your first night at the resort?"

Melvin stirred a packet of sugar into his cup. "Good. I slept better than I have in years. Sure wish Cal had told us he'd bought this place. We could've been staying here on our fishing trips instead of out at Buck Parker's campground. That place gives a whole 'nother meaning to the phrase 'roughing it.'"

Paula snorted. "You don't wish it nearly as much as I do." She blinked away a tear and breathed in the earthy aroma of coffee. "I still can't imagine why he didn't think he could tell me everything. About his marriage to Melinda. About helping her out when she was sick and the resort was failing."

Melvin's lips tightened into a thin line. "I guess we'll never know. But I suspect he was just trying to protect you."

"I hope you're right, but maybe he just didn't think I could handle it. Did he really think so little of me?"

Delbert rolled his eyes. "You were his world, Goldilocks. I wish you could've listened in on our conversations. He might not have thought you hung the moon, but he damned sure thought you kept it afloat."

"Amen," Melvin said.

Paula patted their hands. "Thank you for that."

They sat drinking their coffees while members of Paula's class flitted about as if in a modern dance recital. Groups formed, broke apart, and reformed. Hugs were exchanged and hands were clasped.   Cheeks kissed and eyebrows raised. Raucous laughter erupted from a nearby table and Paula looked up to find Jake in the middle of the hilarity. She caught his eye, and he offered a wan smile.

"How was your first night in your new home?" Delbert asked.

"Interesting," Paula said. "We had a bit of excitement."

Melvin's eyebrows shot up. "Really? What happened?"

Paula recounted the sheriff's theory of the marauding raccoons and the predatory bobcat, finishing with, "At least that's what Sheriff Hill believes took place."

Squinting, Delbert asked, "But you don't?"

With a shiver, Paula frowned. "I bought it at the time, but the more I think about it, I can't help thinking that he was wrong. I'm positive I heard a woman scream."

"We'll keep an ear out for anything that might relate to the events of last night," Delbert said.

Melvin nodded. "I have really big ears."

Paula laughed. "Maybe they'll come in handy. Thanks, guys. It's probably just my imagination getting away from me, but I won't have any peace until I know that all the women on the premises are accounted for."

Delbert downed the last of his coffee and stood. "Speaking of women, I'm going to go see if Sherry is up."

"I know Sue Ann is still huddled underneath the covers, but I'll go roust her out of bed," Melvin said.

"You two might get a better reception if you take your wives some coffee. Remind them about the lunch adventure, okay? Cassie and I are taking our cars and planning to leave at 11:15 or so."

Melvin doffed his cap. "We'll do that."

CHAPTER TWENTY-FIVE

As Delbert and Melvin sauntered off to coerce their wives into leaving the comfort of their beds, Paula took a deep breath and rose to make the rounds among her classmates. *Where to first?* A woman waved her over and Paula smiled. "You're Rudy's wife, right?"

Shaking hands with Paula, the woman said, "Yes. Deb Sinclair. Rudy was telling me that you're a part owner of this place. We really love the vintage feel of the resort, and the surrounding area is so pretty."

Paula beamed. "I'm glad you like it."

"I wondered if you're going to the lunch and plant thingie today. I forget what Rudy called it."

"Burke's Bouquets. I volunteered to drive a group over there. You're more than welcome to ride with me."

"Cool. Rudy's going to play golf and I didn't want to be stranded."

"We wouldn't dream of stranding you. Just warn Rudy that we're going to let you in on all his secrets."

Deb rubbed her hands together. "Oh, goodie. I know he couldn't have been nearly as perfect as a teenager as he'd have me believe."

"Oh, you have no idea. Just don't tell him you're riding with me. He might decide to ditch the golf game and run interference."

"Rudy? Miss a chance to play golf in October? No way. We live in North Dakota, and there's already snow on the ground, so he's chomping at the bit. He's been practicing faithfully since the reunion was scheduled."

Paula chuckled. "In that case, I'll dust off my memories and pull out the best ones for you."

"Thanks," Deb said. "I'm going to go look around the resort for a bit. Which way is the lake?"

Paula pointed her off in the right direction. "It's just beyond those trees." After Deb left, Paula sidled over to the group where Jake was talking music with Ray and Cassie.

"There's my partner in crime solving," Ray said. "I've just been telling Cassie and Jake about our early morning adventure."

Paula hugged him. "I'm so grateful that you heard it all, too, Ray. I'd never have been brave enough to walk to the office in the middle of the night by myself. And I'm still not so sure the sheriff was right about it being raccoons and a bobcat."

Cassie's eyes flitted between Paula and Ray. "Um, y'all were the only two that heard anything?"

Paula narrowed her eyes at Jake who ducked his head. "Apparently."

Barking out a cough, Cassie said, "Hey, Ray, can I ask you a question about tonight's talent show? I think I need a partner for my act."

Ray nodded. "Sure, but first, Jake, thanks for the use of your tools."

"You're welcome. Hope you found everything you needed."

As Cassie led Ray away, Paula grabbed Jake's arm, steering him to the picnic table beneath the Clyde tree. "Okay, mister. Where'd you go last night? I was worried."

Releasing a long breath, Jake sank onto the bench. "I'm sorry I worried you. I guess I just panicked. I bunked out in my van. It wasn't so bad."

"You just panicked? If it hadn't been for Ray's camper being so close to mine, I'd probably have huddled under the covers for the rest of the night, scared to death. I don't get it. What would it hurt if folks knew you were staying with me? This isn't the dark ages and we're adults, after all. It's absolutely nobody's business where anyone's staying. For all they know, we might have planned this. As *friends*."

Hanging his head, Jake mumbled something under his breath.

Exasperation flooded Paula's chest. "What was that you said?"

"I said I don't deserve a friend like you. I shouldn't have come."

Paula's shoulders sagged as she lowered herself onto the bench next to him. "Come here, you big dummy." She wrapped her arms around him. "I'm glad you're here. And you are my friend. Besides, if you weren't here, who'd help me prepare an act for tonight."

Jake ran a hand over his face. "You do have a point there."

"Why don't you move your stuff back into the motorhome? We can practice afterward."

"Oh, about that. I checked with the front desk. A room opened up this morning. Arlene had an emergency and had to go home early, so..."

Paula flashed back to the image of Arlene cozying up to Andy the night before. "Interesting. But, how fortunate for you."

"Yeah, it sure was."

"We still need to practice. Can we do that now?"

"Sure. I promise you'll be a huge hit, and it'll only take a few minutes for you to perfect your act."

Paula shook off the tingle of unease and tousled Jake's hair. "Okay, let's get it over with. I've got lots of other fish to fry today."

CHAPTER TWENTY-SIX

Still giggling from her practice time with Jake, Paula strolled to the office. *We might not win tonight, but he did create the perfect act for us.* She glanced at her watch. *Eleven on the dot. Plenty of time for some snooping before the group needs to leave for lunch.*

Inside the office, Paula helped herself to a cup of coffee and opened the computer. She scrolled through the records for departures where Arlene's stood out as the lone entry. *Arlene checked out this morning. Hm. Andy's still here. Maybe he'll have some insight into why she decided to leave.* She typed a note into her phone as a reminder.

Paula, engaged in scrolling through future reservations, jumped when a hand landed on her shoulder. "Whoa!" Coffee splashed on the counter, missing the computer keyboard by inches.

McKenzie said. "Oh, sorry. I didn't mean to scare you."

Paula wrapped McKenzie in a quick hug then grabbed a paper towel and began mopping up the mess. "It's so good to see you. Even if you did just age me by ten years."

Once the spill was cleaned up, Paula hugged McKenzie a second time then looked her up and down. "So..."

McKenzie beamed, twirling in a full circle for Paula's inspection. "Yes, I'm showing. But just barely. And I haven't had morning sickness in a while. I feel good."

Paula pulled up a second stool. "You look good, too. Sit. Your mom tells me that Delilah hasn't been informed yet."

Grabbing a book of sudoku puzzles from beneath the counter, McKenzie began doodling in earnest, her pencil scratching images in the margins. "No. Jeffries hasn't told his parents yet. He has his reasons, I know, but it's making it harder to be around her. I love Delilah, and I don't want her to figure things out before we have a chance to tell her our plans."

Resting her chin on her folded hands, Paula asked, "So, what reasons does Jeffries have?"

"He'll graduate in December, and he's gotten a couple of job offers, both in Dallas. He wants his folks to know he'll be able to take care of me and a baby, and he can't really do that until he starts earning a paycheck."

"I thought he wanted to come back to Happy Vale and work for his mom. That's what she's expecting, too, isn't it?"

McKenzie scribbled a sad face on the cover of her book and punctuated it with exclamation marks. "She is, but his mom can't pay him enough to support a family. And a big city restaurant can."

Paula groaned. "Oh. I hadn't thought about that." After a moment of thought, she raised a finger. "Okay, maybe I'm asking something that's totally out of line, and tell me to butt out if that's the case, but what about the inheritance you received from your paternal grandfather? Wouldn't that be more than enough to sustain you for a few years, until Jeffries can support you?"

McKenzie's feet swung back and forth underneath the counter. "He won't even think about using that money. Jeffries is so independent, and he wants to succeed without using my funds. I'm feeling more than a little guilty. Like I'm keeping Jeffries from his dreams."

Paula covered McKenzie's hand with hers. "I talked to Jeffries last night. His eyes lit up when he told me how beautiful you are. It's obvious that he's excited about you and the baby. You and that baby *are* his dreams. And you're going to have your esthetician's license soon, aren't you? Maybe he'll work in Dallas for a couple of years and then you two can move back here if you still want to. You can pursue your career and add your income to his. Dallas doesn't have to be forever."

A grin bloomed across McKenzie's face as she hugged Paula. "I hadn't thought of that. That's something to look forward to. I'm so glad you're going to be here to help Mom out. That was another of my worries."

"I'm so happy to be here. And please, try not to worry about anything." Paula glanced out the window where women were gathering in front of the office like colorful birds on a clothesline. She tapped on her watch. "Oh, I'd better get a move on. Those ladies out there are expecting me to take them to lunch. We'll talk later, okay?"

As Paula headed outside, she caught a glimpse of McKenzie doodling hearts and flowers in place of sad faces. *That's better.*

CHAPTER TWENTY-SEVEN

Paula skipped down the steps and into the middle of a heated conversation.   Weaving through the gathering of chattering women, she located Cassie and sidled up next to her. "What's up?"

Cassie pulled her aside. "Vanessa Allen said she's been looking for Arlene all morning. She's tried calling her, but the calls go straight to voicemail. When she went to Arlene's room to remind her about lunch, Jake Martinez was moving his stuff into the room that was Arlene's. He told her Arlene had checked out."

Scanning the assemblage, Paula nodded at a woman who stood wringing her hands in the middle of the pack of women. "Vanessa's the one with the spiky blonde hair, right? Wasn't she a brunette in high school?"

"Yep on both counts. Judy held up her picture at the meeting last night. She and Arlene were tight back in the day. Vanessa said she and Arlene had a beer last night before turning in and made plans to ride to lunch with us today."

Paula bit her lip. "Hm. Jake told me Arlene's room had opened up this morning. I wanted to talk to Melinda about

Arlene's departure, but McKenzie was manning the office. I'll touch base with Melinda when we get back this afternoon."

Cassie wiggled her eyebrows. "You going into amateur sleuth mode again?"

Paula dug a toe into the dirt. "No. Well, maybe."

"And what's up with Jake saying he didn't know anything about the disturbance in the campground last night?"

"So weird. I'll tell you all about it later. Let's get a move on. We're going to Mighty Fin's for lunch, right?"

Cassie signaled with a thumbs up. "We are. Want me to get everyone's attention?"

"Have at it. I'm going to run back to my campsite and drive my car up here. Can you finagle the seating arrangement so Vanessa is in my car?"

"No problem. I excel at finagling."

CHAPTER TWENTY-EIGHT

Paula returned to the parking lot to find that Cassie had managed to wrangle Vanessa into the group traveling in Paula's car, and for the distraught woman to ride shotgun. Giving an approving nod, Paula counted heads as she checked names off the sign-up list. *Nine total without Arlene. Sure hope she's okay.*

Paula followed Cassie's car onto the highway and considered the best way to get everyone talking. "Vanessa, Sue Ann, have y'all met Rudy's wife, Deb yet?"

The women introduced themselves and Sue Ann, in her slow as molasses drawl, asked, "Now, where do you all live?"

Deb said, "Rudy and I live outside of Bismarck, North Dakota."

"Oh, wow, I figured y'all were in Dallas. What do y'all do up there?"

"Rudy's the head of the performing arts program at the University of Mary, and I teach drama at a local high school. He likes to joke that I do all the hard work and, by the time students get to him, he can just coast."

Sue Ann asked, "How can you handle the winters up there? Melvin and I still live in Dempsey and, even there in the Texas panhandle, it gets too cold for me sometimes, and I know we don't come close to having the kind of winters y'all get."

Deb said, "I'm originally from North Dakota. All my family is there. I love the winters, but Rudy keeps hoping he'll find a position in the south—somewhere he can play golf year 'round. It's just that he has tenure now and it's hard to leave."

Paula said, "I imagine so. Vanessa, how about you... Vanessa?"

"What? Oh, sorry. I, um, I live between Dallas and Wylie."

"Oh, do you live near Arlene?" Sue Ann asked, giving Paula the sudden urge to kiss her.

Vanessa's voice trembled. "Yeah. We're about thirty minutes from each other. Y'all, I'm so worried. She wouldn't have left without telling me."

As they drove through Happy Vale, Paula noted the "Under New Management" banner fluttering over the IGA grocery store's sign. With a shudder, she recalled the harrowing events of the previous July when a pair of local teenagers, one of whom worked for his mother at the small grocery store, had terrorized female-owned businesses in the towns near Toledo Bend Reservoir, including the Happy Valley Resort. *I wonder where Rodney is now. Prison?*

Shaking off the memory, Paula said, "Vanessa, when did you last talk to Arlene?"

Vanessa shifted in her seat. "After the music wrapped up last night, I found her, um, she was visiting with Mr. Lewis. Y'all remember him?"

"Oh, yeah," Sue Ann said. "How could I forget?"

"Is he the cute curly-haired guy? The one with glasses?" Deb asked.

"That's him. We all had crushes on him in high school," Sue Ann said.

Vanessa twisted a strand of hair between her fingers. "But it was more than a crush with Arlene. She and Mr. Lewis had an affair."

CHAPTER TWENTY-NINE

Air whooshed from Paula's lungs as she absorbed the revelation.   From the backseat, Sue Ann uttered an incomprehensible sound. Forcing herself to concentrate on the road between Happy Vale and Hemphill, Paula glanced at Vanessa. "An affair? You're certain?"

Vanessa gave a decisive nod and Sue Ann said, "I'm having trouble believing this. Mr. Lewis and Arlene?"

Vanessa half-turned in her seat. "Believe it. Mr. Lewis asked me to take notes to Arlene between classes during study hall almost every day senior year. I know I shouldn't have read them, but I was a teenager and curious. Not to mention a little bit in love with him myself. Y'all, those notes were pretty graphic, at least to my seventeen-year-old mind. I knew it was wrong, and I told Arlene that she needed to end it. She claimed I was just jealous, and if I'm being honest, she wasn't exactly wrong about that. Mostly, though, I thought she might get expelled if anyone besides me found out. She was already in trouble over the drinking incident on the school trip."

Questions swirled through Paula's mind. "How long did this *affair* last?"

"Most of senior year. Arlene went to stay with her older sister in Dallas that summer and I guess that was the end of it—

We stopped speaking after I threatened to tell Mr. Landers, so I don't know that for certain, though."

"Why didn't you tell?" Deb asked.

Vanessa shrugged. "Because she was my closest friend. My only friend, really, and Mr. Lewis was the best teacher I'd ever had, I guess. I know I should have told, but I was trying to preserve some shred of a relationship with Arlene. In the end, it didn't matter because she stopped hanging out with me anyway."

"It's hard knowing the right thing to do when you're seventeen," Sue Ann said.

Deb barked out a laugh. "Hell, sometimes it's hard when you're in your thirties."

Recalling the emotions surrounding her budding relationship with Mark, Paula thought, *That's for sure.* As she maneuvered into the parking lot of Mighty Fin's Paula weighed her next question. "Obviously you two made up. What changed?"

Vanessa smoothed a shaky hand through her hair. "One day in the middle of my sophomore year of college, she contacted me out of the blue and told me I'd been right. That she should have listened to me. I don't know exactly what happened, but I have my suspicions."

Paula clicked off the ignition. *I wish I had another few miles alone with Vanessa.* "I'd be interested in hearing those," she said. "Later?"

Vanessa nodded. "For sure, but could y'all keep what I told you to yourselves? I shouldn't have said anything about their relationship. I'm just concerned about Arlene."

"My lips are sealed," Sue Ann said.

Deb said, "Buttoning my lips right now."

Patting Vanessa's hand, Paula said, "I promise I won't say a word."

CHAPTER THIRTY

Paula's mind buzzed with worry. She passed a basket of bread to her left and attempted to pay attention to the conversations swirling around her. The mural-like view of Lake Toledo Bend rippling in the sunlight outside the oversized picture window failed to bring her out of her reverie. *Arlene and Mr. Lewis? Senior year? He could've gone to jail for that!* She made eye contact with Vanessa, sensing that the other woman shared her feelings. *She is really struggling.*

As she picked at a salad, Paula half listened to the banter circulating the table while picturing Arlene and Andy, their heads almost touching in the moonlight. *Were they rekindling an old flame or arguing? Had he cupped her cheek in affection or in an attempt to control her? And why had Arlene left the resort this morning without telling Vanessa?*

Upon hearing her name, Paula startled. "Huh? What?"

Cassie made a goofy face at her from across the table. "Earth to Paula. Sherry asked you about the talent show tonight. What are you doing for your talent? Have you had an opportunity to practice?"

"I'll be ready, but I'm not telling a soul what my act is. What about you, Cassie? Since you aren't allowed to sing, whatever will you do?"

"I figured I'd do a little juggling," Cassie said.

Paula asked, "Oh? The naked kind?"

The group turned their attention to Cassie and Paula bowed out of the conversation as Cassie recounted her experiences of learning to juggle with the Natural Jugglers of America.

Deb's eyes widened. "So, you're telling us that these folks don't wear *any* clothing when they juggle?"

Cassie said, "Oh, there'll be an occasional hat and sometimes they might wear a scarf or socks, but otherwise, they don't wear a stitch."

Brushing a crumb from her blouse, Judy Sinclair peered at Cassie through her glasses. "I'm trying hard to imagine this type of performance. Or maybe I'm trying to shut out the images of such a thing. So, should we be prepared for nudity in your act tonight?"

Cassie smirked. "I'm not saying. Just bring plenty of dollar bills to vote for me. I'm in it to win it, you know."

Paula snorted. "I'm providing blindfolds for the crowd. Just in case."

"If I were sitting closer, I'd kick you," Cassie said.

Paula blew a kiss Cassie's way and motioned for their server to bring their checks. "I chose my seat wisely, then. Are y'all ready to move on to the nursery?"

CHAPTER THIRTY-ONE

On the way to Burke's Bouquets, Paula's thoughts continued to swirl around the mystery of Arlene's disappearance. *It's probably nothing, but what if she needs help?* As she asked herself the question, she pulled into the parking lot, stopping in front of the charming cottage-style gift shop. A sense of peace and well-being settled over her. *There's something about this place that comforts me.*

Strings of pumpkin-shaped lights twinkled from the windows as Shirley Burke emerged from the main door to walk a path lined with jack-o-lanterns carved in designs worthy of display in an art exhibit. *Shirley's the true work of art, though.* Like a vision from another realm, her welcoming arms opened wide.

Amused, Paula watched the reactions of the ladies in her car. From the passenger seat Vanessa gasped. Paula said, "That's Shirley, the owner and head gardener. She's pretty special."

The women spilled out of both cars, gravitating to Shirley like butterflies to a black-eyed Susan. Paula and Cassie held back, relishing the wide-eyed wonder on their friends' faces.

"Glad we decided to do this," Cassie said.

"After I returned to Dempsey, I thought maybe I'd just dreamed up how special our friend Shirley is. From the looks on everyone's faces, I realize it wasn't my imagination.   Even Vanessa appears more relaxed in her presence."

Shirley gestured to Paula and Cassie to join the group, then drew them each into a hug. "So good to see you both again," she said in her proper British accent.

"Thank you for having us," Paula said. "You've met the others already."

"I have, and if I understand correctly, most are women with whom you went to school. How lovely that you could all be together on this beautiful autumn day. Please, do come in and I'll show everyone around."

Deb snatched a wicker shopping basket from a stack beside the door. "I sure hope we're allowed to buy something today."

Shirley's lilting laughter filled the room. "Oh, I hope so, too."

With her guests trailing in her wake, Shirley escorted them through the gift shop, a work room, and on through a greenhouse where the visitors oohed and ahh-ed over the array of jewel-colored koi jostling for attention in the small creek that wound its way through the room. She opened a side door onto a cobblestone path. "Ladies, this way."

Paula noticed Vanessa holding back and matched her pace. "Hey, are you okay?"

Vanessa raised an eyebrow. "There's nothing I can do for Arlene right now. I've tried calling her phone and her husband's, too, several times. Nothing. If I don't hear anything back by tonight, I'll contact the sheriff's office. Doesn't she need to be missing for twenty-four hours? I think that's the rule."

"Oh, I believe that's a myth. How about we notify the local sheriff immediately? I have his number stored in my cell phone."

Vanessa clutched at Paula's hand. "Thank you, but let's wait until we get back to the resort. Maybe give her more of a chance to contact us?"

Extracting her hand from Vanessa's desperate grip, Paula asked, "Have you mentioned anything to Andy, er, Mr. Lewis, about her departure? Surely he'd be wondering where she's gone."

Vanessa's shoe disturbed a small stone that went skipping ahead of them on the walkway. "No. This is going to sound awful, but I kind of wonder if he's the reason she's gone missing. I mean, if she's truly missing, and he's had something to do with it, I sure don't want to put myself on his radar."

A jolt of shock shot through Paula. "Oh. I hadn't considered that. You don't have any real reason to believe he might want her gone, though, do you?"

With a shake of her head, Vanessa said, "No, I guess not. They just seemed so into each other earlier in the evening, and then, she backed way off. She wouldn't say why, so I was left to speculate."

As they drew near the other women clustered around Shirley in the formal garden, Paula stopped. "Earlier, you said you had your suspicions about the end of Arlene's affair with Mr. Lewis..."

"I did and do. I think Arlene was pregnant."

Paula's mouth went dry. Her next words came out in a croak. "Do you have any evidence to back up your suspicions?"

"Only a hunch, really. She went to stay with her sister in Dallas the day after graduation, supposedly to help said sister out by babysitting for her. The thing is, Arlene's sister has never lived in Dallas, and she didn't have kids at the time."

CHAPTER THIRTY-TWO

Paula had at least a dozen questions for Vanessa dancing on the tip of her tongue, but Shirley forestalled her asking them, calling out from the gazebo where a riot of autumn colors beckoned in the afternoon sun. Paula patted Vanessa's arm. "Can we pick this up later? We'd better catch up or Shirley will send her bees for us."

At Vanessa's look of alarm, Paula said, "No worries. They're mostly friendly bees."

As they joined the group, Shirley gestured to where a colorful mix of small containers, a couple of bags of potting soil, and a variety of plants sat on a long table. "I thought it might be fun for you each to take home a little souvenir of your visit to my shop. Mind, you don't have to, but for those who do I've selected some plants and decorative items to make them uniquely your own. Pull up a stool and feel free to let your creative juices flow."

The chatter of excited women jostling each other for a place at the table while wrangling for the container of their choice filled the garden.

Shirley said, "Cassie, would you mind getting everyone started? Paula, if you'd be so kind as to help me fetch some wine from the house, I'd appreciate it. I feel like a bit of wine does elevate the creative process."

Tapping Cassie's shoulder, Paula asked, "Save me a spot?"

"Sure, Goldilocks."

Paula hurried through the garden after Shirley, catching up to her outside one of the massive greenhouses.

Shirley paused beside the door, taking Paula's hand in hers. "How are you dear? I have missed having you and your friends around."

Paula squeezed Shirley's hand. "I'm doing well. I've just moved to Happy Vale, so I hope to see a great deal more of you from now on."

"Oh, I'm so glad to hear that. We'll have to let the bees know, won't we?"

Paula's eyebrows shot up. "Should I invite them to my housewarming party? I was going to invite you, but I'm not sure the bees would be all that popular with the other guests."

With a chuckle, Shirley led the way inside. "I shall attempt to keep it a secret from them, then."

They gathered bottles of white wine from a small refrigerator. "I have reds in the gazebo already, but these needed chilling." Shirley paused mid-step and took a long look at Paula. "Something's amiss. You don't seem yourself if you don't mind me saying so."

Paula sighed. "It's probably nothing, but one of the reunion guests checked out abruptly this morning without telling anyone she was leaving, and her friend, Vanessa--the one with the frosted-blonde hair--is concerned. The guest, Arlene, made plans to come with us today, and she's not answering her phone."

Shirley tugged on a delicate earlobe. "Hm. Normally I'd say it's nothing to worry about but trust your instincts. They've worked for you in the past."

Offering a sheepish grin, Paula said, "They've also led me down the wrong path a time or two, so..."

Shirley loaded a cooler with several bottles of white wine and hefted it. "I don't think this is too heavy."

Taking it from her, Paula's eyes went wide. "Almost, though."

Suppressing a laugh, Shirley said, "Then, I'll carry it out, if you'll get the tray of glasses and nibbles from the table just over there."

On their return to the garden, Shirley said, "I had a thought. Do you think I should read Vanessa's tarot cards while she's here? We might see if something pops up that would shed light on her friend's disappearance. I can pull a few of the other guests, as well, so she won't know I've singled her out."

Giving Shirley a sidelong look, Paula considered the idea. "It couldn't hurt, right?"

CHAPTER THIRTY-THREE

The conversation around the worktable was convivial as Paula wiggled onto the seat beside Cassie. She perused the remaining items available for her project, tapping a finger against her chin. "Hey, if no one's going to use that little red truck as a planter, I'd sure like to give it a go."

Sue Ann, her brow furrowed, passed the truck to Paula. "Aww. It looks a little like Cal's old Ford, doesn't it?"

Turning the planter in her hands, Paula blinked at the weight of unexpected tears welling up in her eyes. "Why, yes. Yes, it does."

She swiped at the tears with her sleeve as she added potting soil to the bed of the truck. *Hm. Which plants? Something I won't kill outright would be nice.*

From the corner of her eye Paula observed Shirley tapping Judy on the shoulder. Judy responded to Shirley's whispered words with a quizzical tilt of her head, then excused herself to follow their hostess. Paula kept her head down. *How silly is this that we're searching for answers in tarot cards. Still, Shirley's reading in July was right about me getting a kitten. And maybe about finding love, so...*

Cassie elbowed Paula. "Hey, you're being awfully quiet."

"Oh, I'm trying to decide which plants I won't kill within the next few days."

With a snort, Cassie said, "Sure you are. But, since that's your story, did you put some little rocks beneath the potting soil? That'll help whichever plant you choose drain more efficiently."

"*Now* you tell me." Paula dumped the soil into another container and gathered a handful of gravel.

From across the table, Deb waved an empty wine glass in Paula's direction. "You promised to tell me all about Rudy as a high schooler. Maybe while Judy's gone?"

"Oh, boy, where to start?" Paula asked.

Cassie cocked an eyebrow. "Maybe with the most epic, yet most awkward high school performance of *Romeo and Juliet* ever."

Deb rested her chin on steepled fingers. "Oh, do tell me more."

Sherry Derryberry stopped working on her planter and said, "It was only natural since Judy and Rudy were by far the best actors in our class that they were cast as the title characters."

"Oh dear," Deb said. "They've never mentioned that episode."

Cassie scooped some potting soil into her planter, mashing it down with her fingers. "I played Juliet's nurse. I saw the faces the two made at each other before each kiss. Masterful acting, really. Their lips never touched, but the audience couldn't tell that. And the twins' faces offstage? Hilarious. Fake retching. Middle fingers displayed."

"I can't imagine how they pulled that off. I'm a high school drama teacher. I'd never dream of casting siblings to play those roles."

"Dempsey high is a very small school. And male actors weren't exactly easy to come by," Paula said.

"Rudy capitalized on the whole thing when the two ran for class president against each other and one other kid. Rudy's campaign signs read, *I kissed my sister for you.*" Sherry said.

Paula chuckled. "And Judy's signs said, *I kissed my brother, so you don't have to.* The election ended in a tie between the two. Our class sponsors might have been a bit nervous about a runoff campaign, so they declared the two co-presidents."

Deb took a long drink of wine. She squinted at the hedgehog planter she had filled with a variety of succulents. "So that's how that came to be. Nothing those two have done would surprise me. I'll have to find a creative way to incorporate this new information. Hm. Does anyone think this hedgehog looks a little bit like my husband? Oh, here comes my sister-in-law. Don't tell her what you told me, okay?"

Amid a chorus of tipsy giggles, Judy returned to the table. Shirley tapped Vanessa on the shoulder and led her to the far side of the garden. Paula craned her neck to follow their progress until the two were out of sight. Pouring herself a glass of wine, she sidled over to Judy. "What do you think of our Shirley?" she asked.

"I think she's not quite of this world," Judy said. "Straight out of a fairy tale. Thanks for arranging this."

Paula waved her off. "Our pleasure."

Sue Ann asked, "Do y'all remember when we roomed together on the band trip? The one to Dallas?"

"Of course," Cassie said. "We stayed at the Adolphus hotel and ran around the halls all of Friday night with a group of guys from, where was it? Dumas? Mr. Weber was fit to be tied when he found out we'd gotten zero sleep the night before our performance."

"Even Paula came along for that adventure," Sherry said.

"I was just supervising, if you recall."

Deb patted Paula's hand. "I was always the unofficial student supervisor in my class, so I know exactly what you mean. After all, someone had to play the grownup in the group."

Paula nodded. "Exactly so. Heaven knows what trouble the girls might've gotten into without my over-developed sense of responsibility."

"Hey," Sherry said. "As I recall, our self-designated *supervisor* fell asleep during the performance of our final number on Saturday morning and snored during a rest."

Judy chortled. "I always wondered who that was. After all these years I now know it was Perfect Little Paula Purdy who blew that rest."

Eager to change the subject, Paula asked, "Remember when Jake published an article featuring dirty limericks in the school paper? Y'all should ask him how he got away with that little escapade."

Cassie flicked a clod of dirt at Paula. "Nice try, Goldilocks."

Paula ducked. "There once was a girl named Cassie, who tended to get a bit sassy..."

"Okay, okay. Let's not revisit that particular limerick," Cassie said.

Adding a small turtle figurine to her planter, Sherry asked, "What time are we getting back to the resort? Sue Ann and I need to put some finishing touches on our costumes for tonight's talent show."

Paula did a doubletake. "You have costumes?"

"Sure, doesn't everyone?" Sue Ann asked.

"Not me," Cassie said with a straight face, eliciting more tipsy giggles.

Judy shook a mocking finger at Cassie. "I'm not letting *my* husband watch *you* juggle in the nude."

"Remember, I'm supplying blindfolds," Paula said. "We have to even out the playing field for those of us not baring it all tonight."

Amid the merriment, Vanessa made her way back to the table without a word. As she resumed her place on a stool, her eyes were cast down and the hint of a frown hovered on her face. She remained silent as she worked on stuffing potting soil into her arrangement. From behind Vanessa, Shirley cocked her head at Paula, mouthing the words, "Very interesting."

Wiping her hands on her jeans, Paula stood. "Is there a place for me to wash up?"

"Of course," Shirley said. "Come with me."

Paula downed the remainder of her wine as Shirley led her to a wash station in the work room.

"I suppose I should've had you all do your projects in here, but it's so lovely outside I didn't want to waste the day."

Paula dried her hands and leaned against the basin. "You made an excellent executive decision. I'm dying to know what was so interesting about Vanessa's reading."

"Oh, I'm afraid I can't tell you that. Confidentiality, you know, but maybe she'll tell you herself."

"Hm. But you learned something?"

"Perhaps. Perhaps not. Again…" Shirley spread her hands. "I hope I am interpreting the reading wrong. I want to read up on the cards' meanings tonight. There very well could be something I've gotten wrong. It's all very nebulous, though. Not an exact science."

Paula let out a breath. "Okay. I understand, but you've really got my curiosity up. By the way, this was so nice. A great mixer for the women. Thank you for agreeing to host us."

"Absolutely my pleasure. I'm thinking about offering more events like this. I've been toying with the idea of providing gardening lessons, as well. Would you be interested?"

"I would. I need a hobby, and maybe I could plant a small garden at my campsite. Make it feel more like home."

At a rap on the door, they turned to find Cassie's dirt-stained face pressed against the glass. "Do come in," Shirley said.

"Everyone's about finished with their planters. Would it be okay if I directed them here to clean up?"

"Of course," their hostess said.

As Cassie left, Shirley caught Paula by the sleeve. Paula remained frozen in place as Shirley seemed to weigh her next words. With a decisive nod, Shirley said, "I believe there is one thing I can say about Vanessa's reading without violating her privacy. I'm more certain now than I was before that you should follow your instincts. Something has happened to your friend, Arlene. I'm almost positive. And perhaps others are in danger, as well. Please be careful, my friend."

CHAPTER THIRTY-FOUR

Paula shaded her eyes from the sun. A smile tugged at her lips as the women said their goodbyes to Shirley, exchanging hugs and promising to return if they were ever in the area. Only Vanessa remained aloof from the others, leaning against Paula's car. Paula joined Vanessa and unlocked the car door. "I noticed you were one of the lucky ones who had their cards read by Shirley. She read mine when I was here in July. Wasn't it fun?"

As Vanessa opened the door, she fumbled her planter, a terracotta pot adorned with depictions of ladybugs. Paula snagged the pot as it fell from Vanessa's hands.

"Whew. Thanks, Paula. Good save. What was it you asked?"

"About your tarot reading. Wasn't that why Shirley pulled you aside?"

"My tarot cards? Yeah. It was kind of fun."

Paula suppressed a frown. *She doesn't look like a woman who's had fun. Poor dear is worried sick.* "Let's get you back to the resort. We'll see if there's any word from Arlene, but I think for your peace of mind, we need to call the sheriff, regardless."

Vanessa slid into the passenger seat, gripping the planter with both hands. She cast a pointed look at the women gathered around Shirley. "Thank you. I'm not functioning very well. And

I think you're the only one besides me who's concerned." She looked at Paula through a sheen of unshed tears. "Arlene wasn't exactly loved and accepted by the girls at Dempsey High School, but then you probably knew that. But, if you'd practically grown up with her like I did—seen the kind of family life she had, you'd understand why she acted out in some inappropriate ways."

Paula thought back to Arlene's reputation as a girl who was up for anything. Images floated through her mind. *Arlene tangled up with a boy behind the football stadium. If I hadn't dropped my glove from the bleachers, I'd never have witnessed that little vignette. And that afternoon senior year when I was working as an aide in the school office, and a drunken Arlene stumbled into the room, her face streaked with tears. The secretary called her parents, but they never showed up. Mr. Landers had to take her home.* Coming out of her reverie, Paula said, "That's all history, though. Water under the old bridge. Arlene's a member of our class, and I'll be worried sick until we know she's okay."

Vanessa ducked her head and scratched a fingernail against her planter. "Thank you. That means so much."

Patting Vanessa's shoulder, Paula excused herself to say her goodbyes to Shirley. "Thank you again. I'll be in touch to invite you to my housewarming."

"I'm looking forward to that," Shirley said. She clutched Paula to her chest, and whispered in her ear, "But please remember what I said. Be alert. Trust your instincts."

CHAPTER THIRTY-FIVE

A wayward beanbag landed on the hood of Paula's car with a decisive thump as she maneuvered through the resort's parking lot. She hit the brakes and gave a rueful shake of her head. "Sorry about the sudden stop. Looks like the cornhole tournament's in full swing."

Deb snorted. "Be glad they're playing horseshoes *behind* the resort."

Chuckling, Paula said. "For sure. How about I let y'all out here?   There's no need for everyone to ride out to the campground with me."

As the car came to a stop, Ray jogged by to snag the beanbag. "Sorry about that. I'm not winning," he said with a hint of pride, then jogged away again.

Vanessa remained in the car while Deb and Sue Ann said their goodbyes.   "I'd like to come tour the motorhome everyone's talking about, if that's all right. Can I call the sheriff from out there?"

"Sure. Let's hope I can make it home without another beanbag attack. Or worse."

They parked without incident and Paula opened the door of the motorhome to find Star perched on the kitchen table.

Paula set her new plant on the narrow windowsill above the sink and turned her attention to the cat. "Somebody's hungry."

With an indignant meow, Star stalked away.

"She's adorable," Vanessa said.   She waved a hand around the room. "And so is your place. You're really going to live here?"

Opening a can of cat food, Paula said, "I am. At least for a while. Since my husband died, I'd just been rambling around my home in Dempsey. When Cassie moved to Dallas and didn't plan on coming back there, I knew I needed a new start in a new place." Star wound around her ankles.

"But why here of all places?"

Paula gestured for Vanessa to take a seat at the table. "Want something to drink? It's a long story, but the short version is that my husband bought this place shortly before he died. He didn't have an opportunity to tell me about his purchase before he passed away. When I found out he'd sold off most of our property to raise the necessary funds, I thought he had some secret life going on. Fortunately, that wasn't the case."

"Wow. So, *you* own the resort?"

Paula slid a bottle of water across the table. "For now, but Melinda and I are going to officially be partners going forward. We're signing the paperwork this weekend. She'll continue to manage it and I'll help out wherever she needs me."

"That's cool." After taking a sip, Vanessa checked her phone. "Still nothing from Arlene. And her husband hasn't responded to any of my texts. You're sure I should call the sheriff's office?"

"That seems like the logical next step. I'll call if you want. It won't hurt to put Arlene on their radar. You don't happen to know what kind of car she was driving do you? He'll want that information."

Vanessa nodded. "That, I do know."

Paula dialed the sheriff's office. When the dispatcher answered, Paula gave her name and asked if she could speak with Sheriff Hill.   After a minute spent listening to country western elevator music, she was relieved when the sheriff's gruff voice came on the line. She put her phone on speaker so Vanessa could join in.

"Ms. Paula. What's going on now? More unruly raccoons disturbing the peace?   Maybe you've decided to adopt the bobcat?"

Paula rolled her eyes eliciting a laugh from Vanessa. "No, sir, but we've got a possible missing person."

"Do tell."

"I've got you on speaker and the woman's closest friend, Vanessa Allen, is here with me. She can give you all the details."

As Vanessa responded to questions from the sheriff, Paula jotted down notes of her own:

- *Arlene and Vanessa shared a beer, maybe two, in Arlene's room around midnight on Friday.*

- *Arlene's clothes were hanging in the closet and her toiletries were scattered all over the counter when Vanessa was there.*

- *Arlene was excited about all the activities planned for the reunion, including the trip into Hemphill for lunch and a visit to a local nursery.*

- *She'd planned a big surprise for the talent show and couldn't wait to strut her stuff but wouldn't let Vanessa in on the secret.*

- *They'd said their 'goodnights' a little after one, planning to meet for breakfast, and*

Vanessa returned to her room on the other side of the resort.

- *Arlene didn't show up for breakfast and didn't answer a knock on the door.*

- *Vanessa wasn't too concerned until she went to remind Arlene about lunch and Jake Martinez had moved into Arlene's room. He said she'd checked out early that morning and Melinda Arnett let him know a room was available.*

Sheriff Hill asked, "Ms. Paula? You still there?"

"Yes. I was writing notes to study later."

"Why am I not surprised?"

Paula grimaced at the hint of amusement in his voice.

He asked, "Have you had an opportunity to look through the resort's records?"

"Just briefly, and the computer did show that Arlene checked out. I wanted to ask Melinda if she'd spoken to Arlene this morning, but she wasn't in the office, and I didn't have time to wait around. We had a trip to Burke's Bouquets planned and I didn't want to hold the group up since I was one of the drivers."

After mumbling a mild curse, the Sheriff said, "Pardon my French. I hate computers. Ms. Vanessa, what was your friend Arlene driving?"

"She had one of those SUVs. A Lexus. It's a deep red."

"Ma'am, I know it's a long shot, but I don't guess you know her license plate number?" he asked.

Vanessa smirked. "That I do know. It's HOTX3. Texas tags."

Paula added that to her notes. "Sheriff, do you think maybe that scream from last night wasn't a bobcat? That maybe that was Arlene?"

A sigh came through the speaker. "Ms. Paula, I think your imagination is running away with you. Why don't y'all talk to Ms. Melinda and get the information you wanted about Ms. Arlene's abrupt departure. I'll bet you a dollar to a donut that she had some emergency back at home and didn't have time to cross all her i's and dot all her t's."

Paula fought back a growl. "But you'll still put out an all-points bulletin on her car, won't you?"

"I've issued an alert. Fortunately, her car will be easy to spot if she's had car trouble or some such thing. But my money's on her being at home taking care of something or someone who needed her on short notice."

The women exchanged shrugs.

Paula said, "I sure hope you're right. Thank you. We'll talk to Melinda and if she has something relevant to add to the case, I'll get back to you."

"I'd expect nothing less from you, Ms. Paula."

CHAPTER THIRTY-SIX

The staccato clank of horseshoes against metal, punctuated by peals of laughter, rang from every corner of the campground as Paula and Vanessa made their way to the office. The women fielded invitations to join in the action. "I'm not any good at horseshoes," Paula said with a shake of her head.

Brad Higgenbotham elbowed his partner. "Neither is this old fart."

Paula scanned the crowd for anyone who might have information about Arlene. She nudged Vanessa. "Do you think maybe Jake spoke to Arlene before she left? I mean, since he was moving into her room."

"Hm. Maybe. Do you want to talk to him first?"

Paula slowed her pace as she considered the idea. "Let's hear what Melinda has to say. She could easily put an end to all our speculation."

"True."

Melinda glanced up from the computer as the women entered the office. "Hey, Paula, I have some mail for you. Just a sec."

"Thanks, but can I pick that up later?" Paula asked. "I was just wondering about one of the guests. Arlene Davis? Did you talk to her when she checked out this morning?"

Pursing her lips, Melinda said, "No, but she left a note taped to the door saying she needed to go home. She'd paid in advance, but the note said she didn't want a refund for the remainder of her stay, which was kind of odd. Why?"

Taking turns Paula and Vanessa brought Melinda up to speed with their concerns.

Melinda slid open a drawer in the counter. "I kept her note. Hm... Here it is."

Vanessa read over the ragged-edged note and handed it to Paula, who glanced at the curves of Arlene's handwriting. "This was taped to the door? Did you yank the tape off?"

"I guess I could've cut it off, but I didn't think about doing that until I'd already torn the paper. Her message is intact, though. Believe it or not, she used duct tape."

A chill coursed through Paula. *Duct tape. Just like Jake used. What was that he said? That a real man always has duct tape handy? That's bound to apply to most of the guys here. I wish I had a sample of her handwriting.*

"Paula, what's wrong? Melinda asked.

"Oh, nothing. I just had a random thought. Do you mind if I keep the note? I think the sheriff might be interested in seeing it."

"Certainly. Oh, that reminds me, I also got a call from Sheriff Hill this morning. He said he'd paid a visit out here last night."

Paula related the tale of the raccoons in the trash can and the sheriff's theory about a bobcat. "I just can't help but think that the scream I heard was human. But I'm not a country girl, so what do I know?"

Melinda pursed her lips as if in thought. "I hope the sheriff was right. I'd hate to think anyone was in trouble... Hey, look who just pulled in."

CHAPTER THIRTY-SEVEN

Paula tucked the note inside the pocket of her jeans. She hurried after Melinda down the steps of the cabin and through the narrow makeshift pathway between the cornhole games, leaving Vanessa behind. Dodging flying bean bags from both sides, they arrived at the door of a massive motorhome as Zeke Fitzgerald helped his bride, Martha, exit the conveyance. Melinda threw her arms around her mother while Paula kissed Zeke's grizzled cheek. "It's about time you two got here," Paula said.

Zeke ran a hand through his copper hair and winked. "I'd have been here two hours ago, but my wife had other ideas."

"Now, honey, don't go telling these girls about our conjugal stops along the way."

Covering her ears, Melinda said, "Mama, I swear..."

"No swearing, sweetheart. I taught you better than that."

Paula chuckled and kissed Martha. "Good to see married life hasn't changed you any, sweet lady."

Zeke wrapped an arm around Martha's waist. "I'll tell you ladies something; it's sure changed me. For the better."

Melinda ducked as a bean bag soared through the air, landing next to Paula. "Let's get you all out of harm's way," Melinda said.

"I'll stay here with Paula unless you need my help," Martha said. "We need to catch up."

Zeke pecked Martha's cheek. "I'll get us all situated. Visit all you want, my love." He helped Melinda into the passenger side and blew a kiss to Martha as he navigated the motorhome through the festivities.

Elbowing Martha, Paula smirked. *"My love."*

Martha beamed. "Isn't he wonderful?"

"He sure is. Come tell me all about your honeymoon in Paris."

Arm in arm, they strolled across the parking lot, all but oblivious to the activity going on around them as Martha regaled Paula with a verbal snapshot of dining in French restaurants and savoring crepes from a street vendor, visiting the Louvre and meeting sidewalk artists, exploring neighborhoods, and touring all the places Martha had always dreamed of seeing. "Paula, it was beautiful. The entire trip was better than I ever could have imagined. And, you know how you always hear how rude Parisians are? It's just not true. We met such kind people there."

"I'm sure that had a lot to do with who you and Zeke are. In my experience, lovely people tend to meet other lovely people."

They climbed the steps to the office and met Cassie, who stood with her arms crossed over her chest. Her toes tapped out an impatient rhythm. "Martha Fitzgerald, I thought you'd never arrive."

Paula stepped away, taking a seat in a rocking chair, as Cassie and Martha caught up on each other's adventures. Listening to their chatter, she scanned the parking lot, searching for Vanessa. *I hate that I left her so abruptly.* She caught a glimpse of Vanessa leaning against a giant oak, watching a cornhole match involving Ray and Jake. Paula pulled Arlene's note from her pocket. *What if Arlene didn't leave this message? What if someone who routinely uses duct tape to solve his problems did? Someone like Jake... But why? For a room? No, that'd be silly. Sheriff Hill knows what he's talking about. I'm letting my imagination run wild... Still, I should tell him about the note.*

CHAPTER THIRTY-EIGHT

Ducking inside the office, Paula made a call to the sheriff, leaving a message with the dispatcher. Once she'd disconnected the call she sat, drumming her fingers on the counter. *I wonder if Melinda threw the duct tape away. It's worth a look.*

The small trash can behind the counter was brimming with scraps of paper, Styrofoam coffee cups, and a copy of the local newspaper. Paula knelt on the floor to look through the day's castoffs, rescuing coupons for coffee filters and cat food from the stash. The duct tape, adhered to the bottom of the plastic trash bag, tore the bag as Paula ripped the tape off. "Dang, I'll need to get a new trash bag."

"Are you reduced to dumpster diving now?" Melinda asked, startling Paula.

Paula jumped. "Oh! That is what it looks like, isn't it? I thought I'd see if the duct tape from Arlene's note was in here. When I removed it, I tore a hole in the plastic bag."

"Here, I'll get a new one and a baggie for you to put the tape in; although, it's just going to stick to that, too. How about we stick the tape onto a piece of cardboard?"

"That'll do."

When Melinda returned, Paula laid the tape on the cardboard, careful to touch only the edges.

Holding open the baggie for Paula to drop the potential evidence into, Melinda said, "You're being so cautious, but you know I've had my fingers all over that tape. If anything bad has happened to your friend, I'm liable to be the one arrested."

Paula narrowed her eyes. "Let's hope this is just a case of my imagination on overdrive, but young woman, where were you last night?"

Melinda's hands flew to her hips. "Officer Paula, I'll have you know that I do have an alibi, and a gorgeous one, at that."

The realization that the alibi came in the form of Cassie brought an unexpected blush to Paula's cheeks. "That's good. Not, of course, that I really thought you were guilty of anything, and you know, um, well, it's always good to have an alibi."

With a rueful chuckle, Melinda patted Paula's hand. "I didn't mean to conjure up any salacious images. And you can rest easy, we watched old movies and ate popcorn until just after midnight. We thought about calling you, but it was kind of late when we started watching. No hanky panky involved."

"It's okay. I guess I still have some hang-ups about, you know. You and Cassie...You two have every right to some hanky panky."

Melinda bumped Paula's hip. "I'd be surprised if you didn't have some hang-ups. C'mon, let's put this in the safe. Maybe the note, too?"

Paula plucked the note from her back pocket. "Good idea. Separate baggies, though, okay?"

"We either need to limit your access to crime dramas or enroll you in the police academy."

A chuckle escaped Paula's lips. "The first one's not going to happen, and I might be a little past the age of the average rookie police officer, so we need a third option."

Laying a hand on Paula's shoulder, Melinda said, "I'll put my thinking hat on. Oh, before you leave, I've got your mail under here somewhere and that hardware for hanging your painting of the lake... Ah, there it is."

CHAPTER THIRTY-NINE

Paula browsed through the mail, tossing everything into the trash bin except a bill for her annual subscription to the *Dempsey Times*. She tucked that envelope into her pocket as a line of cars pulled into the parking area, stopping outside the ring of cornhole enthusiasts. "That must be the golfers returning from their rounds," she said. "I'd better go make the circuit and see what's going on before I head back to my campsite. I have a few final touches to make in my act for the talent show."

Melinda snorted. "Oh, that's all Cassie could talk about last night."

Squinting her eyes, Paula focused on Melinda. "She is keeping her clothes on for her performance, right?"

Melinda settled onto a stool behind the counter and shrugged. "She'd better, but who knows with that one? So, what's your talent?"

Paula fluttered her eyelashes. "I'll never tell. You'll just have to be there."

"I wasn't sure if outsiders would be welcome. I mean, it is *your* class reunion and all."

"Neither Cassie nor I brought guests, so you can be hers, and if Martha and Zeke want to come, they'll be mine, not that anyone would mind if you were there anyway."

The phone rang and Melinda answered with a cheery, "Happy Valley Motor Inn and Resort. Melinda speaking. How may I help you?"

Paula wiggled her fingers in a goodbye and slipped outside where the finals of the cornhole tournament were in full swing. Slipping between taller spectators she made a place for herself near the action next to Ray. "You didn't make the finals?" she asked between throws.

Ray ducked his head. "The bean bag that landed on your car was one of my better attempts, so no. But Jake did."

"Who's his partner?"

Pointing to the far side of the play area, Ray said, "Larry Jones. They're playing against Seth and Bobby Joe Cagle. Band Geeks versus Jocks. A match for the ages."

"I believe I'll root for the Band Geeks," Paula said.

"We geeks have to stick together. Hey, I understand Arlene checked out this morning. Kind of unexpectedly I hear."

Paula nodded. "Yeah. How'd you know?"

"Vanessa told me. She asked if I'd talked to her this morning."

"Were you and Arlene close?"

Crimson spots bloomed on Ray's face. "At times."

An image so sharp it might have been from a Technicolor movie popped into Paula's mind. *Arlene wrapped around a tall, dark-haired boy behind the bleachers. Heavy breathing. Moaning, even. Oh, my. That was Ray. The same Ray who'd been out and about at two a.m. with me on Friday night.*

Paula hoped her face didn't reveal her thoughts. "Oh?"

"Yeah. I have some really good, yet really awkward memories of those days."

A cheer went up from the spectators, and Paula forced herself to pay attention. "Darn it. Looks like the Jocks won."

"Oh, that's just game one. They've got to win two games out of three. I'm still counting on the Geeks."

"Yeah. Me, too," Paula said. "So *did* you talk to Arlene before she left?"

"Naw. She barely gave me a nod yesterday. She was fixated on Mr. Lewis. Just like she was senior year."

"So, were you jealous of him?"

"Hell, yes. But then all the guys were. Except maybe Seth because he had Cassie. And you can't tell me you didn't have a thing for Andy."

The emphasis Ray put on Mr. Lewis's name irked her, but Paula was unable to pinpoint why. *I did have a thing for him...but I wasn't letting him grope me behind the stadium.* Paula surveyed the grounds. "Where is Mr. Lewis anyway? I'd like to ask him if he spoke with Arlene, but I haven't seen him today."

Ray shrugged. "He might've gone to play golf. Check with Rudy. He'll know."

CHAPTER FORTY

Paula discovered Rudy holding court in the hospitality room where the golfers gathered to relive their exploits on the links. She accepted a Shiner from one of the men with a nod of thanks and listened in on Rudy's recounting of a three-foot breaking putt he missed by a mere millimeter. Paula waited for Rudy to finish his story to a chorus of commiserating groans, then crooked a finger to get his attention. "Sorry, y'all. I need Rudy for a second."

Rudy excused himself and followed Paula outside. "Hey, everything okay?"

Paula said, "I just wondered if Mr. Lewis played golf with you all today. I wanted to ask him something."

Scratching his head, Rudy said, "No, but yesterday he was gathering a group to go with him to NASA's Columbia museum in Hemphill. Let me think who signed up. Oh, Jerry Pagac was one, and David Wayne, I think. I haven't seen either of them since we got back from the golf course, so maybe they're still in Hemphill."

Paula sighed. "Okay. Thanks."

A cheer went up from the cornhole spectators and Rudy scanned the parking lot with humor sparkling in his eyes. "Sure looks like everyone's having a good time."

Paula surveyed the area. The golfers were enjoying their replay of the day's match over beer and bourbon. The cornhole tournament appeared to be a rousing success. The clank and clang of horseshoes, along with the occasional curse, emanated from the campground. "Yeah. You're right." *Maybe I'm making too big a deal out of Arlene's early checkout. I'd like to enjoy my reunion, too.*

Rudy asked, "Is your act ready for tonight? From the chatter that's going around, it's sure to be an epic evening."

"Oh, I'm ready. I'm really hoping to win one of those speech trophies of yours."

Rudy threw his head back and laughed. "That's the spirit. I'd better get back in there to square up on all my bets and make sure they're keeping their stories straight."

"If golfers are anything like fishermen, I wouldn't count on it."

As Paula left Rudy, she resolved to focus on having fun. She inhaled a cleansing breath and exhaled for a count of ten as she jogged over to the cornhole tournament, arriving in time to cheer for the Geeks as they took the second game.

The third game drew most of the class to spectate. Newcomers jockeyed for position as the Geeks battled the Jocks to a tie at the end of the game.

"Now what?" Paula asked as Cassie joined her.

"They'll play until one team outscores the other."

Tensions increased as, round after round, neither team could gain an advantage. Paula kept a close eye on Seth who might as well have been engaged in quarterbacking the NFL championship game, so focused was his attention on the goal. His eyes narrowed and his jaw tightened as he let the beanbag fly.

For his part, Jake maintained a cool detachment, launching one bag after another with a casual air, to all appearances unaware that anything was on the line. In the tenth round, Bobby Joe overshot the hole on his throw allowing Larry

Jones to sink the winning point. Groans went up from half the crowd in counterpoint to the cheers from the other half as the Geeks claimed the trophy.

Money changed hands among Paula's classmates, and she chastised herself. "Darn, I should have placed a bet on the Geeks."

Cassie waved a five-dollar bill under Paula's nose. "I'm rich. Rich, I tell you."

Paula rolled her eyes and elbowed Cassie as the contestants slapped each other's backs and peppered one another with rounds of good-natured ribbing. "I was worried Seth might not lose with grace. Maybe he's not as volatile as I thought."

"I meant to tell you that he apologized to me earlier today. Said he felt like an ass for behaving the way he did yesterday. I think maybe we can be friends now."

"Good. I hope he meant it," Paula said. "Hey, I need to go check on the cat and practice my act a little. Want to come along?"

Cassie paused for a moment, then shook her head. "I think I need to work on polishing my act, too. I'm going to pester Zeke for some suggestions. It's not easy perfecting a juggling act inside a motel room, you know."

"Just keep your clothes on, okay? I'm not sure this class is ready for nude juggling."

With a wink and a giggle, Cassie wiggled her hips and sauntered away leaving Paula to wonder just how crazy the Anything But Talent Show was going to be.

CHAPTER FORTY-ONE

Alone for the first time since leaving her motorhome earlier that day, Paula scrolled through her texts hoping for a word or two, even an emoji, from her favorite doctor. *Hmm. Nothing from Mark. Maybe he regrets sending me that letter. Maybe I practiced all that blinking for nothing. Maybe he's ravishing his dad's cute, young nurse, even as I waste away... Or maybe I think too much.* She shook off the negative thoughts, replacing them with a memory of the kiss she and Mark had shared not far from where she was standing at that moment. *Mm, that's better.*

Her feeling of bliss evaporated into thin air in the space of a breath. *What the...? Why's the door to my motorhome open?* She caught the door as it swung back and forth on a lazy trajectory. *I'm sure I latched it when I left, but then...* Her heart clenched. *Where's my Star?* "Star? Star, come!"

Clasping her hands to her chest, Paula stood on the bottom step and peered around the corner into the motorhome. *Oh, mercy! What in the world?* Like a magnet, her eyes were drawn to her belongings scattered across the floor. Her breath caught in her throat at the sight of the contents of a file scattered across the counter. A pair of jeans, pockets turned inside out, had been thrown onto the bench where Jake had slept. The few pots and pans she owned, minus their lids, were turned upside down on the table.

The cold hand of shock pushed Paula to the floor where she began frantically gathering her clothes into her lap. *Wait! This is a crime scene.* Standing, she backed away. *So, what do I do next?*

A tiny meow sounded from the bathroom. Paula slumped against the wall as tears welled in her eyes. She opened the door, scooping Star into her arms. She sobbed into the cat's fur. "Oh, sweetie! Thank goodness you're here."

Star purred as Paula snuggled her close. Paula asked, "Who did this girl? If only you could talk..."

Paula kissed the top of Star's head, then pivoted and faced the mess in her bedroom where drawers gaped open exposing underwear and nightgowns. She grasped at her left hand, feeling the comforting presence of her wedding rings. A new sob escaped her lips. *Oh Cal, I'm so glad I've never taken my rings off. What if someone had taken these?*

Wriggling out of Paula's grasp, Star jumped onto the bed where Mark's letter lay atop a jumble of bedclothes. Paula breathed a sigh of relief and folded the letter into neat thirds, then tucked it inside her back pocket.

A new fear rocked her. *My photo albums!* With frantic fingers, she opened a storage cubby and blew out a breath. *All three, present and accounted for.* She lifted one album, opening it to a photo of her mother holding baby Paula on her hip. "Lord, thank you for keeping these safe."

Okay, who was in here and what were they searching for? Her hands trembled as she dialed the sheriff's office and left a new message. *Sheriff Hill is going to think I'm nothing but trouble.* She attempted to slow her breathing as she loaded Star into her carrier, locked the door behind her, then headed out in search of Cassie.

CHAPTER FORTY-TWO

Hurrying through the campground on her way to Zeke and Martha's motorhome, Paula carried a mewling Star. Patting the top of the carrier, Paula said, "Shh, girl, you're safe. We're both safe." Star curled into a ball and grew silent. *Wish I could do the same.*

Hearing Zeke's signature guffaw as she approached the motorhome, Paula slowed her pace and steadied her breathing. *No need to upset anyone.*

Arms trembling, she shifted the weight of Star's carrier. "Hey y'all. "Everybody decent?" *Whew, breathe, girl.*

"Hold on a sec," Cassie said. "I don't want you to see my costume."

Paula closed her eyes. "Sure." *How do I tell them without breaking into tears?*

Cassie said, "Okay. The coast is clear. You can come on over."

Releasing a shaky breath, Paula peered around the corner of the motorhome. She forced a lightness into her voice and plastered on a smile. "You're all dressed, then?"

Zeke laughed again and pulled up a chair for her. "Come on, Ms. Paula. Sit a spell. No one's parading around in their birthday suits. At least not yet. Martha's gone in to get us something to drink."

Paula clutched Star's carrier to her chest, as she took a seat. *Am I the only one who knows my knees are knocking?* "A drink sounds good."

"What's up?" Cassie nodded at the cat and smirked. "You taking the cat for a walk?"

Paula's hands tightened on the carrier. She gulped. "Sort of. I didn't know what else to do. My motorhome was broken into this afternoon. I called the sheriff, but he hasn't gotten back to me yet, and...all I could think of was finding you." The dam holding back her tears burst as Paula buried her head in her hands.

Hurrying to Paula's side, Cassie wrapped her arms around Paula's shoulders. "Oh, Goldilocks, I'm so sorry."

Zeke came out of his chair, his hands balled into fists at his side as he paced. "Do you have any idea who might have done this, 'cause I'm ready to kick some ass. What kind of coward breaks into a lady's home like that?"

Paula shrugged. "I don't know. I don't have anything anyone would want. Do I?" She swiped at her eyes. "Sorry, I tried my best not to cry, but..."

Martha emerged from the motorhome, took one look at Paula, and passed a tray of iced teas to Zeke. She knelt beside Paula. "There, there. Zeke honey, I think Paula needs something stronger than tea. Break out the bourbon."

Cassie brushed a tear from her own eye. "Can you tell us what happened?"

After a steadying breath, Paula said, "I'll try. I, um, I came home and noticed the door was open. I'm certain I didn't leave it that way, but I can't remember if I'd locked it or not. I've been pretty casual about that. I mean, we're all friends out here, right? So I wasn't all that concerned with locking up."

Paula accepted a glass filled with amber liquid from Zeke. Taking a hasty swig, she sputtered as Martha patted her back.

"Sip on that. Don't chug it," Zeke said.

Her eyes watering, Paula took a second drink. She held the bourbon in her mouth, then let its warmth slide down her throat. *Oh, that's better.*

"Anyway, when I went inside, it was obvious someone had been there. My pots and pans, and all my clothes were scattered everywhere, and I couldn't find…"

Paula's voice caught in her throat. "I couldn't find Star. I thought maybe she'd gotten out and I couldn't stand the thought of losing my little girl, but whoever broke in must have stuck her in the bathroom. Thank goodness for that, right?"

Zeke offered her a box of tissues.

Paula dabbed at her eyes then realized her hands had steadied. *Must be the bourbon at work.* She took another drink. As she savored the oaky flavor, her eyes grew wide. Paula gasped. "Oh mercy! Cassie, what if all this is related to what went down last night and Arlene's disappearance?"

Cassie's eyes bulged. "Could it be?"

"You two gonna tell us what you're talking about?" Zeke asked.

Paula looked from Martha to Zeke. "In the middle of the night a crash woke me. I got up to look out the window, thinking it might have been raccoons or some other wildlife. But then there was this scream—high pitched, like a woman's."

Martha clasped her hands to her chest. "Oh dear!"

Paula shuddered. "I know, right? Then, a light came on in the neighboring camper. That's my friend, Ray's trailer, so I went out to compare notes with him. We called the sheriff, who came out to investigate. He agreed it was probably raccoons but deduced that the scream was likely that of a bobcat. I'm not saying I don't trust his judgement, but it sure sounded like a woman's scream to me."

"Let me refill that glass," Zeke said.

Paula said, "Thank you, but I'd better not drink any more right now." She pressed the tumbler into Zeke's hands. "Then this morning, we learned that one of our classmates, Arlene, checked out unexpectedly. Her best friend has reason to believe that something happened to her. Maybe this break-in could be related in some way. What if someone's after me? Now I sound paranoid."

Settling back in his chair, Zeke said, "You know, just because you're paranoid doesn't necessarily mean they're not out to get you. What if someone thinks you witnessed some illegal activity last night? Something that might incriminate them. Have you told anyone else that you think this Arlene might have come to some harm?"

"Besides Cassie? Well, her friend, Vanessa, but she's the one who brought it up to me in the first place. And Shirley Burke, but she's the least likely burglar I can imagine."

Martha poured a glass of bourbon for herself. "Tonight, you stay with us. I don't want to think about you all alone in your camper."

Paula shook her head. "Thanks for the offer, but I can't do that. Star's litter box and all... It'd just be a mess. After the sheriff takes a look, I'm sure I'll be just fine."

"I'll stay with her tonight," Cassie said. "And Paula Jean Arnett, don't you dare tell me no."

Paula opened her mouth to protest. *It won't do a bit of good to argue with her*. She raised her hands. "Okay. I probably will sleep better having you there. But I'm not going to let anyone run me out of my own home."

Paula's phone buzzed. "It's the sheriff's office." She wandered to the far side of the motorhome to take the call.

"Ms. Paula? Sheriff Hill here. I'm sending Eugene out to look at your camper. I'm out on a call, but I want someone to make sure it's safe for you to stay there. I trust you to know if that's the case."

Paula blinked away new tears. "Thank you so much. I just feel so vulnerable. The thought of someone touching my stuff, going through my home without my permission, is overwhelming. Whatever anyone might have been looking for, though, they had to be disappointed. No money, no jewelry, no drugs."

Sheriff Hill said, "Can you think of anyone who might want to frighten or intimidate you? It could be that was their intent."

Unable to keep the quaver from her voice, Paula said, "I know you think my imagination has been running away with me, but what if the break-in is connected to the ruckus we had out here last night, and what if the ruckus is connected to Arlene's disappearance? Couldn't that be a possibility?"

With a sigh, the sheriff said, "Pay attention to what the deputy has to say. I'm not ruling out your instincts about last night's occurrences anymore, though. There are too many coincidences for my liking. It's too bad you don't have a man about the house."

"You remember my friend, Cassie, right? She promised to stay with me tonight."

"I'd still rather you had a male around."

For the first time since discovering her home in shambles, Paula's lips curved into a genuine smile. "Well, you've never seen Cassie Campbell wield a baseball bat."

Sheriff Hill laughed. "That's true. I reckon I'll have to use my imagination. Ms. Paula, I'll touch base with you tomorrow unless we discover something before then. Stay safe now. That's an order."

"Yes, sir."

CHAPTER FORTY-THREE

Paula tripped over a fallen branch on the way to her home. Cassie steadied her, while Zeke moved the branch into the underbrush. Pushing her hair back, Paula said, "Thank you. And thank you both for coming with me. I know I interrupted your rehearsal, and as soon as Eugene gets here, y'all can leave me in his hands."

Cassie hitched up her pants and drawled, "Whoa there, little missy. A little lady like yourself needs protection and we're the ones who can provide it."

A tremulous smile hovered on Paula's lips. "Very funny."

"Martha would tan my hide if anything happened to one of you ladies." Zeke grimaced. "I mean women. Sorry, Cassie. Old habits die hard."

Cassie slipped an arm around his shoulder. "For some reason, it doesn't bother me so much when you call me a lady. Just don't let anyone else get the idea that it's okay."

Melinda met them as they approached Paula's campsite. "There you are! I've been worried sick. Deputy Eugene called. Said he was coming out to investigate a break-in. A break-in of all things! What in the world is going on?"

Paula switched the cat's carrier to the opposite hand. She shivered despite the warmth of the afternoon sun. "I'm sorry I didn't call you before you heard the news from Eugene. I should have, but I wasn't thinking clearly."

"Oh, sweetie!" Melinda pulled Paula into a hug. "I'm not upset with you, but I don't even want to think what might have happened if you'd walked in on the burglar."

The color drained from Paula's face. "Mercy. I hadn't really considered that."

Zeke took the cat's carrier from Paula and unfolded a chair. "Sit. Before you fall."

Sinking into the chair, Paula nodded her thanks. "I got really lucky, didn't I?"

Cassie patted Melinda's arm. "I'm staying out here with her tonight. She won't be alone."

Blowing out a breath, Melinda nodded. "Sorry I conjured up such a scary image, Paula. Still, why don't you and Cassie stay with me instead?"

Paula said, "This is my home now, and I'm not letting anyone run me off." *Even if all I really want to do right now is find a corner and hide.*

Hearing a rustling from beyond her campsite, Paula stood and captured Cassie's arm in a vise-like grip.

"Ow," Cassie said. "It's just Ellie and Eugene."

Paula let out a shaky breath. "Right." *Get it together!*

Offering a grim smile, Ellie said, "I'm sorry to hear what happened, but you're in good hands with my, er, with Eugene. I'm going to get on back to the office now."

Noting the deep shade of pink spreading across Eugene's face, Paula hid her amusement behind a cough. "Thank you."

"Ms. Paula, what do we have going on here?" Eugene asked.

Paula waved at her home and unlocked the door, allowing it to swing open. "I came home to this sight after hanging out with my friends for a while."

"Hm," Eugene said. "Why don't you stay out here while I look around? Then I'll have you come in and we'll determine if anything is missing."

Paula nodded and began wringing her hands when Eugene disappeared into the camper.

Cassie smirked. "I hate to be the one to point this out, but you're fidgeting."

Trust Cassie to make me smile at a time like this. Paula grinned and shoved her hands into her pockets. "And now I'm not." *What's taking Eugene so long?* When the deputy peered around the door, Paula glanced at her watch. *Only fifteen minutes? How can that be?*

Cassie slipped her arms around Paula, and said, "We'll stay out here with Star, but call us if you need us."

Paula gulped. "I will."

Eugene stood beside a jumble of clothing. "So, Ms. Paula. Can you give me an idea of when this might have occurred? And, just for the record, none of this was scattered about when you left your trailer this morning, correct?"

Paula's knees wobbled as she joined him. "I'm not a great housekeeper, but I assure you none of my clothes were on the floor and all my cookware was stashed in the cabinets. I've only spent one night in this place, so it was still very organized." She paused, fighting against the tremor in her voice. "Everything was neat as a pin when I left here a couple of hours ago."

Eugene scribbled a few words and perused the room. "We'll probably need to get your fingerprints so we can eliminate them when we run a check. I did pull a few prints from the drawer handles and the closet." He nibbled on the end of his pencil. "Can you think of anything a burglar might've been looking for?"

Placing her hands on her hips, she surveyed the place section by section. The watercolor of the two fishermen Melinda had given her was likely the most valuable thing she owned besides her wedding and engagement rings, and those were accounted for. She shook her head. "I can't imagine what they thought I might have of value."

"Did you take anything from the room before you called the sheriff's office?"

"Just this letter from Mark, er, Dr. Fields." She dug the letter out of her pocket and handed it over with quivering fingers. "It was tossed onto a pile of clothing."

"And where was the letter when you left earlier?"

Paula pointed to the bedside table. "In that drawer."

Eugene jotted a note in his book. "I took prints from the handle. Was the letter folded in that manner when you found it?"

"No, I folded it like this so I could carry it in my pocket. It was spread flat on top of the clothing."

"I'm going to need it for evidence." Using his fingertips, Eugene plucked the letter from her hands, then placed it in a baggie.

Paula fought the urge to snatch the letter from the deputy. "Will I get that back? It's, well, it's special."

Eugene tapped the bag. "I promise you'll get your letter back." He took another look around. "Are you positive nothing is missing?"

Paula took a long look around. "As far as I can tell, all they did was rifle through my stuff."

"Has anyone besides you been in the motorhome?"

Blowing out a trembling breath, Paula ticked the names off on her fingers. "My friends, Sue Ann Atkins and Sherry Derryberry. Their husbands, Melvin and Delbert. Cassie and Melinda. Seth Boone was out here yesterday; although, he didn't come in. Oh, Vanessa Allen and I called Sheriff Hill from here earlier today to report a concern about a classmate who's gone missing. Oh, and Jake Martinez was here quite a bit yesterday. He stayed for part of the night."

Eugene choked on a bit of eraser.

Paula patted him on the back. *I'd better set the record straight...* "Jake slept on the couch for a while but moved into his van after the disturbance. He's checked into a room now." *Great, Paula, now you've made Jake a suspect.*

Eugene said, "I'll be sure to get a statement from him. He folded the small notebook shut and stuck it inside his shirt pocket along with the well-chewed pencil. "We may need to fingerprint your friends. Let me run what I've got and see if they match anyone in the system."

Paula clutched at his sleeve. "Before you go, do you think it's safe for me to sleep here tonight? Cassie's offered to stay with me."

"I don't know why not. It looks like whoever ransacked your place was thorough. Just make sure you lock up, okay?"

She shook Eugene's hand. "I promise. Thank you. Let me know if you get anything from those prints."

"I will, but don't forget, we might need yours, too."

As he left the motorhome, Eugene nodded to the others gathered there. "Looks like I'm leaving Ms. Paula in good hands. Take care, y'all."

Paula waved goodbye. She straightened her spine and gestured for the others to come in. Managing a weak smile, Paula said, "Y'all might as well come in and see what a disaster this is. I have to give Eugene credit, though. He's a lot more confident when the sheriff isn't involved, and he doesn't blush as much without Ellie around."

With a laugh, Melinda said. "That's good to know." As she came face to face with the magnitude of the mess in Paula's motorhome, Melinda's laughter died. "Oh no."

Cassie slipped in behind Melinda, and said, "Damn it! I can't believe someone from our class would do this. This has to be the work of a stranger." She drew Paula to her side.

Tears weighed heavy in Paula's eyes. *No. Crying won't help a thing.* She took Cassie's hand. "I wish I could believe that, but I can't shake the feeling the break-in is tied to Arlene's disappearance and the alleged bobcat in the night. Someone was looking for a specific item or items, I think."

With a click of her tongue, Cassie said. "Regardless of who did it or why, it looks like a tornado blew through."

Wrapping Paula in a hug, Zeke said, "I've seen worse. We can put this to rights in no time. You lead, Ms. Paula; we'll follow."

CHAPTER FORTY-FOUR

Paula slumped at her kitchen table surrounded by her friends. Sipping on a Shiner, she surveyed the newly restored room. *Zeke was right. It didn't take much to put everything back in place.*

"Thank you all for the help. I promise from now on I won't leave home without locking the doors."

Zeke patted her hand. "Good thinking, and you're welcome. You still don't think they took anything?"

With a shake of her head, Paula said, "If anything's missing, I sure can't tell what it is. That's one more good thing about living in a camper—fewer possessions."

As Zeke and Melinda stood to leave, Cassie said, "I'm going to stick around. You shouldn't be alone."

Paula took Cassie's hands in her own and squeezed. "I'll be fine. Go work on your act. You're going to need to be at the top of your game to beat me tonight."

Cassie gave her the side eye. "Oh, yeah? We'll see about that. C'mon, Zeke. We have work to do."

After they left Paula locked the door and opened Star's carrier. The cat glared at Paula and stalked away, her tail whipping from side to side.

"Sorry, girl, it was for your own protection." Paula dropped a handful of cat treats into Star's bowl. "See, I'm not the bad guy... But if I'm not, then who is?"

Paula fought down a jolt of panic. *Stay busy. That's the ticket.* Combing through her purse, she found a scrap of paper and began jotting down the names of those who'd been inside her motorhome. She crossed Cassie and Melinda off with a stroke of her pen. Then Sue Ann and Sherry. *Those are the easy ones. Same for Delbert and Melvin.*

"Star, what about Vanessa?" Paula shook her head. *That's ridiculous. She is worried out of her mind about Arlene. Unless maybe she thinks I have information I'm not sharing, but that makes no sense.* Paula crossed Vanessa's name off the list.

She tapped her pen against the paper. *Jake? Had he been one of the many guys involved with Arlene back in the day? Had she loved him and left him? Is that why he's so sad?*

With a graceful leap to the tabletop, Star flopped down on top of Paula's list and swatted at the pen. Paula held the pen out of the cat's reach and said, "I don't think that's it. Jake's sadness is too raw to have been festering for all these years." *But I do have his tube of antibiotic cream if the sheriff needs it for a fingerprint match.*

Star attacked the list with a vengeance and Paula wrestled it from her claws. "Yes, kitty, I wondered if he was coming back into the camper last night. Had he been up to some mischief? Something that would result in a scream? But why?" She scratched through Jake's name, then added it back in. *Just in case...*

A knock at the door sent her heart into a gallop.

"Paula? You in there?"

Jake!

She slipped the list into the under-table storage cubby and eased off the bench.

Looking out the window, Paula spied Jake standing a respectful distance from the door, a bouquet of wildflowers in his hand. *He certainly doesn't look like a bad guy.*

Paula plastered on a smile and opened the door. "Hey Jake. Come on in."

"Is this a bad time? I thought I heard you talking to someone."

Paula swallowed hard and ducked her head. "Just me and the cat for now. Cassie's coming back any minute, though." *Small white lie, but I can't be too careful.*

He handed her the flowers. "Oh, that's cool. Here, these are for you. An apology for my behavior last night. I was a complete imbecile."

She searched his face for any hint of discomfort or guilt and found none. Paula expelled a shaky breath. "Thank you, these are lovely. Let me put them in a glass. I don't have a vase, so…" Paula rinsed out an empty tea bottle. *What's he doing here? Could he be checking out the aftermath?* Carrying the glass to the table she said. "Have a seat. Beer?"

"No, thanks, but If you've got a Dr. Pepper, I'll take one of those."

"Oh, as long as Cassie Campbell is my best friend, I'll always have Dr. Pepper on hand."

He snorted. "She is a fiend. Hey, are we still good to go with our act tonight?"

Sitting across from him at the table, she picked at the label of her beer with a fingernail while studying his eyes for any hint of remorse or culpability. "Sure. I think it'll be a winner, especially if we can go on last." She inhaled and considered her next words. "So, I have to ask you something."

A guarded look came into his eyes. "Um, sure."

Paula crossed her fingers beneath the table. *This might be a really bad idea.* "Last night when I woke up to the clatter of trash cans and came to investigate, you were already up. Were you coming in from outside? Because it kind of looked like you were."

"Yeah. I'd gone over to my van to get my earbuds. I couldn't sleep and didn't want you to be bothered by my music. Why?"

"You claim you didn't hear the scream. Both Ray and I heard it and I just thought it was weird that you didn't."

He pointed at his ears. "I heard the crash but put the earbuds on right after that. I must've just missed the scream. What was it anyway? Did the sheriff have an answer?"

Paula suppressed a shudder. "Oh, probably just a bobcat." *But maybe it was Arlene and maybe you wanted her room.* "Did you happen to talk to Arlene before she left this morning? I mean, did she know you needed a place to stay?"

He lifted a shoulder. "I can't imagine that she'd have known. Unless maybe you mentioned it to her. And Melinda's who told me a room came open. She had me on a waiting list. I didn't even know it was Arlene's until Vanessa told me. Why the third degree?"

"Because I'm a little worried about Arlene. Vanessa said Arlene was all excited about today's activities and even had an act planned for tonight. Vanessa was with her late last night, and as far as she knew, Arlene was going to be here the entire weekend."

Jake held up a hand. "Wait. You think something's happened to Arlene and that *I* might have gotten rid of her in order to move into her room? Really?"

Paula winced at the hurt in his voice. "Oh, Jake, I'm so sorry. That does sound dumb, doesn't it? I'm just rolling all these ideas around in my head. Plus, I'm operating on very little sleep. And, on top of that, someone broke in here while I was at the cornhole tournament and trashed the place." She pressed her palms against her eyes.

Jake's head turned on a swivel. "Oh, Paula, that's awful. Wha-- I mean who might have done something like that? And in broad daylight? Was it a robbery?"

She pushed the beer away with a grimace. "I have no idea why anyone would break in or who would do such a thing. As far as I can tell, though, nothing is missing. Whoever trashed my camper seemed to be searching for something, and I can't for the life of me think what that might be."

He frowned. "You know, it's not a good idea for you to be out here by yourself tonight. I'll stay if you'd like."

Paula shook her head. "Thanks for offering, but Cassie's going to stay with me." *Besides, I'm still not totally certain that you aren't the bad guy.*

Jake stood and finished his soft drink. "Are you sure? Don't hesitate to bring me in as reinforcements if you need me. I'm your guy."

"I think having Cassie here will be sufficient. She's not a person to be trifled with, you know." *And neither am I. And where did you disappear to anyway while the sheriff was here last night?* A dull throb began to pulse through her head.

CHAPTER FORTY-FIVE

After Jake's departure, Paula remained at the table, massaging her temples with a slow, steady pressure. *Wish this danged headache would go away. So many questions. Jake seemed genuinely surprised about the break-in, though. Is he an accomplished actor as well as a musician?*

Star mewed and Paula ran a hand over the cat's silky fur. Adding Andy Lewis's name to her list, Paula said, "Girl, I still need to visit with Mr. Lewis. He hasn't been in my motorhome, but he might hold the key to Arlene's whereabouts."

Recalling Vanessa's concerns about their former teacher, she said, "Only in my wildest imagination can I consider Mr. Lewis as a bad guy. I'll pin him down for some questioning at supper tonight, though."

Paula took two aspirin and attempted to shove her worries to the back of her mind. *I still need to come up with something to wear tonight.*

As she looked through her closet and storage drawers in search of a suitable outfit for her act, her hands began to shake. Flopping onto the bed, she thought, *Not that long ago someone else was in this very room, going through my clothes. Why? What if they make another attempt while I'm out this evening?*

Stop it! Maybe Delbert or Melvin could be talked into checking on things out here from time to time. I'm sure they will if I ask. The thought calmed her nerves, allowing her to focus on finding something to wear.

She shimmied out of her jeans and checked the pockets. Her fingers latched onto a piece of paper. Paula frowned. *Arlene's business card. Forgot I slipped it in there.* She flipped the card over and studied the large block letters crowded together. *Arlene's personal information.* Paula tapped the card against her chin. *Hm. This doesn't look at all like the writing from the note Arlene left taped to the door of the office.*

Opening the drawer of her bedside table, Paula dropped the card inside, then snatched it back. *No, this needs to go into the safe along with the rest of the evidence.* She shoved the card inside the pocket of a short black skirt and pulled on a rich green sweater. Black tights and a pair of black Converse sneakers completed her ensemble. Examining her reflection in the bathroom mirror, she nodded. *Emerald and Ebony--Dempsey school colors. Quite appropriate for our talent show act. Now, if I can just put all the drama out of my mind for a couple of hours...*

After grabbing a Shiner and a Dr. Pepper, Paula locked her door and checked it twice. She followed her nose to the barbecue meal being served near the Clyde tree. Scanning the small crowd that had begun to gather, she couldn't find Andy Lewis. *Where is that man?*

Cassie waved her over to a table. "Hey, is that Dr. Pepper for me?"

Scooting onto a seat, Paula said, "Absolutely. It's the least I could do after you volunteered to be my guardian angel tonight."

"Glad to do it." Cassie popped open the Dr. Pepper and asked, "How are you doing, Goldilocks?"

Paula shrugged. "Honestly? My nerves are on edge, and I'm ready for a distraction from the break in and everything else that's happened in the past twenty-four hours."

Cassie made a goofy face. "Well, you're in the right place."

Paula giggled. "Can you keep that up for an hour or so?"

"Nope, that was it. By the way, you look particularly adorable. Just like you did senior year," Cassie said.

Paula pulled at the hem of her skirt. "I think this outfit might be from that year. The sweater might have a few holes in it, and this skirt is a little too snug. Remind me not to bend over. Besides, this is my costume. Where's *yours*?"

Mischief gleamed in Cassie's eyes. "Costume? What costume? I don't need no stinking costume. C'mon. Let's join the buffet line; I'm starving."

With heaping servings of barbecue brisket and all the fixings on their plates, the women found a table near the concrete slab-turned-makeshift stage. As Paula spread a napkin across her lap, Ray and Jake joined them.

Ray jerked a thumb in Cassie's direction. "Cassie's a shoo-in to win the talent show tonight. Just wait 'til you get a load of our act. She's going to knock everyone's socks off. I'm just glad she's letting me be her wingman."

Jake threw back his head and cackled. "I beg to disagree. Paula and I are going to astound the crowd. We'll bring tears to everyone's eyes."

"That bad, eh?" Ray smirked.

Paula relaxed and enjoyed their easygoing banter. *Surely Jake couldn't be involved in Arlene's disappearance, or the break in at my trailer and continue to chatter on this way. And maybe Arlene did check out and go home. With the exception of what happened to my place, there's been no concrete evidence of foul play.*

A tap on her shoulder brought her back to the real world, and Paula looked up into Mr. Lewis's eyes. He raised a single eyebrow. "Paula, Rudy said you were looking for me."

CHAPTER FORTY-SIX

Paula dabbed at the corners of her mouth and eyed Mr. Lewis. *Vanessa probably wouldn't think this is the wisest course of action, but I'll be careful.* She excused herself from the table. "Guard my plate, please. I'll be right back, y'all."

Keeping pace with Paula, Andy asked, "Is it something serious?"

Paula thought, *Just in case Andy is a bad guy, I want to be somewhere public, but not too public. Hm.* "I just have a few questions, and I'd prefer to ask them in private. Could we step into the office for a few minutes?"

He nodded, a slight frown on his unlined face. "Sure, whatever you need."

Paula led Andy through the living area and into the office where McKenzie was on duty scrolling through the reservations screen. "Hey, McKenzie, would you mind if I use the office? I'll keep an eye on things while you're gone?"

"Sure. I'll grab a plate of barbecue if that's okay. Be back in a minute."

Paula patted McKenzie's shoulder. "Take your time."

When McKenzie left, Paula gestured to one of the chairs while she sat on a stool behind the counter.

With a nervous chuckle, Andy peered up at her. "For some reason I feel exactly like I did when I confessed to Mr. Landers on senior skip day all those years ago. Surely I haven't crossed a line this time."

Paula twirled a strand of hair around her finger and made eye contact with him. "Well, do you have anything to confess today?"

"Such as?"

She held her breath. "Such as, when was the last time you talked to Arlene Davis?"

His face grew crimson. "We talked a little bit while the music was going on last night, but I left her at her motel room door around ten, I think. Why?"

Paula tapped on the counter. "Do you know where she is now?"

"Why would I know? Isn't she out having fun at the barbecue? We said our final goodbyes last night. I told her I had no time for her nonsense."

Her brows knit together. "What kind of nonsense?"

The man's shoulders slumped. "I suppose there's no harm in telling you now; although, I'd appreciate it if you didn't make this common knowledge."

Paula narrowed her eyes. "I guess that depends on what you reveal, doesn't it?"

His right knee began bouncing up and down like a yo-yo on speed. "Hm, yes. I understand your point. It's just not something I'm proud of. All these years later, the whole thing seems like a bad dream. You see, I was involved with Arlene that first year I taught." He took a deep breath and looked away. "We became intimate. There I was, barely older than you kids and she was hard to resist."

Her eyes widened. She held her breath. *I already knew this stuff but hearing it from him makes it real...oh mercy!*

Andy splayed his hands wide. "I know, I know, I was supposed to be the grown up in the equation. I knew better, but

I was lonely in a town where I had no friends, and she seemed so mature. So experienced. More so than many of the women I'd dated in college."

Recalling her own state of innocence at the same age, Paula shook her head. "But she was only seventeen. And you were her teacher. *My* teacher."

Andy lowered his head into his hands. When he raised his eyes again, his expression was bleak. "I am truly sorry that I betrayed that relationship. The one I'd developed with the students at Dempsey High. I lived in constant fear that someone would discover what was going on. But every time I tried to end things Arlene became hysterical. Initially, she threatened to hurt herself. When I didn't give any credence to her threat, she claimed she was pregnant with my child and said if I left her, she'd make her pregnancy public."

"And was she? Pregnant, that is?" Paula asked.

Andy's chin dropped to his chest. When he looked up, tears glistened in his eyes. "I have no idea. She didn't go through with the threat, though, because I reassured her that I wouldn't break things off. That I would be there for her, regardless. That I loved her. And perhaps I did, just a little, but it would've meant the end of my teaching career if I acknowledged our relationship. I could've been sentenced to prison. I couldn't have handled that."

He shifted in his seat and offered a grim smile. "My hands were tied. But I gave her a good deal of money. Money I'd saved to make a down payment on a home in Dempsey. And I didn't press her on the pregnancy story, fearing she'd get spooked and start spreading tales about us. Anyway, Arlene's mother died toward the end of senior year, and her father shipped her off to Dallas the day after graduation. Apparently, she found someone else there and that was blessedly the end of our unfortunate relationship. I was out several thousand dollars, but I still had my career and my freedom, so I chalked the whole thing up to lessons learned."

A door opened and closed in the cabin's living area, and Paula braced her arms against the counter. *Maybe I have time for one more quick question.* "Last night I saw you and Arlene. While most everyone was gathered in the campground listening to Jake and Cassie, you and Arlene were, well, it was tough to determine exactly what you were doing. So, I must ask—did you threaten her?"

Andy's eyes widened. "Threaten her? Hardly. I did ask how she was doing and if indeed she'd been pregnant when she left Dempsey. She hemmed and hawed and tried some of her seductive powers on me and I finally said 'enough' and bid her adieu. I've spent this entire day avoiding her."

"So, you don't know?"

He huffed. "Know what?"

Paula traced an invisible question mark on the counter. She paused, then said, "That Arlene checked out in the wee hours of the morning."

Snorting out a laugh, Andy said. "You're serious? So, I maintained my distance from her and the resort this entire day for nothing?" The look of disbelief on Andy's face appeared genuine. *But then he is a writer. Don't they make stuff up for a living?*

CHAPTER FORTY-SEVEN

Paula watched Andy through narrowed eyes as he left the office. He greeted Sue Ann and Sherry and shook hands with their husbands.   He threw his head back in laughter over something Sue Ann said. *Unless Andy's a total sociopath, I don't think he could possibly be that casual. Not if he'd had something to do with Arlene's abrupt departure anyway.*   By the time McKenzie joined her, Paula's list of potential suspects no longer included their former teacher.

Eyeing McKenzie's plate piled high with barbecue and potato salad, Paula remembered her own dinner. *I'll bet it's cold by now. Darn.* "Do you know the combination to the safe? I need to put something in there for safekeeping."

McKenzie stuck her fork into the potato salad. "Sure. Mom told me about the break in at your camper. I can't believe someone would do that."

Paula grimaced.   "I'm struggling to understand how anyone I know could've done that to my home. I feel so violated."

"I get it," McKenzie said. "Someone smashed a window on my car while I was in class one afternoon. There wasn't much in there of value, and I had my purse with me, but I still fantasized about ways of catching them for months. I wanted them to pay for what they'd done to my car."

Paula moved so McKenzie could access the safe. "I totally get that. I just want to know *why*. Why my place?"

While McKenzie unlocked the safe, Paula labeled an envelope as EVIDENCE.

"Wow, this looks official," McKenzie said.

"I do my best. Say, before you close the safe, let me take a look at one of those baggies." Examining the container with Arlene's note tucked inside, Paula scrutinized the handwriting. *It's as elegant as I remember. Totally unlike the angular scribble on the business card.*

She placed both pieces of evidence side by side on the counter for McKenzie to compare. "Do these appear to have been written by the same person?"

McKenzie shook her head. "Not at all. I mean, my handwriting is never quite the same two days in a row, but it's never *that* different."

"That's what I was thinking." Paula slipped the business card into the envelope and placed it inside the safe along with the note, stepping aside so McKenzie could seal the items inside. "Thank you. I feel better knowing everything's in one secure place."

She turned to walk away, but McKenzie caught her by the sleeve. Paula hesitated at the sight of McKenzie's trembling lips. "Oh, what's wrong, sweetie?"

McKenzie's voice quivered. "Um, Jeffries and I are hoping to tell his parents about the baby tonight. Wish us luck?"

Paula wrapped McKenzie in a hug. "I don't think you'll need luck, but I'll wish it for you two anyway. I don't know his dad at all, but Delilah thinks the world of you, and she loves her son. She might be shocked at first, but remember, so was your mom."

McKenzie's face broke into a smile. "And now Mom's buying booties and blankets and suggesting possible names."

"Exactly. I'll be thinking about you tonight, but you'll be fine."

CHAPTER FORTY-EIGHT

As Paula left the office, her phone dinged, and she pulled it out of her pocket. *Miracle of miracles, a text made it through.* She glanced at the name and squealed. *Mark! It's about time. Now, what does my Dr. Hunky have to say?* She made a beeline for the nearest picnic table where she plopped onto the bench and opened the text:

> *"Hey Paula, I'm trying to be a good boy and not bother you during your class reunion, but I just wanted you to know I'm thinking about you and missing you. Counting the days until I can see you again. It's a good thing I have ten fingers, because that's the goal I have in mind. Ten days, not ten fingers. I already have the fingers. Keep working on those blinks. Keeping with the theme, ten blinks would be a nice round number, though. But, in this case, the more the merrier. Yours, Mark."*

All thoughts of the day's drama flew out of Paula's mind. *Break in? What break in?* Her shoulders relaxed as the tension she'd held inside all day melted away like butter on a warm biscuit. *Ten days? I can do that standing on my head! Now, how to respond?*

> "Hey Mark, sometimes being a good boy (or girl) isn't all it's cracked up to be. I miss you, too. Ten days, eh? Whew. My blinking is coming along just fine, thank you. So far, I'm up to...Oops, gotta go. I'm performing in a class talent show tonight. Wish me luck."

He responded within seconds.

> "You don't need luck. Ask Cassie or Melinda to get your act on video for me, okay? I hate that I'm missing it, but ten days. Soon. Your bad, good boy, Mark."

A delicious shiver coursed down Paula's spine. She texted a kiss emoji, pocketed her phone, and hurried to the campground where the alluring aroma of barbecue was still drawing folks to dinner.

CHAPTER FORTY-NINE

Paula returned to the table with a goofy grin on her face. Even seeing that her dinner plate had been cleared away failed to dampen her mood. *Still, Cassie doesn't need to know I'm letting her off the hook.*

Poking out her bottom lip, Paula said, "Okay, I thought I left you in charge of guarding my barbecue."

Cassie wagged a finger in Paula's direction. "Chill, girl. I covered your plate in foil and put it in the refrigerator in the cabin. It'll be waiting on you after the talent show, but I did fetch another Shiner for you."

Paula blew Cassie a kiss and settled onto the bench beside her. "Thank you. To be honest, I think I'm too nervous to eat right now anyway."

With narrowed eyes, Cassie said, "You don't look quite as glum as you did earlier. Did something happen I should know about?"

Paula arched an eyebrow. "I heard from a certain doctor."

"Oh? And what did this certain doctor have to say?"

Paula held her hands up, her fingers splayed wide. "Ten days. Mark said he'd be here in ten days."

Cassie's eyes danced. "No wonder there's a smile on your face. Have you thought about how you'll welcome Dr. Hunky home?"

Fanning herself, Paula said, "Oh, maybe once or twice."

"You're turning red, Goldilocks. Now maybe you'll be able to relax and have fun this evening.

Paula took a long pull from her beer. "Maybe. I'm going to see if Melvin and Delbert will check on my motorhome a few times. And it might be a good idea to get someone to walk out there with us after the talent show."

Jake tapped Paula's shoulder. "Speaking of the talent show, I think it's time we jockeyed for a good place to sit."

Paula said, "Oh, good idea. Would you and Ray mind fetching the folding chairs from my campsite, please? Grab all six of them in case we need extras."

After Jake and Ray left, Paula leaned in close to Cassie. "I interrogated Mr. Lewis."

"You did what? Why?"

"Long story, but Vanessa had a feeling that he might be behind Arlene's disappearance."

"I don't understand. Why in the world would Mr. Lewis be connected to Arlene?"

Paula lowered her voice to a whisper. "They had an affair senior year. Very sordid. She threatened to rat him out to the school, but Arlene's dad sent her off to Dallas after her mom died. And maybe Andy didn't want her to tell people at the reunion."

Cassie's eyes grew as big as saucers. "An affair? Are you kidding me? Holy cow. You actually confronted him?"

"I did. And now I don't think he had anything to do with Arlene. He's been avoiding the resort all day because he didn't want to run into her again. I believe him."

Cassie's jaw dropped as Jake and Ray returned. "Later, Goldilocks. I need details."

Paula rapped on the table and stood. "You now know just about everything I do. Oh, there's Melvin. I'm going to go ask him if he'll check on my house this evening."

LESLIE NOYES   197

CHAPTER FIFTY

After touching base with Melvin, Paula noticed Vanessa standing alone beside the Clyde tree and made a detour in her direction. "Why don't you come sit with Cassie and me? Jake and Ray are hanging out with us, and we've got plenty of room for you."

"Are you sure?" Vanessa asked. "I don't want to impose on anyone."

Waving her hand, Paula said, "I wouldn't have invited you if I didn't want you there. We'd love to have you. Please?"

Vanessa shared a shy smile and nodded. "Thank you."

As Paula and Vanessa approached, Ray stood. "Here, Vanessa. Take my chair. I'll scoot down one."

Paula watched their interaction. *I wonder if Vanessa knows about his past with Arlene. I'm certainly not going to tell her. Although, who knows where Ray was when that scream rang out through the woods? He had plenty of time to rush back to his camper and emerge all innocent in the aftermath. Hm. Stop it. Stop looking for suspects everywhere.*

Once Ray settled into his chair, Paula said, "Hey, Ray..."

Cassie shushed Paula as Judy Sinclair strode onto the makeshift stage and took the microphone from its stand.

"Good evening, everyone. Welcome to the first, and depending on how things go, maybe last, Anything But Talent Show. First, a round of applause for Hall Brothers' Hill Country Barbecue. That was good stuff, wasn't it? Thank you, guys."

Judy adjusted the microphone as she waited for the applause to die down. She displayed a jar in spokesmodel fashion. "Now, if I may have your attention, please notice the jar I hold in my hand. This one will join ten others at the front of the stage. Each jar has a photo of a classmate or classmates who'll be performing tonight. Their names are on there, as well, just in case the actual people no longer look like they did senior year. You get to vote on your favorite act by placing money in the jar featuring your choice. Oh, and my brother tells me you can vote for more than one act. In the end, the act with the most money in their jar wins the competition. But all the proceeds go to funding our next reunion. Don't be tightwads. Vote early and vote often."

Taking a photo from her pocket, Judy adhered it to the jar and placed it alongside the others. "That's me, in case you wondered."

Rudy hit a switch and fairy lights blinked on across the campground. He claimed center stage and waved at those assembled. "Thank you, Sis. Everyone, I'll be acting as master of ceremonies tonight, while running the spotlight and keeping the microphone working. I didn't want to take a chance on winning this thing and having to cart one of my trophies back home."

Ray said, "Likely story!"

Rudy grinned and flipped Ray the bird, then said, "We drew numbers from a hat, and it looks like my talented sister, Judy Sinclair is up first. Judy, the stage is yours, yet again."

As the sun set over the campground, Judy returned to the stage, performing the complicated cups song from the first *Pitch Perfect* film with a saucy flair. *Dang, she's good,* Paula thought, as Judy snapped the final cup in place.

The audience erupted in applause while many of Paula's classmates hurried to drop dollars into Judy's jar. Rudy made a show of adding a twenty-dollar bill.

Jake nudged Paula. "We can beat that."

Snorting, Paula said, "Glad you're confident. Besides, it's not about winning, it's about supporting the reunion fund."

"Speak for yourself. I need a win."

Sue Ann and Sherry, wearing rhinestone studded flapper dresses, performed a cheeky song and dance number to the old Shirley Bassey tune, *Big Spender*. When Sue Ann peered over her shoulder and delivered a come-hither look to the audience, Paula leaned into Cassie. "I had no idea those two had it in them. Hold my place, I'm going to vote for them."

Valynda Jean Baker, one of the sweetest, shyest kids in school, appeared from the edge of the stage swathed in jewel-toned scarves with bells jangling on her fingers and toes. As she worked the crowd to a Shakira song, Valynda, whose stage name was Sheba, drew her audience into the joy of her belly dance routine with her radiant, confident smile. For the grand finale, Valynda stepped onto the stage and manipulated a half dollar coin the length of her abdomen using nothing except her stomach muscles.

Paula made a grab for Jake's sleeve as he and Ray stood to contribute money to Valynda's jar, along with most of the other males in the audience. "Don't you know she's our real competition," Paula said with an exaggerated pout.

Jake grinned. "Like you said, it's all about adding to the reunion fund."

Paula shooed him away with a laugh as old drinking buddies, Roy Oldham and Max Fields took to the stage to do a redneck version of Abbot and Costello's "Who's on First" routine. *Oh mercy, they're perfect*. Wiping tears of laughter from her eyes, she handed Cassie five dollars. "Can you go put that in their jar for me?"

By the time Rudy announced Cassie and Ray as the next to last act of the evening, the jars all brimmed with money. Cassie rubbed her hands together and blew out a breath. "Whew. Here goes nothing."

Paula pressed her hands together and inclined her head. "Good luck. Or break a leg. Whichever is appropriate. And for heaven's sake, leave your clothes on!"

CHAPTER FIFTY-ONE

Paula shivered, whether in anticipation of Cassie's act, her own impending performance, or the change in temperature as the stars appeared in the night sky, she wasn't sure. Melinda slid into Cassie's vacant chair and waved to her sweetie. Paula peered around Melinda to find Martha perched next to Vanessa.

"Where's Zeke?" Paula asked.

Martha pointed at the stage. "He's a toady."

Melinda whispered in Paula's ear. "I think she means 'roadie.' Zeke's helping out with the act."

Paula chortled. She realized her knees were bouncing up and down and pressed her palms against them, willing the nerves to stop. She tapped Jake's shoulder. "I'll be glad when we get this over with."

"Relax. Our act will be the perfect dénouement to the evening."

"Ooh, I'll bet all the girls go crazy when you speak French."

Jake snorted and put a finger to his lips. "Here they go."

Ray strode across the stage wearing a cape over his jeans and t-shirt, with a top hat completing the outfit. "Ladies and Gentlemen," he said. "Your attention please."

With Zeke's assistance, he stretched a paper banner featuring an oversized, multi-tiered birthday cake painted in bright, primary colors across the stage. "It is with great pride that I present to you Cassie Campbell, juggling for the very first time in her birthday..."

Paula and Melinda exchanged wide-eyed looks.

"She wouldn't dare, would she?" Paula asked.

Melinda shrugged and covered her eyes.

"...tuxedo!" Ray finished with a flourish as Cassie broke through the banner wearing a black tuxedo jacket, shorts, and black tights. To Lesley Gore's song, "It's My Party," she juggled a trio of bedazzled party hats that sparkled under the lights as she twirled them in intricate patterns. Ray tossed her his top hat and she added it into the mix.

Paula pried Melinda's fingers away from her eyes then clapped her hands and attempted to whistle through her teeth. The music ended with all the party hats nestled inside the black top hat. Cassie bowed once and held up a finger. "What's a birthday cake without candles? Let's light this place up."

Zeke offered Cassie a pair of small tiki torches painted to look like birthday candles then lit them, while keeping another for himself. He backed away, leaving Cassie in the spotlight.

Directing a pointed look at the donation jars, Cassie said, "I do expect my jar to fill up now." She sent the two torches aloft to Katy Perry's "Firework." Once she established a rhythm, she caught the third torch from Zeke, never missing a beat. High tosses. Low tosses. Behind the back tosses. She whirled in a full circle with all three torches in the air as if suspended on a wire, and caught them, one by one, as they descended, blowing them each out in turn. The audience, roaring with applause, rose to its feet as Cassie curtsied.

Scurrying to the stage, Paula dropped twenty dollars into the jar. "Awesome performance!"

Cassie's eyes sparkled as she hugged Paula. "Thanks. Your turn to break a leg, Goldilocks."

CHAPTER FIFTY-TWO

The caterpillars wriggling in Paula's stomach morphed into monster-sized butterflies as she and Jake waited for Zeke and Ray to clear the stage for her act. Wondering if an actual broken leg might be preferable to following Cassie's performance, Paula motioned for Jake to hurry. "Let's get this done before I lose my nerve."

Jake strapped on his guitar and gestured to the crowd. "Savor the spotlight a little. And if you need to, picture the audience naked."

Paula sputtered, recalling her attempts to do just that while preparing to speak at Martha and Zeke's wedding over the summer. "That never works for me. It just makes me break out in fits of giggles. I prefer to picture them knitting."

"Knitting, eh? Whatever floats your boat. Ready?"

She gave a shaky nod and held herself stiff as a board as Rudy announced their act. "Fellow classmates, I would hate to follow that act, but that's just what these next folks are about to do. Give a big hand to our final performers of the night, Paula Purdy Arnett and Jake Martinez."

As applause rang out, Paula joined Rudy and Jake on the stage, her thoughts juggling about like so many tiki torches. *Why can't I be more like Cassie? Wait, am I supposed to say something first? Maybe. What, though? Remember to picture them knitting; they're all knitting. Sure wish Mark was here to knit.*

Rudy adjusted the microphone for her and offered a reassuring nod. "You'll be fine," he whispered, as he left the stage.

Jake strummed a soothing note on his guitar. "You all know they've saved the best for last this evening. Get those dollar bills ready because you're in for a treat. Paula and I have been practicing this act for what, Paula, three hours now?"

Paula gulped. "More like one and a half."

The crowd tittered and Jake spoke as he continued strumming. "The thing is, this is a class reunion, y'all. And it's all about friendship and unity and pride in our school. Coming together to celebrate and reminisce about our pasts, catch up on our presents, and speculate about our futures with those who knew us way back when. Before we were doctors or teachers or whatever it is that we are now. You're each something special to us because you're part of our shared history. And I don't want to wait forever until we're together again. So, even if you don't vote for us, put a dollar in somebody's jar so we can do this again real soon."

Paula sensed an aura of peace flow through the campground as classmates shared hugs and a few tears.

With a showman's sense of timing, Jake waited until the crowd was focused only on the stage. "Paula, you ready?" he asked.

She took a deep breath and found Cassie and Melinda, Zeke, and Martha in the audience. "I am."

"Now Paula is going to do something that no one, not even she, thought possible. She's going to sing our school song backwards. If you think you can sing along, once she gets started, join in."

A deeper hush fell over the crowd while Jake performed a drum roll on the body of his guitar. He counted off, "One, and two, and…"

Paula pivoted, and putting her back to the crowd began singing the opening notes of "Dempsey High Forever."

Laughter rang out in the audience and Paula winked at Jake as his voice and the voices of others joined hers. Soon, everyone who remembered the words was singing along. As they reached the last two lines, the voices from the crowd began to dwindle until only a few stragglers remained singing, "The emerald and ebony, true to you we'll ever be..."

She became distracted by people buzzing with talk instead of harmonizing on the final words. *Have they all forgotten how the song ends?* Puzzled, she looked to Jake who shrugged and motioned for her to turn around.

There, appearing as hunky as he was in Paula's dreams, stood Doctor Mark Fields. He sported a look of love in his eyes, a hundred-dollar bill in one hand, and the jar with her photo on it in the other. "Best act ever," he said, dropping the bill inside the jar.

She blinked as if her life depended on it.

CHAPTER FIFTY-THREE

Wrapped inside the warmth of Mark's embrace, Paula forgot everything around her. The roar of applause, coupled with hoots and catcalls urging them to 'get a room,' soon reminded her that she was still on stage. She pulled away with a reluctant sigh and brushed a finger across his lips. "Hold those thoughts."

Jake sidled up next to her. "We really should take a bow."

Unwilling to let go of Mark, Paula held on to his hand as she and Jake bowed.

"Thank you, thank you very much," Jake said, channeling Elvis. "And don't forget to vote."

Rudy reclaimed the microphone, reminding everyone they could continue to cast ballots for the next fifteen minutes. "So, if you need to fetch more money from your room, don't waste any time.   While you're waiting for the results, help yourselves to the desserts Delilah from Oaks on Main brought out this afternoon. And there's still plenty of beer and other refreshments in room twenty-three. Just be back here for the results in thirty minutes. Oh, if you volunteered to count money, meet me back by that big oak tree. The one with the face on it."

To Paula's ears, Rudy's voice registered as a vague buzzing in the background. Mark kept an arm wrapped around her waist as her classmates scattered for the intermission. *Mark's here. He's really here!*

Taking Mark's hand, Paula smiled. "Mark, come meet my friend, Jake Martinez. Jake, this is Mark Fields, my, um, special friend."

Mark's eyes twinkled as the men shook hands. "Pleased to meet you, Jake."

Oh, he found that amusing, eh? We'll just have to define our relationship a little better.

With a whoop, Cassie claimed Mark for a hug. "It's about time you returned to us."

Melinda and Martha took turns kissing Mark's cheek, as Zeke shook his hand. "A man can't hardly cut through all these women to say hello to a friend," Zeke said.

Throughout it all, Mark held on to Paula. *Like we're each other's lifelines.*

"Paula, did you know he was going to be here?" Melinda asked.

Her eyes shining with tears, Paula shook her head. "No. Ten days. He said ten days. Mark, you said ten days!"

His lop-sided grin sent a delicious warmth coursing through Paula's veins. "I can leave and come back next week if that'd make you happy..."

Paula buried her face in his chest. "Don't you dare!"

Melinda smacked her own forehead. "Oh, Mark. I'm afraid I've let someone else have your room. The resort is full and...If I'd known you were coming..."

Mark shot Paula a questioning look. She put a hand on Melinda's arm. "He'll have a place to stay. I've got plenty of room." *Who is this brazen woman who's taken over my body and brain?*

"Hm, guess you won't need *my* protection tonight," Cassie said, her lips curled up in a mischievous grin.

Paula winked. "I guess not." *There she goes again. I do believe I like this new, bolder version of me.*

Martha whispered in Mark's ear, and his face took on the color of a ripe pomegranate. "Absolutely," he said. At Paula's raised eyebrows, he squeezed her close. "Maybe I'll tell *you* later."

"Mark, have you had anything for dinner?" Melinda asked.

"No, well, yes. I don't know. I just wanted to get here. At any rate, I'm not hungry right now."

"There's leftover barbecue in the cabin's fridge. Help yourself when you're ready. Um, Cassie? Mom? How about you and Zeke come help me in the cabin while the votes are being counted."

Paula sent an appreciative look Melinda's way, realizing she'd managed to give her some alone time with Mark. She led him to the edge of the campground, out from beneath the lights. "Well?" she asked, peering up at him through a veil of lashes.

"That's a really deep subject," he said, eliciting a full-throated laugh from Paula. "Oh, how I've missed that sound."

She pinched his arm.

"Ow, what was that for?"

"I needed to see if it's really you. I feel like maybe I fainted on stage and bonked my head open, and now I'm in the middle of a concussion-induced dream. But, no, you're here."

"I can provide even more proof." Mark cupped her chin and bent to kiss her, his lips warm and familiar.

A cough from nearby caught Paula's attention and with a reluctant sigh, she broke off the kiss. "Yes?"

Vanessa stood at her elbow, with eyes downcast. "Sorry to bother you. Do you have a minute?"

Paula said, "Vanessa, this is Mark Fields. Mark, Vanessa."

After the two shook hands, Paula asked, "So, any news from Arlene?"

Vanessa shook her head. "No, and it's closing in on twenty-four hours that she's been missing. I just feel like if she were okay, we'd have gotten word by now."

A whippoorwill called out, sending a shiver through Paula. She clasped Vanessa's hands. "Let's stay positive."

"I'm trying, but then I heard that someone vandalized your camper today, and I can't help but think it's all connected. What if you went missing, too?"

Holding up a hand, Mark said, "Wait a minute. What happened? I thought Cassie was kidding about you not requiring her protection."

Paula took his hand and dropped a kiss onto his knuckles. "They didn't exactly vandalize it. I mean, no harm was done. But someone seemed to be searching for something. Whatever it was, they didn't find it. Nothing was missing."

Mark's eyes held Paula's. "Still, I hope you called the sheriff."

"Of course, I did. I'm beginning to accrue frequent caller points."

He wrapped his arms around her. "I'm so glad I listened to my instincts and drove straight through."

Resting her chin on Mark's chest, Paula said. "Me, too, even though I'm in absolutely no danger."

Vanessa huffed. "So very sorry to bother you. Now that your man's here, I guess everything is different. Looks like I really am the only one who cares about Arlene after all. It's like high school all over again." She stalked away without looking back.

"Wait," Paula said. "That's not..."

Mark pulled Paula into his chest, kissing the tip of her nose. "She needs to cool off a little, and I think you need to bring me up to speed on what's been going on."

"I will. Later. But look, Rudy is getting ready to announce the results."

CHAPTER FIFTY-FOUR

Paula grasped Mark's hand and navigated their way through the maze of chairs. She avoided the questioning looks in the eyes of her former classmates. *Most of them only found out yesterday that I lost my husband. They probably think I'm a hussy now. But it's been over a year since Cal's death. Surely this is okay.*

Jake sat in Paula's chair, so Cassie moved over a seat as Paula and Mark approached. "Thanks," Paula said. She surveyed the empty seats on their row. "Hey, where did everyone go?"

Cassie adjusted her headband and scooted her chair closer to Paula's. "Martha was tired. She went on to bed, but Zeke is hovering around somewhere. He's just certain I'm going to win, and he wants to be here to celebrate with me. Melinda had to take a call, so she's in the office."

"What about Vanessa?"

"She stormed off saying this was all a sham. I was going to ask if you knew but..."

Paula shrugged her shoulders. "I know she's concerned about Arlene but, beyond that, I've got nothing. Oh, look. Rudy's at the mic."

Clearing his throat, Rudy tapped the microphone. "I don't know about you all, but I thought our Anything But Talent Show was a resounding success. I certainly enjoyed it. Give everyone who performed a big round of applause."

He shuffled a set of note cards and rearranged them to his liking. "Okay, before I announce the winner or winners, I wanted you to know that we earned enough from this event to fund another reunion. Thanks to your generosity and your participation tonight, we ended up adding a little over two thousand dollars to our class coffers."

Rudy paused as applause broke out in the campground. "The funds will be deposited into the class's savings account at the First National Bank of Dempsey. Helen Parker has done a great job of managing that account over the years. How about a hand for Helen?"

Paula joined in the applause, waving to Helen across the sea of classmates.

"Now, I know you're all eager to discover who took the honors in our first, and now hopefully not last, Anything But Talent Show. The top three acts will each receive one of my old speech trophies. Lucky ducks. But only the first-place act will win a weekend at this resort along with a meal at a local restaurant. It's a great prize."

Cassie clutched one of Paula's hands, while Mark held on to the other, offering a reassuring squeeze.

"Okay, here goes. In third place, Paula Purdy Arnett and Jake Martinez. Come up and get your trophies."

To the sound of enthusiastic hoots Jake escorted Paula to the stage where Rudy kissed her cheek and presented the trophies. "Well done. You two stay up here, okay?" Rudy said.

Paula moved to one side of the stage to stand next to Jake and winked at Mark who gave the pair a standing ovation.

"We'll get 'em next time," Jake said.

How can he be so upbeat and still have that desolate look in his eyes? What kind of tragedy has he faced? Still, it's a good thing he moved out of my camper. I doubt Mark would take kindly to sharing my space with me and another man tonight.

The thought that she'd invited Mark to share her motorhome filled her with an anticipation she had not experienced since losing Cal, bringing a glow to her cheeks and a warmth to other parts of her anatomy. *Oh mercy.*

Rudy consulted with someone offstage and nodded. His mellow voice rang out across the campground. "I've been told that I need to stall for a minute while those counting the votes do a recount for second and first places. It's a tight race, and they want to be certain before giving us the results. I do know that third place wasn't that far behind in the earnings. In fact, there was only a difference of about thirty dollars between first and last places. I'd call that a success."

Paula and Jake high-fived.

Rudy surveyed the audience, waiting for their attention. "I've been part of several conversations that began with the words, 'remember when', since arriving at our reunion, but one of the best was, 'remember when all hell broke loose in Freshman biology class?'"

Laughter erupted from the crowd and Rudy raised his hands. "I see some of you know where I'm going with this. For those who didn't attend Dempsey High, perhaps your significant other has told you about the day all ninth graders dreaded— Earthworm Dissection Day. But in case they haven't, it was a tradition that on that momentous day each year, the cafeteria ladies would serve spaghetti. One section of biology was taught immediately before lunch, so the students who'd just been slicing and dicing into slippery, slimy, earthworms went directly to the cafeteria where they were met with a meal of slippery, slimy earthworm-looking noodles. Our freshman year, that half of the class survived the whole thing without incident."

Someone snickered and Rudy paused. He peered into the crowd. "But those who had biology immediately after lunch didn't fare quite as well. Oh, yes. I was part of that group and, wisely, I refused to eat anything but my salad that day, having had a heads up from a buddy in the morning class. But my sister? That's another story."

"Rudy, are you sure you want to go there?" Judy asked, her voice rising above the laughter.

"Yes, yes I do. You see Judy loved spaghetti. It was her favorite school lunch. Upon fetching my tray from the lunch ladies, I said, 'Sis, I'm not all that hungry. You want mine?' Following my lead, several others donated their spaghetti to Judy, and I don't think she turned a single offer down. As the legend goes, my sister was late to class that day. She rushed into the room just as the bell rang, and sat down by her lab partner...Who was that? Ah, yes, Ray Landry. Tell us, Ray, what was it you did then?"

Ray raised a hand, his thumb and forefinger pinched together. "I held up an earthworm and said, 'Hey, I saved you some spaghetti...'"

"And then?" Rudy asked.

"And then I pretended to swallow it."

"And, Sis, what happened next?"

Judy stood in the crowd, a hand on each hip. "I threw up. And then someone else did. And then their lab partner followed suit. Even Coach Pearson lost his lunch that day. Soon it was hard to tell the earthworms from the regurgitated spaghetti."

Surveying the crowd, Rudy asked, "If you lost your spaghetti that day, raise your hand."

Paula giggled and raised her hand. Cassie's hand shot up, as did a good many others. Mark laughed with Delbert and Melvin, neither of whom had been in the same graduating class as their wives.

Rudy cleared his throat. "And that, ladies and gentlemen is known as the Day the Spaghetti Came Up in Dempsey."

With chatter erupting throughout the crowd, Paula elbowed Jake. "You didn't puke?"

"I had an orthodontist appointment. Missed the whole thing."

Rudy accepted a note card from one of their classmates. He glanced at it and said, "Why don't we have the top two acts come on up here and we'll find out which is which. Okay, in no particular order, Valynda Jean Baker, come join us. And, Cassie, you and Ray."

Paula clapped and attempted to whistle as the three contestants gathered at center stage. She crossed her fingers for Cassie's act and held her breath as Rudy consulted his cards once again. *Please, no more stories.*

"Could I get a drum roll?" Rudy asked. From the audience came the sound of hands slapping against chairs and thighs and anything else that might mimic a drum sound. "And second place goes to…Cassie Campbell and Ray Landry. That means, Valynda Jean, you are the winner of our very first Anything But Talent Show."

Those on stage surrounded Valynda Jean with hugs and kisses, and the once timid girl graced the crowd with one more swish of her hips, while awarding both Ray and Jake a scarf from her costume.

It really was a perfect ending to the show. Making eye contact with Mark, Paula crooked a finger in his direction, but as he rose to join her, flashing red lights filled the campground and the sound of sirens drowned out the sounds of merriment.

Two sheriff's department cars pulled up as near the stage as possible. The door to the first car opened and Sheriff Hill emerged from the driver's seat. He strode onto the stage and took the microphone from a bewildered Rudy. "Excuse me, folks. I'm Sheriff Hill of the Big Lake County Sheriff's Department. I'm sorry to interrupt your shindig, but this afternoon, we located Arlene Davis. She is currently in the hospital in Hemphill where she remains in critical condition. We have reason to believe that Ms. Davis was the victim of foul play."

CHAPTER FIFTY-FIVE

Paula's gasp joined that of the others in the campground. She searched the crowd for Vanessa and found Ray consoling her, his arms wrapped around her. Andy Lewis, on the other side of the audience, appeared stunned. Beside her, Jake had gone rigid. She whispered, "Do you know anything about this?"

"No. Absolutely not. It's just that..."

A grim look on his face, Sheriff Hill said, "It's likely that the last person or persons Ms. Davis spoke to are here at this gathering, and in order to get a handle on who did this, we need to speak to each one of you. For now, we'd like you to go back to your rooms and we'll question you in turn. If you're staying out in one of the campers, though, we ask that you come into the main cabin. Ms. Melinda has given us permission to use her living room and office and that'll facilitate the process. The Sabine County sheriff's department was kind enough to loan us some deputies, so this should go fairly quickly. No one leaves the property until we've questioned everyone, and then not until we give the okay. Understood?"

There were a few grumbles, but no one protested outright.

Paula asked, "Sheriff, can you give us any information about where you found Arlene or what happened to her?"

"At this time, all I can say is that she's lucky to be alive."

A lump formed in Paula's throat as Mark threaded his way through the throng of folks hurrying to their rooms to take his place by her side. He held her close, stroking her back. "You have a lot to tell me, it seems."

She snuggled into his embrace. "Yeah, I do. We have plenty of time, don't we? Of course, since you weren't here when Arlene went missing, I'm sure Sheriff Hill would let you go. There's no reason for you to stick around for the questioning."

He smoothed a thumb across her cheek. "Hush. You're reason enough to stick around. I'm not leaving you. Besides, you offered me a place to sleep tonight. It'd be pretty rude of me to just leave. Wouldn't it?"

The twinkle in Mark's eyes ignited a flame in her veins. Her voice took on a sultry twang. "Very rude."

Paula watched as Cassie approached Sheriff Hill. She spoke to him, and he nodded. As the sheriff left, she joined Paula and Mark. "I asked if it'd be okay if I joined the campers in the cabin. He said that'd be fine. Shall we get this over with?"

With a nod, Paula looked around the immediate area and headed toward the cabin trailing behind Cassie and Mark. A determined looking Seth Boone strode past Paula and placed himself between them. He looked Mark up and down, his words falling like bricks in the fall evening. "So, *this* is the guy you've taken up with?"

Patting Seth's shoulder, Cassie took a deep breath and released it. "Not that it's any of your business, but no. He's my friend. If you'd been paying attention, you'd know he's Paula's guy. Not mine."

Mark extended a hand. "Yep, that's me. Paula's Guy."

Seth raked a hand through his hair. His eyes searched Cassie's. "I'm sorry. I've tried to stay away, but it's eating me up inside. I guess I thought if I had a face to pin on the guy who took my place, I could get over you."

Paula's heart raced as Cassie straightened her spine and faced Seth head on. In anticipation of her best friend's next words, Paula pressed close to Mark and held her breath.

Cassie took Seth's hand, fastening her eyes on his. "Seth, I should have told you a long time ago, but there was no easy way to do it. There is no guy. I'm gay. I'm in love with a woman. As much as I enjoyed being your girl in high school, we were never meant to be."

Paula focused on Seth's face. When an ear-to-ear grin appeared, she expelled a held breath.

"Oh, that explains so much," Seth said. He whooped and picked Cassie up, spinning her in a circle. "I always thought there must be something wrong with *me*, when all this time it was *you*. I mean this all makes perfect sense because I'm kind of a great package."

With a look that asked, "Is this guy for real?" Mark squeezed Paula's waist and tugged on Cassie's shirt. "I think we need to get inside so the sheriff can get started. Nice to meet you, Seth."

Paula peered over her shoulder at Seth, his arms raised high above her head in victory, a look of wonder on his face. He crowed, "Y'all! After all these years, it wasn't me, it was her!"

CHAPTER FIFTY-SIX

Inside the cabin, Paula looked over the crowd of twenty or more people scattered about the living room. She waved to get Melinda's attention and pointed to the kitchen, mouthing, "We'll be in here."

Paula retrieved barbecue leftovers from the refrigerator and motioned for Mark to sit. "I'll warm this up. It won't take but a minute."

Melinda joined them, catching Cassie up in a hug as the microwave dinged. "I'm sorry I wasn't around to hear the results of the talent show. I was busy dealing with the sheriff. Did you win?"

Cassie's shoulders slumped. "No, we came in second."

Melinda said, "That's great. But now I wish I'd thrown more money into your jar."

Cassie offered a weak smile. "Oh, thanks. I was happy with the outcome."

Melinda held her at arm's length. "Wait. What's up? You look rattled."

Ducking her head, Cassie said, "I can't imagine why. One of our classmates might have been attacked by another of our classmates, I'm about to get questioned by the police, and I just announced to Seth that I'm gay."

Melinda blinked. "Oh. Put that way, you have every right to be rattled. But you told Seth? Really? That took courage."

Cassie wrapped her arms around her chest. "It didn't feel courageous; it felt more like desperation. Can we sit? I'm a little shaky."

Melinda sat and pulled Cassie down beside her. "Of course. I'm here now."

Paula grimaced. "Seth wasn't exactly gracious about Cassie's news. He implied there was something wrong with her. Mark kept me from slapping him upside the head."

"But," Cassie held up a single finger. "On the bright side, I think that's it. I never have to deal with Seth Boone again. And that feels good."

Paula patted Cassie's back then retrieved the plate from the microwave. "I think we'll all feel better if we have something to eat".

"So, who's going to tell me what's going on here?" Mark asked.

Paula placed a plate in front of him. As she reheated her meal, she and Cassie took turns telling him about the disturbance in the campground the night before, Arlene's unexpected departure, and Vanessa's worry over her friend's oddly timed absence.

"Remind me—is Vanessa the one who stormed away over your lack of concern for Arlene?" Mark said.

Paula sat across from him and tore a slice of Texas toast in half. "That's her. She thinks Mr. Lewis, that is Andy who you haven't met yet, might have had something to do with Arlene's leaving in the early morning hours. He was our high school sponsor."

"And Paula says that Andy had a fling with Arlene in high school," Cassie said, her eyes wide as she stole a bite of brisket from Paula's plate. "Can you imagine?"

Melinda's jaw dropped open. "What? A teacher and a student? I mean I've read about that kind of stuff in the news, but it actually happened in your town? Wow."

Mark wiped the corner of his mouth. "But why, after all these years, would he have a motive to harm her?"

Leaning in close, Paula spoke in a voice pitched just above a whisper. "Because Arlene might have been pregnant when she left Dempsey. She accepted quite a bit of money from Andy to keep quiet about their relationship, and she wouldn't confirm or deny that she'd had his child."

Mark waved his fork in the air. "That seems pretty flimsy, though. If Arlene hadn't made a move to out her teacher in all these years, why would she now?"

They sat in silence picking at their meals. Paula sighed. "You're right. I don't really suspect Andy anyway. I just want this solved. Poor Arlene. Regardless of what she might have been up to in high school she didn't deserve this. Remember, the sheriff said she's lucky to be alive."

Cassie said, "Tell Mark what happened to your motorhome this afternoon."

"He knows," Paula said. "Vanessa brought it up."

Mark covered Paula's hand with his. "If whoever did that also attacked this Arlene, you could be in real danger."

With a wave of her fork, Paula dismissed the notion. "Seems like they were looking for something, but they didn't take a thing."

"Any idea what that something might have been?" Melinda asked.

After considering her answer, Paula grimaced. "No, and there's no reason to believe that what happened in my home has anything to do with Arlene; although, I really think the two events must be related. But other than Vanessa, no one except me was paying much attention to Arlene's absence. In fact, if it hadn't been for Vanessa, I doubt anyone would've given Arlene's unexpected departure a second thought. So, if the vandalism was connected to Arlene, wouldn't they have searched Vanessa's room instead of my place?"

Melinda shrugged. "Maybe your place was easier to search. Vanessa's room was probably locked, and it's in the main area of the resort, where someone might spot an intruder."

Blowing a stray hair off her face, Paula said, "True."

The kitchen door opened, and a female deputy strode into the room. "Which of you is Ms. Paula Arnett? We're ready for you."

CHAPTER FIFTY-SEVEN

Following the uniformed woman, Paula's mind bubbled with questions she would love to ask the officer. *This probably isn't the time or the place to ask her how she got into law enforcement, but maybe she'll give me her card and we can have coffee one day.*

The woman paused outside the office, allowing Paula to precede her into the smaller room. This time, Paula took one of the chairs against the wall while the deputy took her place on a stool behind the counter. *No wonder Andy felt like he was being interrogated this afternoon.* Paula offered a nervous smile. "I hope something will turn up tonight that can help you find out what happened to Arlene."

The officer jotted something on a notepad and looked down at Paula as if noticing her for the first time. "Ms. Arnett, I'm Lydia Gray, a deputy with the Sabine County Sheriff's office. Thank you for your time. We'll make this process as easy as possible."

Fighting back a gulp, Paula nodded. "Yes ma'am. I appreciate that."

"Now, when did you last talk to Arlene Baxter Davis?"

"I talked to her yesterday afternoon. In the parking lot. We caught up on each other's pasts for about ten minutes or so, then someone else came along and she gravitated to them."

"During those ten minutes, did she mention being worried that someone might be looking for her or out to harm her?"

Raising her hands, Paula said, "No. It was just stuff like 'where do you work,' and 'where are you living now?' That sort of thing."

Deputy Gray took a pair of glasses from her pocket and arranged them on her nose. "And who was the person who interrupted your talk with Ms. Davis?"

"Um, let me think. There were so many classmates coming and going. Oh, wait, it was Vanessa Allen. She's probably Arlene's closest friend from our class and she's been worried sick all day."

"And that's the last you spoke with Ms. Davis?"

Paula tapped her finger on her temple as she thought back over the previous day. "Yeah. I think so. I saw her last night, though. We had a campfire and live music while we all visited."

"And who did Ms. Davis visit with?"

Heat rose to Paula's face. "Andrew Lewis. He was our senior class sponsor."

The officer scribbled something then looked up.

Hm. Officer Gray has gray eyes. Go figure.

"Ms. Arnett, when did you last see Ms. Davis in the company of Mr. Lewis?"

Paula closed her eyes, trying to recall if she had paid any attention to the time. "I'm not sure, but it was full dark. Maybe nine-thirty or ten? They were at the edge of the campground, away from the music."

"How would you describe their interaction?"

Oh wow, how will I describe it? "Well, um, they were having what looked like a deep conversation. Their heads were close together."

"Did Mr. Lewis touch Ms. Davis?"

Paula closed her eyes and recalled Andy's fingers cupping Arlene's face. "Yes."

"And how would you characterize that contact?"

Without hesitation, Paula said, "Tender. I've thought about it since she left so abruptly, wondering if Andy, Mr. Lewis, that is, might have meant to intimidate her, but it was a tender touch. I thought they were moving into the shadows to kiss."

"Is there any reason you thought Mr. Lewis might have meant her harm?"

Paula shook her head. "Not at the time."

"But now you do?"

"No. I mean I considered it after I learned they had a past together, but I talked to him this afternoon and asked if he'd had anything to do with Arlene's disappearance. He appeared genuinely surprised that she'd left. He claimed he'd spent the day avoiding her."

"And you believe him?"

Paula met the deputy's eyes with conviction. "Yes. I do."

Deputy Gray looked over her notes and tapped her fingernails on the counter. "Okay, I think you can go. Just don't leave the premises until Sheriff Hill gives the okay."

Paula rose and made it halfway to the door when Deputy Gray said, "Oh, I'm sorry. Ms. Arnett. Paula? I have just one more question. Where were you last night?"

"In my motorhome. Except for a brief time when Sheriff Hill came out to investigate a suspicious noise in the campground. Ray Landry, he was in the camper next to mine, and I alerted the sheriff and walked through the area with him."

"And what did you find as you walked with Sheriff Hill?"

"That the noise was likely due to raccoons digging through a trash can, and that the scream we heard might have been a bobcat. The sheriff found tracks, but I—"

"Other than that, were you alone all night?"

Paula took a deep breath and fought the urge to clasp her hands. "For part of it. Jake Martinez was staying in my little guest nook, otherwise known as the dining area. He didn't reserve a room in time, and I let him stay with me. But he left while Ray and I were busy with the sheriff. That would've been around 2:40-ish."

Jotting down a note, Deputy Gray asked, "Did Mr. Martinez say where he went?"

"I didn't ask. Jake was kind of self-conscious about having to stay with me. I just figured he bunked in his van for the rest of the night. It was parked on the far side of my camper, but he moved it this morning."

The officer peered at Paula over the rim of her glasses for what felt like an eternity. Paula held her breath as she peered back. *I've watched my share of Criminal Minds, lady.* After several seconds, she asked, "Will that be all?"

With a curt nod, Deputy Gray dismissed her.

CHAPTER FIFTY-EIGHT

Making her way through the living area, Paula realized the number of people milling around had dropped during her interview with Deputy Gray, leaving only six or so remaining to be questioned. She reviewed the officer's questions in her mind. *I wonder why she didn't ask for details about Mr. Lewis's past with Arlene. Maybe they've already gotten that information.* Ray waved her over.

She tried for a light tone as she approached him. "Hey, have you already been in the hot seat?"

He shoved his hands into his back pockets. "No. I think they have a list, and I must be way down the ladder."

"The experience wasn't all that awful. I think I'm going to head out to my motorhome now. Last night's antics and this evening's excitement have worn me completely out."

Ray's eyes narrowed. "If you'll wait until I'm finished here, I'll walk out to our campsites with you. If someone from our group hurt Arlene, it might be safer if you had an escort."

"Thanks, but with all these police officers hanging around, it'd be rather foolish for someone to try anything. Besides," Paula said, nodding at Mark who was making his way toward them. "I've already got an escort."

Ray cocked an eyebrow. "I can see that now. You be safe, okay?"

"I will. You, too."

Mark nodded at Ray and extended a hand to Paula. As he steered her toward the back door, he asked. "All through?"

"I am. Did you have to talk to anyone?"

He lowered his voice in a conspiratorial manner. "I didn't want anyone to think I was a suspicious character, so I spoke briefly with Deputy Eugene."

"Oh, is that so?"

His voice grew husky. "Yeah. I told him I'd keep an extra close eye on you. We should err on the side of caution. Just in case, you know."

A heady, liquid heat flowed through her limbs. "Oh. That sounds like a good idea. Erring on the side of caution, and all."

They left the cabin, stepping into the mild night. After a few paces, Mark came to an abrupt stop, standing toe to toe with Paula. His hazel eyes searched her face. "Cassie gave me directions to your motorhome, so I moved my car around to your site earlier. Before we head out there, though, are you sure you're okay with me staying? With you? All night?"

Paula stood on her tiptoes and wrapped her arms around his neck, kissing him as if his lips were water and she a vagabond who had spent a week crawling across the parched desert on her knees in search of a drink.

When they parted, he took her hands in his and squeezed. "So, was that a yes?"

Paula returned the squeeze. "Most definitely. Yes, it was a yes."

He narrowed his eyes and offered a fake scowl. "Then why in hell are we standing around out here? We've got a lot of time to make up for. Let's get a move on."

CHAPTER FIFTY-NINE

Outside her motorhome, Paula held up the key and jingled it. "Remember when you had to help me unlock my door when we were here for Martha's wedding?"

Mark held out his hand and she dropped the key into his open palm. "Remember it? I replay that scene in my mind all the time. Sweet little inebriated Paula broached the subject of kissing me."

A pout on her lips, Paula said, "And you resisted my offer."

He unlocked the door and stood aside for her to enter. "I didn't want you to regret anything that might have come out of that. And I wanted you to be, well, *you* when we finally had the opportunity to be together."

She swayed against him. "You are such a good man."

He took her hand and nodded toward the bedroom. "And you are definitely you tonight. In here?"

"Yes, please."

The cat, curled up in the middle of the bed, opened one sleepy eye and yawned. "This must be Star," Mark said, petting the cat. Star jumped off the bed and ran into the kitchen, disappearing beneath the table.

Paula slid the door closed behind them. "I believe she understands we need some privacy."

With a smoldering smile, Mark said, "Wise cat." He held out his arms and Paula melted into him.

CHAPTER SIXTY

A persistent purring followed by a masculine chuckle roused Paula out of a deep sleep. She opened her eyes to find Star kneading Mark's chest while he scratched the satisfied cat behind the ears. Paula studied the pair with contentment. She examined her feelings. *Should I feel guilty about last night? No. No guilt. This all feels perfect.* "Mm," she mumbled. "After just one night you've brought another woman into our bed. I guess that's what I get for falling for a hunky doctor."

"I tried to talk *you* into sleeping on my chest, but *no*, you wanted a pillow and a mattress and all that other fancy stuff. Star loves me."

Paula smirked. "Watch this. Star, baby, are you hungry?" Star meowed and darted into the kitchen area. Paula kissed Mark and took Star's place atop his chest. "I won't be distracted by the promise of food."

He wiggled his eyebrows. "Mm. Let's test that out. Paula, are you hungry?"

"Only for you." At Mark's husky groan, she thought, *There's that crazy, brazen Paula again. I'm really beginning to like her a lot.*

* * *

Paula and Mark loved, and snuggled, and dozed until Star demanded to be fed. Paula pulled on a robe and hurried to placate the adamant cat with a can of the feline's favorite delicacy. She put on a pot of coffee and peered out the window where all seemed peaceful. *Maybe they've figured out who hurt Arlene. I sure hope she's made it through the night okay. Maybe we can go to the hospital this morning.* When she returned to the bedroom with two cups of coffee, she found Mark propped up against the headboard, scrolling through his phone.

"Working on a Sunday, Doctor?"

He accepted the coffee with a kiss and patted the mattress beside him. "Checking on Mom and Dad. Apparently, they're fitting right in at Hidden Pines. Mom said they were getting ready for church."

Paula perched beside him and smoothed back a lock of his hair. "I still can't believe you found them an assisted living center near Happy Vale. And that you kept the whole thing a secret from me for weeks."

Putting his phone away, Mark stroked Paula's leg. "Honestly, we didn't know if we could get them into Pines until a week ago. And then we had to settle everything in Phoenix and arrange for a moving truck. I didn't want to get your hopes, or mine, up in case everything fell apart." He chuckled. "My sisters all came to help with the moving process, and they accused me of trying to toss heirlooms out the window so I could get here faster. I'm not sure some of that didn't happen."

A warm glow spread through Paula. "I can't wait to meet your parents. So, are they all still in the area? Your sisters, I mean."

"Everyone had to go straight back to their homes except for Janie. She flew back to Dallas with us and plans to fly back to Cleveland once Mom and Dad are settled. I want you to meet her before she leaves."

"I'd like that."

"I guess I should let you know that, even though she's the youngest of the four, Janie is the tough one. She never married because, according to the other sisters, no one ever met Janie's outrageously high standards. And I think she's been tasked by sisters one, two, and three, with interrogating the woman who has captured their baby brother's heart. I'm not sure what the officer put you through last night, but I guarantee my sister will be tougher."

Paula rolled her eyes. "Surely, you're exaggerating?"

Mark shrugged, but a mischievous half-smile lay on his lips. "Don't say I didn't warn you. She's a middle school principal. Need I say more?"

A knock sounded at the door and Paula gave Mark a quick kiss. "Be right back." She closed the bedroom door behind her as a more urgent knock sounded.

"Goldilocks, open up."

Paula opened the door to find Cassie pacing back and forth across the campsite. "What's the matter?"

"Get dressed and come to the office! Jake's being arrested on charges of kidnapping and attempted murder!"

CHAPTER SIXTY-ONE

Paula scurried back to the bedroom and rifled through her closet while Mark looked on from beneath hooded lids. As she scrambled into a pair of jeans and an old sweatshirt, Paula ruminated on how best to bring him up to speed on Jake. *What if he takes this all the wrong way? Better I tell him than someone else who might put a different spin on it.*

Mark extended a hand. "Penny for your thoughts."

She sat and pressed her lips to his knuckles, then said, "I don't want you to find out from someone else, but Jake stayed here on the night Arlene went missing. And now he's being arrested. I need to go set things straight."

His eyebrows knit together. "What do you mean by 'stayed here'? Like *here*, here or at the *resort* here?"

Paula snuggled against him. "He didn't have the funds to get a room until it was too late, and all the rooms were taken. I let him sleep on my foldout bed in the kitchen area. He moved into Arlene's room when she left."

"Oh."

"Mark, he's an old friend who needed a place to stay. I couldn't stand the thought of him sleeping in the back of his old van."

He waved his hands. "I meant, oh, in that case, you can vouch for him."

Paula kissed him. "I love that you trust me on this. But to answer your question, not really. Not for the entire night, anyway. Jake was gone when I got back inside after the sheriff came out to investigate the ruckus with the racoons."

Mark shook his head and pulled a t-shirt on. "If he had anything to do with Arlene's disappearance, you might have been a target, too. I love how kind you are, but one day..."

She plucked his jeans from the floor and handed them to him. "I'm positive Jake had nothing to do with Arlene's kidnapping. He just doesn't have it in him. There's this sadness that surrounds him, but no anger, no animosity toward anyone as far as I can tell."

He buttoned his pants and gathered her close. "I hope you're right. I really do. But I couldn't handle it if something happened to you. I love you."

Her breath caught in her throat. "Is this where I'm supposed to blink a whole bunch of times?"

Mark offered his lopsided grin and tucked a strand of hair behind her ear. "Oh, beautiful lady, don't you think we're passed the blinking stage? You ready?"

She blushed and lowered her eyelashes. "Yeah. Um, let's go see what's going on."

CHAPTER SIXTY-TWO

Paula towed Mark along in her wake as she half-ran to the cabin, weaving through a gauntlet of worried looking classmates. They arrived outside the office as Jake's hands were being cuffed. Sheriff Hill pushed him into the back seat with a firm hand on Jake's head, shutting the door behind him with a decisive shove. Paula closed the distance between them as the sheriff opened his own car door.

Her hands balled into fists at her hips, Paula said, "Sheriff, there's no way Jake had anything to do with Arlene's kidnapping, and he sure as hell never tried to murder her. Ask anyone here."

"Ms. Paula, we have some pretty strong evidence to the contrary. Now, if you'll excuse me…"

Everything Paula had ever garnered from her hours of binge-watching *Law and Order* flooded into her head. "Jake, don't say anything to anyone until you have an attorney. Promise me."

Jake nodded; his eyes filled with bleakness.

"I promise he'll be treated fairly," Sheriff Hill said. "But you may have to accept that your friend is responsible for a pretty heinous crime."

"But I can provide an alibi for him."

"We have your statement. Now, please, let me do my job."

Mark slid an arm around Paula's waist. "Come on, hon. We'll do whatever we can from our end."

They huddled together as the sheriff's car pulled away from the resort. "Now what?" Cassie asked.

Spinning to face her, Paula realized that many of their classmates were gathered nearby, looking to her for an answer. Straightening her spine, she said, "Now we find out what really happened and we free Jake."

CHAPTER SIXTY-THREE

Pacing the perimeter of the cabin with Mark at her side, Paula took vague note of the sheriff's car pulling onto the road as a catering truck entered the resort's parking lot. Her stomach rumbled, even as Jake was being carted to the county jail. *Good grief. Hungry at a time like this? What would Stephanie Plum do?* She stopped her march around the building, holding up a finger. "We need to get an attorney right away. Delbert's here. He'll go."

Mark asked, "He's not a criminal lawyer, is he?"

"No, but he can hold down the fort until we can find one. He might even know someone in the area." She pivoted and headed through the back door of the cabin and on into the office with Mark close on her heels. She found Martha and Melinda whispering over coffee and hot cinnamon rolls. "Hey, mind if I look up a room number in the computer?"

"Not at all," Melinda said. "We're so sorry to hear your friend was attacked. Is there anything we can do?"

"Pray. I think we just need to pray for Arlene and hope that Jake's the man I think he is and wasn't the one who harmed her."

Martha patted Paula's arm. "I can do that."

Paula squinted at the screen, clicking on a name. "I'm going to find Delbert to see if he'll go to the jail until we can get a criminal attorney down there."

Mark said, "Hold on a second. Martha, do you have any more of those cinnamon rolls? Paula's stomach is making weird noises."

"I'm good for now," Paula said. "I'll be back in a few minutes, but maybe you'll grab me one for later?" She jotted down a number as Martha raised her eyebrows at the doctor.

Martha said, "So, Dr. Hunky, did you two work up an appetite?"

Paula winked at Martha. "What happens in the motorhome, stays in the motorhome, don't you know?" *Was that me or my new brazen alter ego?*

She jogged across the parking lot and knocked on Delbert's door. Sherry answered the knock in a short floral robe, her hair in a tight bun. "Hey Paula, come on in."

"Thanks, but I'm looking for Delbert. It's kind of an emergency."

"He went to gas the Suburban up before we head back to Dempsey. I know y'all have some paperwork to do on the resort, but he wanted to be on the road as soon as that was done, and the sheriff okayed it."

Paula's face fell. She pulled her phone out of her pocket and dialed Delbert's number. As it rang, she said, "Jake's been arrested for the attack on Arlene."

The color drained from Sherry's face. "Oh, no. It couldn't have been Jake."

"I don't think so either, but I need to see if Delbert will represent him until we can find a local attorney."

"You know Delbert will want to help. Sit a spell while you call. I'm just going to finish putting my makeup on."

Paula sank into a chair beside the bed. When Delbert answered, Paula said, "Jake's been arrested. They think he hurt Arlene. I'm just afraid he'll unintentionally say something that can be used against him if he doesn't have someone there. Would you mind...?"

"Not at all, Goldilocks. I'll head to the sheriff's office straight away. Would you let Sherry know it's going to be a while?"

"Sure. I'm with her now. Thanks, Delbert. I owe you one."

"You don't owe me a thing. Glad to help. And I think I have an old law school buddy who lives near here. He went into criminal law, if I remember correctly, so I'll give him a call on my way."

A weight lifted from her shoulders. "You're the best. And, for the record, I know Jake didn't do anything to harm Arlene."

Delbert's voice took on a gritty edge. "Whether he did or didn't, he has the right to representation. You just sit tight, and I'll handle the legal stuff."

CHAPTER SIXTY-FOUR

As Paula disconnected Delbert's call, she ticked off choices on her fingers. *Sitting tight is not an option.* "I'll see you later, Sherry." She did her best to ignore the promise of bacon cooking on a nearby grill as she trotted back to the cabin. She met Cassie outside the office door and embraced her then drew back, her lips narrowed. "Where'd Mark go?"

"He put together a breakfast plate for you. He and the food are waiting in the kitchen."

Amid her anxiety, Paula felt surrounded by love. "What a guy, eh?"

Cassie gave her a gentle shove. "Yeah, you're not off the hook for details about last night. But go to your man."

"Grab your plate and come with me," Paula said. "We need a strategy."

"Melinda mentioned you were going to talk to Delbert. Any luck?"

"Yeah, that's squared away, but we've got to learn what evidence they think they have on Jake and then refute it. I have a feeling it's something simple and easily explained and that the sheriff just plucked the lowest hanging fruit."

Paula opened the kitchen door and crossed the room into Mark's arms. "Thank you for thinking of my stomach."

"I know what my woman likes," he said, sliding an arm around her waist.

Their lips met. "You sure do."

Cassie groaned. "Oh, great. Lovebirds. Eat, you two, so we can talk."

Paula slid into the chair Mark pulled out for her and snagged a piece of bacon. "The smell of this stuff cooking almost distracted me from my purpose."

"Coffee?" Cassie asked.

"Oh, yes. Please and thank you," Paula said.

Mark spread strawberry jelly on a biscuit and waved his knife in the air. "Won't the sheriff have to let Jake's attorney know what evidence they have on him?"

"I think so." Paula thought back to the items in the safe. "You know, I don't believe the sheriff ever came to get the note that Arlene left on the door yesterday morning. We should take that to Delbert along with the other stuff we stowed in the safe. Maybe there's something in there that could clear Jake, or at least cast some doubt on the evidence they believe they have."

A tousle-headed McKenzie peeked around the door. "Oh, hi, everyone. Have any of you seen Mom?"

Cassie said, "If she's not in the office, she's out helping Ellie. One of the housekeepers called in sick today."

"Oh, shoot. I'd better get dressed and take over for her."

"How'd things go with Jeffries's parents last night?" Paula asked.

McKenzie's lips slanted down in a frown. "Okay, I guess. His dad wasn't there. Delilah's not exactly jumping for joy, but she wasn't exactly angry either."

Mark looked from McKenzie to Paula. "What would cause Delilah to be angry with you?"

A look passed between the three women in the room. "No one told you?" Cassie asked.

Paula covered her mouth. "I didn't think to tell him."

"Tell me what?"

McKenzie pressed her hands against her stomach. "I'm pregnant. Jeffries and I are going to have a baby."

Mark's eyes grew wide, then softened as he rose. "Wow. May I hug you?"

Paula's eyes stung with tears as he drew McKenzie in close. *He'd make such a wonderful father. Would it be fair to tie him down to someone like me who isn't able to have children? We haven't even discussed marriage or anything beyond the next moment, but maybe we need to talk about the future…*

"I'm sure Delilah will come around. The initial shock will wear off then she'll realize all the joy that will come of this," Mark said. "How far along are you? Have you found an obstetrician yet? I can recommend a good one. Are you getting good prenatal care? Taking your vitamins? I can write you a prescription."

Paula sat back and enjoyed observing as the doctor took over. *I really do love this man.*

After assuring Mark she was doing all the right things to care for the baby, McKenzie left to get dressed.

Paula mulled over their options in silence as she finished her breakfast, then gathered the dirty dishes. She loaded the dishwasher under the scrutiny of the others, then faced them with a decisive nod. "Okay, I'm going to the jail. Maybe Delbert can get me in to see Jake and we can learn why they think he's good for this attack on Arlene. Y'all coming with me?"

CHAPTER SIXTY-FIVE

On the drive to the jail, Paula looked over the three pieces of potential evidence from the safe—the duct tape, Arlene's note, and the business card with Arlene's scribble on the back. With Mark behind the wheel, she gave the items her complete attention. She tapped on the card as a frown hovered at the edges of her lips.

Paula handed two of the baggies to Cassie in the backseat. "Take a look at these handwriting samples. Do they look like they came from the same person?"

"Hm… The one sample on the back of the business card is kind of small. But just at first glance, no, they don't. Where'd you get the card?"

"Arlene gave it to me early on Friday. I watched her jot down the information. Granted, we were standing in the middle of the parking lot, and she was using her hand as a flat surface but, even at that, I can't see her having written the elegant note that was taped to the office door. The beautifully rounded letters in the note and all the sharp-edged ones on the card don't come close to matching."

Mark coughed. "I hate to say this, but wouldn't that just further incriminate Jake. If Arlene didn't leave the note on the door, then maybe he did. Maybe he was emulating what he thought Arlene's handwriting would look like."

Paula bit her lip. "No one knows I have a sample of Arlene's handwriting, except for you two and McKenzie. If we could get Sheriff Hill to take several samples of Jake's handwriting, we might get him to see that Jake didn't plant the note."

"But that means someone else did," Cassie said. "Who? And we don't know what the attacker did to Arlene. Was she beaten? Shot? Strangled?"

Paula shuddered as one image after another flashed before her eyes, each more violent than the last. "Hush. Oh, mercy, I hadn't thought of the possible details of the crime. Poor girl. Maybe there was a weapon left at the scene. There's a whole lot of stuff we just don't know, but I don't believe Jake could've done this. For one thing, there's no motive. At least not one that comes to mind."

"Greed and lust. Isn't that what crime usually revolves around?" Mark asked.

Paula nodded. "And I can't see either of those motivating Jake to harm Arlene."

Mark turned into the county jail parking lot and killed the engine. "Be prepared to be turned away."

Paula smirked. "I'm not too worried about that. I've got Cassie with me. No one says no to her."

CHAPTER SIXTY-SIX

"No? What do you mean no?" Paula scowled, her hands rigid at her sides.

Sheriff Hill peered down his nose at her. "Exactly what *no* always means. You all don't have visiting privileges at the moment. We're still processing Mr. Martinez, and his attorney will see him as soon as we've finished with all the paperwork and such."

Paula elbowed Cassie who went into femme fatale mode.

Cassie's voice took on a husky undertone and her brown eyes widened in feminine innocence. "Sheriff Hill, what would it hurt if we just stayed for a moment to give Jake a little support? I mean, wouldn't you want to know your friends were here for you if the situation were reversed? Please, Sheriff? It would mean the world..."

Holding her breath, Paula thought for a couple of seconds that Cassie's ploy might work until Sheriff Hill shook his head. He waved his hands in the direction of the door. "Nope. Now, you all should head on out. If all goes well, Mr. Martinez can have visitors on Tuesday afternoon. One at a time for fifteen minutes each. That's the rule."

Cassie and Paula exchanged weary shrugs and the sheriff shook his head with an amused huff. "You two make a pretty good team, though. Maybe we should hire y'all to soften up some of our more hardened criminals, not that we get many here in this county."

Mark laughed. "They could do it."

Giving both men a withering look, Paula said, "If we can't see Jake, we can still leave the three pieces of evidence we've collected. I called and left a message with the office, but maybe you didn't get it."

The sheriff pushed his hat back and sat at his desk. "Let me see what you've got."

Paula first placed the baggie containing the business card in front of him. "On Friday, Arlene wrote her personal information on the back of this card for me as we were chatting. Note the handwriting. Very rigid. Blocky."

Putting on a pair of cheater glasses, the sheriff examined the card. "Okay. She had lousy penmanship."

"But look at this note, the one Arlene supposedly left sometime early on Saturday morning." Paula said, placing the second evidence baggie in front of him. She stood back as the Sheriff compared the two.

"I'm no handwriting expert, but these do appear to have been written by two different people; however, that doesn't help your friend at all. It just shows that Arlene didn't write the second note."

Paula huffed out a breath. "I'd be willing to bet this is not Jake's handwriting. Look how consistent it is. All rounded letters. At least get a sample of Jake's writing."

"Pretty please?" Cassie asked with a flutter of eyelashes.

The sheriff threw his hands in the air. "I will do that. And I'll see if someone from the Sabine office specializes in handwriting. Will that satisfy you?"

"For now," Paula said.

"What's your other piece of evidence?"

"Oh, right." She handed him the third baggie with the piece of duct tape. "This was used to tape the note to the office door. Maybe you could get some prints off it."

Pinching the bridge of his nose, the sheriff accepted the evidence. "I will say this. You're persistent. But seriously, Mr. Martinez is in good hands. And you'll get to visit with him on Tuesday if he's still here."

"What do you mean, *if* he's still here? You mean if he's released?" Paula asked.

"There's a possibility he'll be moved to a facility with higher security than we have. If Ms. Davis doesn't survive her injuries, he'll be up on charges of murder."

Gasping for air as if all the oxygen had been sucked from the room, Paula collapsed onto a chair. "Oh. No."

CHAPTER SIXTY-SEVEN

A wave of disbelief crashed into Paula. *Murder? Mercy.* Only Mark's arms kept Paula upright and moving in the right direction as he steered her to his car. She couldn't wrap her head around the possibilities. *What if Arlene died? What if Jake is charged murder? No, I refuse to consider either of those outcomes.* "Mark, can we drive over to the hospital? They took Arlene to Hemphill. I feel like I need to be there."

Mark took Paula's hand in his. "Your wish. My command."

Cassie patted Paula's shoulder as they passed the city limit sign outside of Happy Vale. "You accomplished something back there. The sheriff promised you he'd get a sample of Jake's handwriting and have it checked out. He's a man of his word."

Blinking away a tear, Paula said, "I know he is. I'm just afraid they're so eager to wrap this case up that they'll be swayed by some piece of circumstantial evidence. Hopefully Delbert can give us information about what went down and what they have on Jake."

They drove the eight miles to Hemphill in silence, but Paula's mind swirled in chaos. *Could Jake really be responsible? Did I have a potential murderer in my motorhome overnight? But what about a motive? There is no motive. What if he is a psychopath? No. No. No. Jake did not do this, and we're going to prove it.*

Arriving at the Sabine County Medical Center, Mark navigated into the area reserved for physicians. "I'm going to try and pull some strings so at least one of you can have a few minutes with Arlene. If she's in intensive care, they won't let anyone but family and health care providers in, but I have admitting privileges here, so let's see what I can do. Just stay with me and act like you belong here. I should be able to check in on her regardless, and that might have to be good enough. Okay?"

Both women nodded, their eyes solemn. Paula tiptoed up to kiss him. "Thank you. Can we hurry, though? I'm not crazy about hospitals."

They followed Mark through the halls of the medical center and into the intensive care unit. As Mark spoke with the nurse in charge, Paula and Cassie stood behind him. Paula straightened her spine and attempted to ignore her surroundings. She arranged her face into a look she hoped made her appear professional, even in the jeans and sweatshirt she had donned in haste. Glancing at Cassie, she stifled a laugh. Not only were Cassie's shoulders squared off straight enough that one could have used them as rulers, but her eyebrows were arched in a manner that brooked no nonsense. *Formidable woman. Glad she's on our side.*

When Mark turned away from the desk to face them, his face was grim. "They'll let me in, but no one else. There's a waiting room just outside those double doors. You two go have a cup of coffee and I'll find out everything I can."

Paula's shoulders sagged. "Thank you. Please tell Arlene we're sorry this happened. And that we care about her. I'm not sure she always knew that was the case."

Taking Paula's hand, Cassie sniffled. "What Paula said. But add that we want her to get well soon."

Mark drew them into a group hug. "I'll do all that. You two try to stay out of trouble. I won't be long."

CHAPTER SIXTY-EIGHT

Paula's mind flitted from one idea to another like a restless hummingbird dancing from flower to flower as she paced the waiting room floor. *Who would gain from Arlene's death? Who had reason to hate her? Or maybe it wasn't hate. Maybe there was another motive. Money? Jealousy?* She accepted a cup of coffee from Cassie with a nod. "If Jake didn't have a motive to hurt Arlene, then who did?" Paula asked.

Cassie slid onto a green vinyl sofa, grabbed a magazine from a corner table, and began flipping through the pages. "You're certain it wasn't Mr. Lewis?"

"I was, but maybe we need to take another look at his alibi. He gave her a pretty large chunk of money back in the day to keep her quiet about their relationship. Maybe he wanted her to repay it."

"But she can't do that if she's dead," Cassie said, frowning as she perused the pages of the magazine.

"But maybe things got out of hand. Maybe he just wanted to intimidate her, and it went too far."

"That's a whole lot of maybes."

"Yeah, and he really doesn't seem the type to hurt anyone. Of course, that's what people tend to think until they know better. 'He was a quiet guy. Nice enough to talk to. Who'd have ever imagined he was hiding twenty corpses in his mom's basement?' That sort of thing."

Cassie ripped a coupon from the magazine and brandished it at Paula. "Woo hoo. Two dollars off my favorite shampoo."

Paula narrowed her eyes. "Really?"

"Sorry. It's expensive shampoo. But, back to the topic at hand. The same could be said for Jake, though. Couldn't it? Nice guy. Quiet."

"True. I just can't imagine what sort of evidence they have on Jake. If we only knew…"

Tapping on the metal arm of the sofa, Cassie asked, "Is there anyone else who was involved with Arlene back in the day? Someone who might carry a grudge?"

Paula sighed and settled into a chair across from Cassie. "From what I understand, Arlene was involved with quite a few guys. Even Ray."

Wrinkling her nose, Cassie said, "Ray? Hardly seems like he'd have been Arlene's type. Although, he did date a few girls outside of band. It's that charm of his. He's like a ray of sunshine."

Paula chuckled. "His parents named him well, didn't they?"

"You know, come to think of it, I think even Vanessa dated Ray some. I remember she was his date to the band banquet our senior year."

Paula tried to picture the two of them together, the tall, athletic Vanessa and Ray, the once ultra-skinny poster boy for band geeks, but she came up empty… Until she recalled the image of Ray making out with Arlene beneath the football stadium.

"Oh Cassie, did I ever tell you about the time I discovered Arlene under the bleachers at a football game?"

"If you did, I've forgotten. What happened? Why are you remembering it now?"

"It was late in the season, and bitterly cold, so we had to wear those white gloves for band. I dropped one of mine and Mr. Weber sent me down to retrieve it. Arlene was right under the band section making out, and I mean seriously making out, with someone. It was Ray. I didn't register it at the time, but now, I'm certain. I think at the time I was too shocked."

"Hmm… He certainly got around more than I would have given him credit for. But, Ray, a violent criminal? That's even more far-fetched than thinking Jake might be one."

They tossed ideas back and forth in a game of verbal catch, standing when Mark entered the room, followed by an older, balding man.

Mark's face remained somber. "Paula, Cassie, this is Arlene's husband, Ted Davis. Ted, Paula and Cassie went to school with Arlene."

Shaking hands with the women, Ted said, "Thank you for so much for coming. Please, sit."

Paula perched on the edge of her seat. "We're so sorry for everything that's happened to Arlene. How is she doing?"

"Her doctor seems to think she'll make it. We wondered for a while if that was going to be the case." His face crumpled and his next words came out in sobs. "I knew I should have come to the reunion with her. This never would have happened if I'd been here."

Cassie exchanged helpless glances with Paula and Mark and patted Ted's back. "There, there. You couldn't have known something bad would happen. Don't blame yourself."

Ted sighed and accepted a tissue from Paula. "Oh, I love my wife. She's impetuous and rambunctious and full of life, but she is a magnet for trouble."

Paula took Mark's hand and asked. "Have you spoken with Vanessa yet? She got worried when she couldn't reach you."

"Who? Vanessa? Oh, I don't remember seeing anything from a Vanessa on my phone."

Paula and Cassie exchanged puzzled looks.

Mark grimaced. "We can probably chalk that up to the lousy cell phone connectivity at the resort."

Paula snapped her fingers. "Oh, yes."

A doctor peered around the corner. "Mr. Davis? Good news. Your wife is waking up. She's asking for you."

Ted rose, a look of unabashed joy on his face. "Thank you. Thank you all. Doctor, I'm right behind you."

CHAPTER SIXTY-NINE

A spark of hope flared in Paula's chest. As Ted hurried after the doctor, she hugged Mark and then Cassie. "Good news at last. And now Arlene will be able to tell the authorities who attacked her. She can clear Jake."

Mark rubbed Paula's back. "Don't get your hopes up just yet. Arlene might be a little disoriented. The trauma of last night's events could linger for a while."

"Were you able to find out what happened to her?" Cassie asked.

Mark leaned forward, his elbows on his knees. "This information shouldn't leave this room. Understand?"

Paula crossed her heart and Cassie followed suit.

"Whoever did this made a clumsy attempt to make it look like a suicide. Arlene was found in her Lexus in a wooded area about eight miles from the resort. A hose was fastened to her tailpipe and run through the passenger side window. Then duct tape was used to seal off any places where fresh air might come in—around the hose where it came in through the window, mainly, but also around the other windows. Someone really wanted her dead."

Paula covered her face with her hands and groaned. "Duct tape. Jake had lots of duct tape."

Cassie said, "So, why was it clumsy? How'd they reason that it wasn't really a suicide attempt?"

"Because the idiot sealed the windows from the outside of the car."

Paula sputtered. "Wow. Now, I'm sure Jake didn't do it. He's not stupid."

Mark took Paula's hand in his. "But he might've been inebriated. Maybe he got drunk to get his courage up and wasn't thinking straight. The car apparently reeked of alcohol and there were dozens of beer bottles scattered all over the place. Most of them had Arlene's prints on them, but others were wiped clean."

"So, he was too drunk to know that Arlene wouldn't have been able to seal up the windows from the outside, but not so drunk that he forgot to wipe his fingerprints from the bottles? I just don't get it. What piece of evidence ties Jake to this crime?"

Mark scratched his head. "Good point."

"Was Arlene drunk?" Cassie asked.

"Oh, yes. Way over the legal limit. In fact, that was the biggest medical issue they had to deal with when they found her because whoever left Arlene out there didn't think to check the level of fuel in her tank. The car ran out of gas long before enough carbon monoxide accumulated inside to kill her; although, it did add to her distress."

Paula stood and began pacing with renewed energy. Her eyes grew wide as she stopped in her tracks, holding up a finger. "Wait. It just occurred to me. Jake doesn't drink. Except for soft drinks. He sticks to Dr. Pepper. Let's go tell the sheriff what we know."

"Honey, just because you haven't seen Jake drink alcohol doesn't mean he never does. But like you said, when Arlene wakes up and has her wits about her, she could clear him. Let's just hope she makes a full recovery."

CHAPTER SEVENTY

On the drive back to the resort, Paula worried over parts of the conversation with Ted. *Something just doesn't ring true.* She shifted in her seat to face Cassie. "Cassie, did you think it was odd that Ted didn't get a call from Vanessa or even act as though her name meant something to him?"

"Yes, but as Mark reminded us, cell phone service is a real issue at the resort."

"But she tried while we were at Burke's Bouquets, too. If Vanessa and Arlene are as close as Vanessa says, why wouldn't he know her? It's not like Vanessa is that common a name, and she had his number saved in her phone. Was he playing dumb?"

Mark said, "Okay, just adding my two cents here. The man was distraught."

Paula held up her hand. "What if he knew that Arlene was coming here hoping to get a little action on the side, and he decided that enough was enough? She does have a history of trouble. Ted said that, remember?"

"Yes, but I didn't take it that way," Cassie said. "I agree with Mark. Ted adores Arlene and he was out of his mind with worry."

Paula blew out a breath. "You're right, I suppose. I can't wait to tell Vanessa that Arlene is out of her coma, though.

Maybe she'll forgive me for not paying more attention to her concerns last night."

As soon as Mark's car came to a stop in the resort's parking lot, Paula rushed to the office and logged into the computer. Finding Vanessa's room number, she hurried over and knocked. When no one answered, Paula glanced at her watch and surveyed her surroundings as Mark joined her on the porch.

Mark pecked her cheek. "Melinda caught Cassie and me on our way over here. She's changing bedding in one of the rooms and Cassie stayed to help her. It seems the sheriff gave the okay for folks to leave since they've got Jake in custody. Vanessa may have already checked out."

Paula's shoulders slumped. "This is exactly what I feared would happen. They have Jake in custody and voila, everyone else has magically cleared. Still, I can't believe Vanessa would leave without knowing how Arlene is doing. Besides, I'm fairly certain that's her car under the carport. I'll bet she's around here somewhere."

Mark kicked at a pebble, and they followed its journey with their eyes as it skittered down the porch. "I keep thinking about the person who tried to make the attack on Arlene look like a suicide attempt. They either had to be drunk or just not very bright. And I wonder if the sheriff found tire tracks for another car."

Paula dropped into one of the guest chairs. "Oh, yeah. If it was someone from the reunion, they'd have needed a way back out here. How far from the resort did you say they found Arlene?"

"About eight miles, I think. That'd be a heck of a walk back here in the dark. There had to have been another car."

She cocked her head. "So, a drunken Arlene drove herself out there and someone followed her, sat in Arlene's car with her, and they both drank until what, Arlene passed out? And then the perp hooked up the hose to the exhaust, taped up the car, and drove back to the resort... What are we missing here?

"I think that until Delbert learns what evidence they have against Jake, we're at an impasse, but it wouldn't hurt to put the thought of another car in Sheriff Hill's head."

"You're right. I know he's sick of taking my calls but... Hey, there's Delbert's Suburban."

CHAPTER SEVENTY-ONE

Paula waved Delbert over to Vanessa's room, studying his weathered face for any clues to how his preliminary visit with Jake had gone. As he neared the room, Paula clasped his hand and searched his eyes for news. *Please let him have something good to report.* "Thank you so much for being there for Jake. How'd it go?"

Sighing, Delbert folded his rangy frame into a chair. "First, he wanted me to tell you how much he appreciates your support. And, my attorney buddy, Brady Johnson, is in Dallas until later today, but he agreed to take Jake on as a client. They don't get a lot of criminal activity here, so I think we made his weekend. Uh, sorry. That didn't come out like I intended it. Anyway, he'll be back in the area around five, and he promised to meet Jake as soon as he gets into town."

Paula pulled her hair back, securing it in a ponytail. "That's great news. Can you tell us about the evidence they have on Jake?"

"So, I don't know how much you know about how they found Arlene."

Mark pulled up a chair and sat beside Paula, taking her hand in his. "We went to the hospital. Her husband filled me in on everything he knew. The botched attempt to make it look like a suicide. Arlene's blood alcohol level. The beer bottles that had been wiped clean of fingerprints. The way the hose was taped to the car..."

Paula's eyes pleaded with the attorney. "Delbert, even if Jake was capable of something like this, he wouldn't have been stupid enough to stage a suicide and then tape the windows from the outside."

Delbert held out a calming hand. "I agree, but Jake's given me permission to tell you why they arrested him. Where's Cassie? She's gonna want to hear this, too. Can I get some coffee before I go into detail?"

CHAPTER SEVENTY-TWO

Paula dug through her purse to retrieve the key to her motorhome. Dangling the key in front of Mark, she said, "Why don't you two go ahead. The coffee's in the cupboard above the sink if you want to get a pot brewing."

The men headed off and she stopped outside a room with a housekeeping cart parked on the porch. She found Cassie tucking the corner of a sheet onto the bed. "When you finish with that, come join us in my camper. Delbert's back from the jail."

"Really? Okay, I'll be right there."

As Paula neared her site, she stumbled upon Ray sitting outside his camper, clinging to a beer, his face a mask of sadness. She wrapped an arm around his shoulders. "Oh, Ray. It's going to be okay. Arlene seems to be rousing from her coma and we're going to get Jake out of this mess."

He peered up at her, his eyes shining with what Paula took to be hope. "Thanks. I needed some good news. Is there anything I can do to help?"

"Come with me.   Sherry's husband, Delbert, is an attorney. He's been with Jake this morning and he has some information for us."

They entered Paula's motorhome and were greeted with the welcoming aroma of coffee. Cassie stepped in behind them, helping herself to a Dr. Pepper as Delbert dropped his phone onto the table. Pouring coffees for herself and Ray, Paula took a seat at the table and asked, "What do you have there?"

Delbert's eyes searched hers as he cast a wary glance at Ray.

Paula patted Delbert's arm. "Delbert, this is Ray Landry. He's one of Jake's oldest friends. He should be in on this, too."

The two men shook hands. "Ray, nice to meet you. Jake mentioned your name. Have a seat."

Once everyone was in place, Delbert spread his hands on the table. "Ray, I don't know if you've been staying in contact with Jake these last few years..."

Ray shook his head. "Not really. It almost seemed like he dropped off the face of the earth for a while, but he was the one who contacted me to make sure I'd be here this weekend."

Nodding, Delbert tapped on his phone. He shifted his gaze to Paula. "So, one of the reasons Jake was such a prime suspect is that he's done time for manslaughter."

Paula's eyes blurred. "What? No. That doesn't make sense."

"It gets worse. He was also previously arrested on charges of kidnapping."

CHAPTER SEVENTY-THREE

The world tilted and Paula closed her eyes in hopes it would right itself. She waded through the confusion in the voices of her friends, and her thoughts joined their words. *It just can't be true.* Mark's hand found hers and she held on for dear life. "Oh, Delbert, what have I done? I let him stay here until he had a room. But, still, *Jake*? Our Jake?"

Delbert held up a hand. "He told me everything and I called in a favor so I could corroborate his story before I passed it along to you all. It seems Jake was in a band—"

"Yeah," Ray said. "Fair to Middlin'. They were kind of a big deal for a while. Then they just disappeared from the scene. I kept up with them for a long time. It was cool knowing that I knew their drummer."

Delbert nodded. "Jake said they were riding high for a time and enjoying all the perks that went with that—booze, drugs, plenty of willing women. He fell hard for a girl named Amelia. The only thing was, she wasn't a groupie. No, Amelia was the lead singer's wife. To hear Jake tell it, he didn't care about all the women that threw themselves his way, and he was disgusted that Amelia's husband, Tony, indulged himself in a series of one-night stands when they were on the road."

Paula clutched Mark's hand as if afraid he might drift away. "So, did he confront Tony?"

"If he had, we probably wouldn't be here now. No, he had an affair with Amelia."

"Oh, no," Cassie said, her jaw dropping open.

Paula slumped in her seat. "That's not good."

Dropping his Stetson onto the counter behind them, Delbert said, "He says that Amelia was lonely and vulnerable, and now, looking back, he feels awful for taking advantage of those feelings, but at the time, they were young and ruled by their hormones. Jake and Tony were on a binge at a tavern one night when Amelia met them outside and confronted her husband about his affairs. Then, she threw her relationship with Jake in his face. Tony became enraged. He threatened to kill them both. But he was so stoned that he could barely put one foot in front of the other. Amelia left the bar with Jake, who was also high."

Delbert paused to drink from his coffee cup. With a hitch in his voice, he continued. "They didn't get far. Jack missed a curve, and they crashed head on into a tree doing upwards of seventy. Amelia was thrown from the car. She died instantly."

"Oh, no," Paula said, her words ending in a choked off sob.

Mark pulled her close. "And why was a kidnapping charge involved?"

"Tony maintained that Jake took Amelia against her will, even though there was plenty of evidence that she'd left with Jake of her own accord. Unfortunately, the judge was a good friend of Tony's father, and the charge was only dropped when Jake's attorneys worked out a plea. Jake ended up doing two years in prison on a vehicular manslaughter charge."

CHAPTER SEVENTY-FOUR

Paula fought to think objective thoughts even as Delbert's words burrowed a tunnel in her mind. *Jake's an ex-con*? *And here I am, fighting for his release. Am I just being dense?* She shook her head to dislodge the negative thoughts. *He's done his time, but still...* Paula asked, "So, Delbert, if the kidnapping charges were dropped, why are they being brought into consideration in the attack on Arlene?"

"Unfortunately, there was a piece of hard evidence left at the scene that ties Jake to Arlene."

Paula's shoulders slumped in sync with Ray's.

Cassie asked, "What kind of evidence?"

Delbert took out a pair of reading glasses and examined a photo he'd taken on his phone. "I know I'm not old yet, but apparently my eyes haven't gotten the message. Can one of you take a look at this?"

Cassie gave Delbert a withering look and snagged the phone from his hand. "If you had gone to the University of Texas instead of Texas A&M, you'd know how to enlarge a photo on your phone." She made the photo bigger and shared it with the others. "It's a receipt. What's so significant about it?"

With a good-natured grin, Delbert said, "And if you'd been a Texas Aggie instead of a lowly Longhorn, you might understand the significance." Sobering, he pointed out the date on the photo. "These items were purchased last Thursday at a Lowe's in San Marcos. Let's see, he bought a heavy-duty garden hose, duct tape, a couple of different sized wrenches, and gum. The credit card is in Jake's name."

Ray held up a hand, "Oh, I had a cardboard box with all that stuff in it on Friday night. Jake loaned it to me so I could tinker with some stuff in my trailer. I did the repairs after the campfire that night and left the box outside my camper. I planned on returning it before I went to breakfast the next day, but it was gone when I checked. I figured Jake picked it up."

Mark sat forward. "Did you happen to notice the receipt in there when you were getting materials out of the box?"

Ray bit at his lip and studied the ceiling of Paula's motorhome. "There were a few scraps of paper in there. Might have been a receipt or two. I remember thinking that I needed to buy the guy a toolbox."

Paula grasped Delbert's hand. "So, we need to determine if that box is in Jake's vehicle. Have they already searched his van?"

"They have. I haven't gotten a list of any items they took into evidence, but I'll check for that. Still, whether it's in there or not, that doesn't get Jake off the hook."

Mark stabbed a finger at the photo of the receipt. "Except anyone could've grabbed that box from outside Ray's camper and used the contents to set the stage for Arlene's attack."

Delbert nodded and stroked his chin. "True. But with Jake's record, he's going to need a much better alibi for the goods."

Rising to get the coffee pot, Paula said, "Mark brought up the issue of how Arlene's attacker left the site last night. Were there other tire marks? Maybe it was more than one person involved—one to drive out there with Arlene and another to follow and bring the attacker back here."

"Now that's something Jake and I discussed, and it doesn't seem like the sheriff has yet considered all the ramifications of the way the crime was carried out. It is within the realm of believability that whoever did this rode out there and then walked back to the resort, though. There would have been ample time."

A light went on in Ray's eyes. "Not for Jake! He has a bad knee. Said he was injured in a collision. Oh, damn, you think maybe he injured it the night Amelia was killed?"

A glimmer of hope wound its way through the anxiety in Paula's chest. "I'll bet you're right! That might explain so much. Jake did mention he had a bum knee, and I've seen him limp. Especially when he's been on his feet for a while."

Delbert jotted down a note. "I didn't notice a limp, but then we were seated for the interview, and he didn't mention it. This might be a way to cast doubt on his involvement. At this point, that's a really good thing. There's still room to speculate on his having an accomplice, but nothing about this feels premeditated, and I'd think it would have to be the case for the attackers to coordinate their actions."

Paula's phone buzzed. "Hey, that's Vanessa. I need to go let her know that Arlene's condition seems to be improving." She kissed Mark. "You've got my keys. Would you lock up if y'all leave the camper?"

CHAPTER SEVENTY-FIVE

Hurrying through the campground on her way to meet Vanessa, a jolt of dismay stopped Paula in her tracks. *So many vacant parking spaces. Looks like just about everyone from the reunion has checked out now. And I've been too busy to say my goodbyes.* She entered the vintage-style motel area of the resort, trotted to Vanessa's room, then knocked.

From the other side of the door, Vanessa said, "Just a minute. I'm getting dressed."

Leaning against a support column, Paula caught movement from her peripheral vision and realized that, despite her mild angst at having been abandoned, a few of her former classmates were still wandering around. She hailed Rudy and he jogged over.

"Any news about Arlene or Jake?" he asked.

Paula related everything she thought it was okay to tell him, leaving out Jake's criminal record and the evidence left at the scene.

"Listen, Paula, you and I both know that Jake didn't attack Arlene. There's no way I'd believe he'd hurt anyone. Not on purpose anyway."

"That's what I think, too. We're fighting for him. And as soon as I'm able to visit with Jake, I'll tell him what you said. He needs all the support he can get right now."

Rudy hugged her. "Thanks. Listen, Deb and I have a flight to catch, but give us a call when this gets straightened out, and I have no doubt it will. Here's my card. My personal cell number is written on the back."

Rudy strode away as Vanessa opened the door, her eyes rimmed in red. "Paula, I'm so sorry I was curt with you last night. I feared the worst, and I couldn't bear that no one else was as worried as I was."

"That's totally understandable, and I didn't mean to seem as if I was brushing you off. I've been worried about Arlene, too. May I come in?"

Vanessa stood aside. "Of course. I'm just finishing up my packing. Have a seat."

Paula slid onto the nearest chair while Vanessa folded a blouse, placing it atop a stack of clothing in her suitcase."

"So, there's some good news," Paula said.

"Really?" Vanessa dropped down on the bed next to the suitcase and clutched a pillow to her chest. "I've been afraid to hold out hope."

"Yes. We have it on good authority that Arlene is likely out of the woods."

Vanessa clapped her hands together. "Really? That's wonderful! Let's go visit her."

Paula wrinkled her nose. "Now? There's a good chance we won't be allowed in to see her."

Vanessa stood. "Arlene will want to see me. I'm certain. And I really need to see her. For my own peace of mind. Please?"

"Well, I suppose we could try...Let me go get my car and my purse. Maybe Cassie would like to ride along."

Vanessa closed her suitcase and pulled on a cardigan. "I'd rather not wait. We can take my car. I'll bring you back to the resort after our visit, and then I'll head on home."

Paula knit her brow as her eyes scanned the room. "You sure you have everything?"

Vanessa stuffed the rest of her clothes into the suitcase without bothering to fold them. "I'm sure."

Buoyed by Vanessa's enthusiasm, Paula followed her out to the car, locking the room door behind them.

Sliding behind the steering wheel, Vanessa said, "You'll have to give me directions. I'm not familiar with the area."

"Sure." Paula shoved her phone into her back pocket. "Make a left when you get to the end of the driveway. Then, it's pretty much a straight shot until you get to Hemphill."

Once the Happy Vale city limits sign was behind them, Vanessa broke the silence. "I don't suppose you've spoken to Jake."

"No. We tried to get in to offer him our support earlier, but he was still being processed. We did find him an attorney, though."

"Oh, good. You know, I first thought that Mr. Lewis might be responsible. And I'm still not ruling him out. He and Arlene have such a sordid past, after all."

Paula shifted in her seat. "You don't really think Jake did this either, do you?"

"No, but I think it's someone close to him."

Searching her brain for an answer, Paula asked, "Such as...?"

"Ray."

Paula huffed out an indignant laugh. "Oh, come on. Ray?"

"Maybe you didn't know, but he had it bad for Arlene. Of course, she couldn't resist his charms. Her daddy was awful to her. I believe that's why Arlene was a real sucker for any man who paid attention to her. Anyway, I wouldn't have been at all shocked if they'd arrested Ray this morning instead of Jake."

Ray did borrow that box of tools… But surely if he were guilty, he wouldn't have mentioned having the box in his possession, would he? Why give anyone a reason to think he might have been Arlene's attacker? To throw us off track? No. I can't believe that. Paula shook her head. "I'm not buying Ray as the bad guy. But I'm not buying Mr. Lewis or Jake either. I just hope Arlene's attacker isn't long gone now that the sheriff has cleared everyone to leave."

As they entered Hemphill, Paula's phone buzzed. She pointed ahead and let the call go to voicemail. "Take a left at the next corner. The hospital is at the end of the road."

CHAPTER SEVENTY-SIX

Paula pointed out a parking space near the entrance to the medical center. *Mark led us through the doctor's entrance. We'll need to go the visitors' route.* With gritted teeth, she steeled herself for another foray into the antiseptic world of a hospital. "I really don't like hospitals," she said as they stepped out of the car. "Never have. But since Cal died, let's just say I don't need the reminders."

Vanessa blinked and raised an eyebrow. "Oh, I practically live in a hospital. I'm an RN."

A twinge of guilt hit Paula. "Really? I had no idea. That's quite an accomplishment. I'm sorry that we didn't get to spend more time getting to know each other this weekend. We'll have to stay in touch from now on."

They reached intensive care and Vanessa took over, flashing her hospital identification at the charge nurse while Paula stood by, her fingers crossed. Vanessa said, "I know I'm not on staff here, but my dearest friend was admitted yesterday. Arlene Davis? I was hoping I could see her."

The nurse examined a page on her computer. "Ms. Davis has improved enough that she's being moved to a room just down the hall. Hm, looks like she'll be in 115. You won't be able to see her until she's settled in. Her husband went to get a bite to eat and to bring her some things from the nearest Walmart, so I'm sure she'll appreciate the company when the nurses are through setting up."

Paula said, "Thank you for your help."

They retraced their steps, pausing outside Arlene's new room where a pair of nurses were engaged in inserting an IV and hooking their patient up to monitors.

Vanessa stuck her head in the door. "How's she doing?"

An older nurse said, "Come back in thirty minutes. There's a waiting room down thataway."

Paula caught Vanessa's arm. "I know the place they're talking about. Let's go. We can use this time to visit."

A pot of coffee sat on a table inside the waiting room. Paula helped herself to a cup and poured one for Vanessa. "Sugar? Cream?"

"No, I take mine black."

Paula raised her cup in salute and settled onto the green vinyl couch. "We have that in common."

Vanessa took a sip of coffee and paced. "Not bad for hospital brew. The stuff at Fort Worth General is awful."

"So, tell me about yourself. Did you always want to go into nursing?"

"Oh, yes. From the time I was a little girl. All my dolls had chronic illnesses. What about you?"

With a shrug, Paula said, "I never knew what I wanted to be. I still don't; although, my friends will tell you I'm addicted to cop shows. Maybe I should have gone into law enforcement."

Cocking her head, Vanessa said, "So, if you were in law enforcement, who would be your best guess for a suspect?"

Paula hesitated. *Just how much of what Delbert shared with us should I tell her?* "Hm. If I were approaching this as a police officer, I'd say it was someone who Arlene trusted enough to take a ride with in the wee hours of the morning. A drinking buddy, probably. And someone who wanted her gone but didn't want to make a mess. I mean, this is Texas after all. Everyone and their grandmother owns a gun here. It would have been easier, I think, to have shot her and placed the gun in her hand. Her attacker cared for her on some level. The method they chose would have been painless, I think." She shuddered thinking of how things might have gone had the perpetrator chosen to shoot Arlene.

Vanessa raised her Styrofoam cup in a salute. "Wow, you really do watch a lot of cop shows, don't you?"

"Yeah, I guess I do." Paula flashed a proud smile, then sobered. "I'm so relieved they didn't shoot her. I don't even want to think about where we'd be now."

One of Arlene's nurses peeked around the corner. "Ms. Davis can have visitors now. One at a time, though. And keep your visits short, okay?"

Paula nodded at the door. "Vanessa, you go first. She'll be so happy to see you."

Vanessa blinked tears from her eyes. "No, you go. I need to get myself together. I'm afraid I'll fall apart when I walk into the room."

Wrapping her arms around Vanessa, Paula said, "It's going to be okay now. I'll be back in a few minutes."

CHAPTER SEVENTY-SEVEN

Slipping inside Arlene's room, Paula resisted the urge to hold her breath. *I can do this. That's not my Cal laying there.* She hovered by the door as a nurse adjusted a setting on Arlene's IV. She and the nurse exchanged nods and Paula tried her best to ignore all the medical equipment surrounding the bed as she moved to the bedside. Patting Arlene's hand, she said, "Hey, sweetie. We've been so worried about you."

Peeking out through swollen lids, Arlene blinked. "Paula. Thank you so much for being here. Have you seen Ted? My husband?"

"We met him earlier. Such a nice man. He's been so concerned about you. The nurse in the ICU told us he'd finally gone to eat. He should be back soon."

Tears gleamed in Arlene's eyes. She clutched at Paula's hand. "I don't deserve Ted. Oh, don't shake your head at me. I know what kind of wife I've been. Always looking for greener pastures. While I was hovering between life and death, I had what must have been a dream. You know that light they talk about? And the tunnel? I was there. I was faced with a decision. Stay here or go there. But as bright as that light was at the tunnel's end, Ted's love was brighter. I could see it shining here, right here, not with my eyes, but with my heart. Even after the hell I've put him through. I swear I'm done playing games. I just want to live out my life as Mrs. Theodore Davis and show him what he means to me."

Tears shimmered in Paula's eyes. She squeezed Arlene's hand and offered a hopeful smile. "We don't all get second chances. I'm sure glad you do, though. Do you remember anything at all from last night?"

"It's all foggy. When I close my eyes, I get only shadowy impressions. Sometimes I hear a familiar voice, but I can't pin down who it belongs to and nothing they say makes any sense."

"Then don't try too hard. Just rest and recover. I'll bet it's one of those things that you'll remember when you least expect to."

Arlene's eyes closed and her breathing fell into a steady rhythm.

Poor thing, she needs to rest. Paula extricated her hand from Arlene's and stepped away from the bed as Arlene's eyes fluttered open again.

As if the conversation never lagged, Arlene said, "I'll bet you're right. If I try too hard, it just seems to slip further away."

Paula stepped closer to Arlene. "Give yourself time to heal, sweetie. I'm going to go now, but there's someone else who's been worried sick and is anxious to let you know she's been thinking about you. Bye for now."

Stepping outside the room, Paula took a deep breath. *We were so close to losing her.*

Vanessa met her halfway between Arlene's room and the waiting area. Her eyes searched Paula's. "How is she?"

"Weak but determined. She's going to be good as new. Maybe better than new."

Vanessa offered a tremulous smile and crossed her fingers. "Wish me luck. I don't want to lose it in there."

"You can do this. If nothing else, assume your nursing persona."

Vanessa tapped a finger against her temple. "Good advice. Thank you, Paula."

CHAPTER SEVENTY-EIGHT

Paula heaved a sigh of relief as she entered the waiting room. *Arlene's going to make it. Thank goodness. And that wasn't too awful. Still, I don't want to make hospital visits a routine thing.* She poured a fresh cup of coffee and pulled her phone from her pocket, grimacing when she realized there were multiple messages awaiting her attention. *Oh, shoot.*

She returned Mark's call first. "Hey, Mark, what's up."

"Paula, where the hell are you?"

She blinked. "I'm at the hospital with Vanessa..."

"What? Wait. Hold on a second."

Mark barked something unintelligible to someone on the other end of the conversation.

"What's going on?"

"Is Vanessa with you now?"

Paula frowned. "What? No, but I can get her for you. She's in visiting with Arlene."

"Someone from the Sabine County Sheriff's office is on their way to the hospital. We're on our way, too. Honey, Sheriff Hill is looking at Vanessa as a suspect now. Stay where you are!"

Blood pumped in Paula's ears as she strode across the waiting room. "Screw that! I need to be with Arlene in case it is Vanessa. Don't worry. I'll be casual."

"Damn it, Paula. Don't!"

She disconnected and raced down the hallway, into the room where Vanessa stood beside Arlene's IV, a syringe in her hand.

The tableau shocked Paula into action. "Vanessa! Stop! Don't do this."

Vanessa sneered. "Please, little miss goody two shoes. Don't you dare tell me to stop! You have no idea what this witch has put me through. You're just in time to help me deliver enough digoxin to stop Arlene's heart." Vanessa's finger hovered over the plunger.

Paula growled and launched herself at Vanessa, but the force of Vanessa's fist as it met Paula's chin, stopped her in her tracks and sent her crashing to the floor. Stars circled around her head as it bounced off the tile, taking Paula into darkness with one last thought--*So much for being casual.*

CHAPTER SEVENTY-NINE

A chorus of subdued voices swirled around Paula, mingling with the internal conversation running circles in her head, until she was unsure whether anyone in the real world was speaking or if every word was a figment of her imagination. She opened one eye and the resulting stab of pain forced a single word through her lips. "Ow."

A warm hand gripped hers. "Paula, honey, it's okay. You took a couple of nasty blows to the head. Be still."

"Yes, Dr. Hunky," she mumbled.

Cassie's voice penetrated Paula's thoughts. "Sure seems to me like she has a concussion. Still thinks you're hunky."

Paula chuckled, then winced from the pain and the sudden recollection of events leading to her current condition. "Cassie, how's Arlene?"

"She's going to be just fine, Goldilocks. From what they've been able to piece together, Arlene hit the nurse's call button around the time Vanessa entered her room.

"Must have 'membered," Paula said in a drowsy murmur.

Mark brushed a thumb across Paula's forehead. "Good thing, too, because Vanessa injected Arlene's line with digoxin. Fortunately, you arrived before she delivered the full dose. As much as I want to be furious with you for ignoring my warning, you probably saved Arlene's life."

An attempt to sit up put Paula's head into a spin. She closed her eyes and fell back onto the pillow. "I need to know everything. Has Jake been released?"

Mark rubbed her arm. "All in good time. They want to keep you overnight for observation. You not only got a dose of Arlene's fist, but you hit your head on the way down. A double whammy, at least that's what we in the medical profession call it."

Paula fought against laughing, fearing the pain that would accompany the act. She settled for a pout. "But, no, I want to go home. With you."

"You won't be alone. I'll be here all night."

Cassie kissed Paula's cheek. "Okay, you two. I believe that's my cue to leave. Mark, do you need anything before I go?"

He squeezed Paula's hand. "Thanks, but no. I've got everything I need right here."

CHAPTER EIGHTY

Throughout much of the night, Paula dozed on and off, replaying scenes from her confrontation with Vanessa in a series of hazy dreams. Once, she startled awake with a whimper, certain she had arrived too late to save Arlene, and Mark soothed her worries away with a kiss. Even as she drifted off to sleep again, she felt the peace of his presence. *He's been here all night, either reading or listening to something through his earbuds. I don't think he slept a wink.* For the remainder of the night, she nestled into dreams of Mark's arms wrapped around her.

When the sun came streaming through the window above her bed, Paula groaned, bringing Mark to her side. "The sun. Make it stop."

He chuckled and closed the drapes. "How's that?"

"Mm. Much better. Thank you."

He kissed her forehead. "You're welcome. Good morning, my junior crime fighter. This escapade might have earned you a magic decoder ring."

"Ugh. Please don't make me laugh."

"But that's one of my favorite things to do. Right up there with this." He kissed her again.

Amusement tugged at her lips. "More kisses. Less sunlight. So, what are you listening to?"

"I'm sure you'd find it terribly boring, but since you asked, I'm listening to a lecture on the use of statin therapy in the treatment of women who've been diagnosed with triple-negative breast cancer."

"Ooh, so you *are* more than just eye candy," she said.

"Keep talking like that and I'll have to crawl into that bed with you."

Paula giggled and realized the action resulted in almost no pain. "Hey, I feel better."

He ran a hand down her arm. "I'd have to do a complete exam to confirm that, but..."

"Get me out of here and I'll okay that procedure."

He poured a cup of water from the pitcher beside her bed. "For now, drink this. I spoke with the doctor. If all goes as planned, they'll let you go after he makes his morning rounds. It's still early, though, so you might have a couple of hours to wait."

Paula sipped from the cup. "So, how's Arlene doing?"

"She's great. Are you up for a visitor?"

Paula's eyes narrowed. "Sure. As long as it's not Vanessa."

"Promise," he said with a chuckle. "Be right back."

He returned with Ted who pushed a smiling Arlene through the doorway in a wheelchair. Paula brightened at the sight of her. "Oh, Arlene, you look so much better this morning. Are you going home?"

Arlene rose from the chair and wrapped Paula in an awkward hug. "Thanks to you I am. Maybe not today, but tomorrow if all goes well. Paula, that wouldn't be happening if not for you. You saved my life."

Patting Arlene's back, Paula said, "Nonsense. I hear you saved your own life. I just provided a bit of slapstick to the whole production."

Ted pushed the wheelchair closer. "Sit, dear."

"Oh, you, always fussing over me," Arlene said, a look of unadulterated love shining in her eyes.

Ted said, "Seriously, Paula. You distracted Vanessa from providing a lethal dose; otherwise, even the nurse's quick response might not have been enough to save my Arlene. Without your intervention who knows how this might have turned out? Let's just say the two of us are eternally grateful."

Arlene clasped her husband's hand and gazed up at Mark. "Could we ladies have a moment to ourselves?"

Ted kissed his wife's cheek and nodded. "Sure. Want to get a cup of coffee, Mark?"

"You bet. Ladies, no dancing," Mark said with a wag of his finger.

"Spoil sport," Paula said.

CHAPTER EIGHTY-ONE

As soon as the door closed behind Mark and Ted, Paula extended her hand to Arlene, peering up at her with troubled eyes. Her voice threatened to break as she gave into the worries that plagued her throughout the night. "I'm so sorry I didn't catch on earlier to what Vanessa had in mind. All night long, I pictured how everything might have ended if she'd been able to administer a fatal dose of that stuff. If I'd been a few seconds later, or if... Oh, Arlene..."

Arlene took Paula's hand and squeezed. "Please don't blame yourself for anything. I've known Vanessa since we were little girls, and even I didn't realize she had it in for me until it was almost too late."

"The whole time you were missing, she was worried to the point of distraction. She even flared up at me because she didn't think I was concerned enough. Learning that she was the one who tried to kill you was just surreal. Do you have any idea why she did this?"

Arlene released Paula's hand as she slumped against the back of the wheelchair. "Oh, my stars, Paula, it seems she's had reason to hate me for years. My one true friend and I never understood that our relationship should have kept me from stealing her boyfriends and going out with guys she had crushes on, all the time flaunting my conquests in her face with no regard for her feelings."

"But—why would you do that to a friend?"

"Oh, I have tons of terribly lame excuses, but the main one revolves around my father's hatred of me. He never wanted me and told me nearly every single day of my life that I never should have been born. That he wanted a boy and instead got stuck with me. My mother did everything she could to placate him, and that meant, for the most part, ignoring me."

Paula closed her eyes and pictured her own doting, sometimes infuriating, overly attentive parents. "Oh, Arlene, I'm so sorry."

Arlene sniffled. "Wasn't your fault. But I was all about getting attention—mainly from men, but any attention was welcome. I wanted to be wanted. I needed to be noticed, and I didn't care who I stepped on or what I did to get that attention, even if that meant hurting the only real friend I had. And the whole time, a part of me knew it was never going to be enough."

Arlene's tears began to fall. "And you know what? Vanessa never spoke a word against me or about me, as far as I can tell. I never knew she was harboring such anger, but how clueless was I? Always focused on me, me, me. Oh, what have I done?"

Paula stroked Arlene's hair as both women cried. Paula offered her a tissue from the box on the bedside table. "Here, sweetie, it's going to be okay."

"I sure hope so. We got lucky. If I'd, um, if I hadn't made it, Jake might have been sentenced to prison, or worse, for a crime he didn't commit. When Ted told me Jake had been arrested, I simply couldn't make the connection. I mean, why him? I just barely knew Jake in high school. He was one of the few boys who wasn't on my radar and, as far as I know, Vanessa never had her sights set on him, either. Why frame him?"

Paula shrugged. "That's a mystery. I hope everything will come out when she's questioned. Speaking of which, do you know if she's been arrested yet or if Jake has been released?"

"I haven't had an update on Jake yet. I know there's a manhunt underway for Vanessa, though. For my peace of mind and yours, I hope they find her soon." Arlene took a deep breath, exhaled, and steepled her hands under her chin.

After a moment, her eyes met Paula's. "The reason I wanted to speak with you without the men in here, was to let you know that what I said earlier, about starting a new way of living, I meant that. Ted, heaven help him, has put up with so much. He understands me better than anyone ever has, and I'm going to spend the rest of my life being the best wife possible. I do love him, and he loves me, and that's so much more than some people ever experience."

Adjusting to an upright position in the bed, Paula said, "May I ask you a personal question?"

Arlene placed a hand over her heart. "You saved my life. You can ask me anything you want."

"I know about your relationship with Mr. Lewis. Vanessa told me and he confirmed it. Were you pregnant when you left Dempsey?"

Arlene shook her head. "Only in my imagination. I wanted so badly to have someone to love and to love me. I was such a foolish woman. When I get home, I'm going to write Andy. Repay him every dime he gave me and tell him the truth. He deserves that."

Fresh tears welled in Paula's eyes. "Come here, girl. I need to hug you again."

CHAPTER EIGHTY-TWO

Overcome with gratitude, Paula smiled as she stood outside her camper. *Oh, it's good to be home. And this place really is home.* She dropped to her knees, pressed her lips to the grass, and came up sputtering. "That always looks so romantic in the movies. Now I'm not sure I'll ever rid my tastebuds of the peculiar flavor of grass." She swiped her mouth with the back of her hand.

Beside her, Cassie cackled. "Good grief, Paula. Maybe they shouldn't have let you out of the hospital yet."

"The doctor said I was good to go, and Mark promised he'd keep an eye on me. Where is he anyway?"

Cassie's eyebrows shot up a notch. "An eye, eh? I'm sure he wants to keep more than an eye on you."

Paula's cheeks flushed a delicate shade of rose as she refused to rise to Cassie's bait. "Seriously? Shouldn't he be here by now?"

"Patience. He had some errands to run. Should be here soon. Let's go in and get you comfortable."

Paula handed her keys to Cassie and followed her into the camper as a blur of white raced by. "Oh, dear. Star, I didn't even think about you while I was gone. I'm so sorry, girl."

"I slept out here last night. She was just fine."

Hugging Cassie to her side, Paula said, "Thank you. I feel awful that I didn't worry about her. Star, come here." The cat sniffed at Paula's hand and wound around her legs.

Cassie pointed a stern finger at the nearest bench. "Sit. Doctor's orders. You're not to do anything too strenuous for a week or so. And that includes worrying and thinking too hard. The cat survived. I spoiled her rotten, so it's all good."

Paula slid behind the table where she was joined by Star who landed in her lap with a plop. Cassie started a pot of coffee brewing.

"Don't you have classes or something?" Paula asked.

"Only one class today, and the instructor gave me a pass. She said I could probably teach this lesson myself with one hand tied behind my back."

Kicking off her shoes, Paula rested her head in her hands. "You didn't have to hang around. I'd have been fine."

"I had to make sure, you know, and with everything that went down over the past couple of days, I needed to decompress a little. I'll head back to Dallas once Mark gets here."

Paula shook her head. *Ow! Reminder to self: Don't do that again anytime soon.* "It's still so hard for me to believe that Vanessa attempted to kill Arlene. Not once, but twice."

"And that she tried to frame Jake, of all people, for the poorly disguised suicide attempt."

"Just unthinkable." Paula shuddered.

Cassie poured a cup of coffee for Paula and grabbed a Dr. Pepper for herself. "So, try not to think about it. Your brain needs a rest. I'm cold. Mind if I borrow one of your sweatshirts?"

"Not at all, if you'll bring one for me, too. Look in the storage compartments underneath my bed. Third drawer, I think."

Cassie ducked into the bedroom and, after a few moments, said, "I can't find one."

"Then you're not trying all that hard. Let me help you."
Paula stood as a knock sounded at the door. "That must be
Mark," Paula said, pivoting to greet him. Even though they'd
parted ways less than an hour earlier, the mere anticipation at
being with him again sent heat waves coursing through her veins.
Dang, girl, you really have it bad.

She ran her fingers through her hair. *Sure wish I'd done
something with my hair or put on some makeup, but it's not like
he hasn't already seen me at my worst.* "Door's unlocked. Come
on in."

The door flew open, and the anticipatory warmth at the
thought of being in Mark's arms evaporated into a cold sweat as
Paula came face to face with the woman standing in her
motorhome. "Uh, Vanessa... Wh-what are you doing here?"

CHAPTER EIGHTY-THREE

Paula's heart stuttered, then accelerated into a frantic rhythm. *Am I having a stroke?* She pressed a hand to her chest. *Breathe.* Her eyes were drawn to Vanessa's hands as the taller woman filled the room with menace. *No syringes, thank heaven!* Her voice quivering, she said, "Vanessa. I figured you'd be hundreds of miles away by now."

Vanessa smirked. "And I figured you'd be smart enough to lock your doors at all times by now. Didn't my little break-in teach you anything?"

Paula slid her fingers over her tender chin. *Stay calm. Maybe catch her off guard.* She nodded at the table. "Could we sit? Please?"

In one smooth motion, Vanessa drew a gun from her purse and pointed it at Paula. "You first."

Paula's eyes widened. *Oh, mercy! I'm the one who brought up the idea of a gun.* A simple prayer looped through her mind: *Please Lord, oh please, oh please don't let her shoot me!*

"Okay," Paula said. "I'm sitting. But I can't think with that gun pointed at me." She slid onto the bench and scooted around the table until she was facing the bedroom door. She sent a silent plea to Cassie--*don't try to be a hero.*

Vanessa sat and placed the weapon on the bench beside her. Her eyes roamed over Paula's bruised face, and she chuckled. "I did do a number on you, didn't I? I'm terribly sorry about that, but really there was no need for you to get hurt. If you'd just stayed in the waiting room, I'd be long gone, and you wouldn't look like the loser in a five round boxing match."

Without the gun pointed at her face, Paula took in a shuddery breath and exhaled. Forcing herself to speak in slow, measured tones, she said. "Please help me understand all this. Why the break in? Why'd you try to kill Arlene? And why did you try to frame Jake? As far as we can tell, he had nothing to do with you or Arlene."

With a shrug, Vanessa said, "I guess I should tell someone. Might as well be you."

Paula's mouth went dry. *She's only going to tell me because she's going to kill me afterward.* "Would you like a cup of coffee first? I know I could use one."

"No, but thank you. You always were the polite, gullible little princess. You bought my whole 'Arlene's my best pal and I'm worried out of my mind' bit. I counted on you to throw suspicion away from me."

Paula fought to maintain a steady gaze as her mind urged her to run. She braced herself for flight. *No! Running will only get me killed sooner. Just keep her talking.* "That was pretty clever, I have to say. But again, why did you break in here of all places?"

Vanessa tapped the side of her head. "Think about it. You had that note that I taped to the front door of the office. Or at least I thought you did. I got to thinking that it might lead back to me."

Clutching her hands together on the table, Paula stilled their shaking. "Oh, that makes sense. I appreciate your honesty. And that you made sure that my cat didn't get out. Thank you for that. But why would you want to harm Arlene? I thought you were best friends."

"Because that ungrateful hussy never cared about me. If she had, she wouldn't have stolen my boyfriend—the one guy I really cared about. Of course, he's not without blame either, but Arlene made it so easy. It wasn't enough that she had Mr. Lewis wrapped up in her claws; she wanted Ray, too."

Paula gasped. "You were Ray's girlfriend? I knew you'd gone out with him a couple of times, but..." Again, the vision of Arlene and Ray making out beneath the stadium flashed through Paula's head. *Oh, my goodness.*

A clatter from the bedroom brought Vanessa to her feet. "Who else is here?"

CHAPTER EIGHTY-FOUR

Bile rose in Paula's throat as Vanessa grabbed the gun and aimed the barrel at Paula's head. *Please, no!* She cowered; hiding behind her hands in a clumsy attempt to ward off any bullets that might come her way. "Vanessa, don't shoot! That was just Star, the kitten. I had to spend the night in the hospital, and she's still upset that I left her alone."

At the sound of her name, Star trotted down the hallway and jumped onto the table where she cozied up to Vanessa with a head bump. Vanessa seemed to forget about the gun as she stroked the kitten. She eyed Paula with a smirk. "While you were comfy cozy in the hospital, I was spending the night in my car in the woods waiting for you to return here. All night long, I expected the sheriff department's dogs to catch my scent. Every now and then, I heard a distant bark, but I guess you could say I got lucky. So, in my defense, I might be a bit jumpy. And after all I've been through these last few days, surely you can understand that."

After all she's *been through? Really?* Biting back a retort, Paula managed to plaster a look of understanding on her face. "I do. I really do. I think we're all on edge."

Tears glimmered in Vanessa's eyes as she smoothed a hand over Star's silky head. "I really should have gotten a cat at some time in my life. And this one is so sweet."

Paula crossed her fingers at the white lie that rose to her lips. Taking a calming breath, she said, "She does seem to genuinely like you. That's weird. Usually, I'm the only one she'll respond to. So, about Ray?"

"Oh, yes. Back to Ray. He took me to the band banquet two years in a row. Two years! I thought I meant something to him. But then I made the mistake of telling Arlene and the next thing I knew, she laid claim to him. And because she was my only friend, I didn't fight for Ray. I just added that betrayal to a host of others Arlene accumulated over the years."

Paula spread her hands, steadying them on the table. "But I still don't get it. Please help me understand why you didn't try to frame Ray instead of Jake for the first attack on Arlene."

A rueful chuckle escaped Vanessa's lips. "I thought I *was* framing Ray. On Friday night, I was trying to figure out the best method of getting rid of Arlene. Honestly, Paula, when I arrived at the reunion, I thought maybe I could let bygones be bygones, but there was Arlene, all over Mr. Lewis. And Ray wouldn't even look at me. I kind of had hopes that maybe he and I could rekindle our old flame, but no. I blame her for that, too. Ray's all cheery. Joking with everyone and never once apologized for scarring me emotionally. I decided it was finally time for Arlene to pay for all the ways she hurt me, and if I could take Ray or even Mr. Lewis down, that wouldn't be a bad thing."

Paula wanted to scream, but a little voice inside her head cautioned: *Show empathy. Don't give her any reason to use that gun.* "I think I understand your need for revenge. It had to be hard to deal with that kind of pain for all these years."

Vanessa sighed and batted away her tears. She studied her hands on the table for a moment. When she made eye contact with Paula again, her gaze was solemn. "It was. So hard. Anyway, there I was out wandering the campground in the early morning hours, looking for something that might be useful in doing away with Arlene and, lo and behold, there was this box outside Ray's camper. I couldn't believe my good luck. It was almost a do-it-yourself murder kit—a hose and duct tape. Wrenches, too. I dug through the contents and even found a credit card receipt to leave behind at the scene. I couldn't have asked for anything better." The corners of Vanessa's lips curled up at the memory, sending a shiver down Paula's spine.

"How was I to know the box belonged to Jake? I did feel guilty when I learned they'd arrested him, but I figured they'd sort out the missing box soon enough and Jake would be cleared. And then if Ray took the fall, that'd be great. If he didn't, I was willing to let him off the hook."

Paula repressed a shudder at Vanessa's cold logic. She pressed a hand to her mouth, then said, "Oh, so that was *you* making all that noise in the campground Friday night? *You* knocked over the trash can and woke us up."

Vanessa's hands flew to her chest. "Why would I have done a thing like that? I was trying to be stealthy. But I'll admit that the scream was all mine. A family of raccoons ran between your camper and Ray's with a bobcat on their tails. You'd have screamed, too, if a bobcat appeared out of the dark and missed running you over by mere inches. At that point, I figured everyone in the area would come flying out of their campers. I had no choice but to grab the whole box and run back to Arlene's room."

So, I was right; that had been a woman's scream. If Vanessa kills me this afternoon, I hope Cassie tells everyone I told them so. Stop already with the macabre thoughts! "Do you mind if I get another cup of coffee?" Paula asked. "My head is throbbing."

"Oh, I don't think I'll give you the opportunity to throw hot coffee in my face. I'll get it for you. Just stay where you are."

CHAPTER EIGHTY-FIVE

The throbbing head was no lie. The thoughts battling for attention in Paula's brain were akin to that of a legion of angry, hammer-wielding wasps who had been trapped there and were doing their best to find a way out by battering against the inside of her skull. *Breathe deeply. Just keep her talking. Cassie's here and everything will be okay... But what if Vanessa grows tired of talking and decides to just shoot me instead? Cassie might not know until she hears the gunshot. What if Vanessa discovers Cassie and shoots her, too? What if Mark comes in and she shoots him? No! I'll think of something. I've got to think of something.* Accepting the cup from Vanessa, Paula said, "Thank you. I promise I wouldn't have tried to hurt you."

Vanessa slid back into her seat. "Oh, Paula, we both know the old saying about desperate times calling for desperate measures. Hell, this whole weekend has been a testament to that phrase."

Cradling the coffee mug with trembling hands, Paula took a sip, then said, "There is something that's been bothering me. Several somethings, I guess. You said you and Arlene shared a couple of beers and then you left her..."

"That part is true. When I left her, I went back to my room and I'm ashamed to say, had a bit of a tantrum. Here's Arlene, married to Ted who, by all accounts, is a great guy, but is she satisfied? No. She came here hoping to hook up. Can you imagine the nerve of someone to say that?"

Raking a hand through her short hair, Vanessa choked out a laugh. "And here I am. Never married. Never really had a man in my life after high school. I'm sure a psychiatrist would say that's why I run triathlons. Always running away from my problems. But this weekend, I decided to stop running. Figuratively speaking, that is. I did have to run back to the resort after I left Arlene out in the boondocks on Saturday morning."

That explains that. "But how'd you get Arlene to take you out there in her car?"

Vanessa snorted. "That part was easy. I gave her a note...told her it was from Mr. Lewis, *Andy*, asking her to meet him, just like those days in high school. I'd already gotten her drunk, so she didn't pay attention to the lack of a location or directions. Those beers we'd shared were just the tip of the iceberg. A bottle of Jack Daniels didn't hurt either. She was too drunk to drive so I offered to take her out to meet him, then she could ride back here with him. Only..."

"Only there was no him out there."

"Bingo!" Shifting to accommodate Star who was curled into a tight ball on her lap, Vanessa tapped a finger on the tip of her nose. "I sat pretending to drink with her until she passed out. Lord, but that woman can hold her liquor. I was beginning to think I was going to have to hit her over the head with one of the wrenches from the murder box. That would have been a lot faster, but she was my friend after all. I really did want to make her death as painless as possible."

Vanessa stared into Paula's eyes with renewed interest. "You know, you weren't far off in your assessment of Arlene's assailant. I did care for her, and I didn't want her to suffer. It would have been so much easier if that wasn't the case. I'd brought my gun with me, you see, as a last resort."

Paula swallowed hard and schooled her face to hide the horror of that casual statement. *This woman needs some serious help.* "So, you dropped the receipt in the car before you hooked the hose up to the exhaust, then taped everything up from the outside, knowing that no one would buy Arlene's death as a suicide?"

"Yeah. Like I said before, I was flying by the seat of my pants. I wanted her dead, and I'd be okay with Ray taking the blame." Vanessa's nose wrinkled. "She really should be dead, you know. I just don't understand how she survived."

Paula weighed the consequences of telling Vanessa where she had gone wrong. *Maybe I should let her reach her own conclusion...* "How long did you two sit out there with the car running? If it took her a long time to pass out..."

Vanessa smacked her own forehead. "I'll be damned. That stupid gas-guzzling SUV. Ha. It must've run out of fuel. Go figure. I suppose that failure's on me." She leaned forward on the bench and eyed Paula across the table. She lifted the gun from the bench and cocked it. "But what happened in the hospital, Paula, that's all on you."

CHAPTER EIGHTY-SIX

Paula's eyes widened as she shrank away from the pistol aimed at her head. An odd detachment overcame her even as she broke out in a cold sweat. *Oh, this is it. I'm going to die.* "Vanessa, please. I'm begging you. Please don't pull that trigger. As of this moment, you haven't done anyone permanent harm. Right? You could walk away with nothing more than probation. I'll vouch for you."

Vanessa rolled her eyes. "That's what you think, eh? I'll lose my job, my nursing license, my reputation. No. I think you need to pay for your actions, and don't worry your pretty little head; I'll make it quick. I'm sure a good girl like you will go straight to heaven, too. And about your kitty? I'll just take her with me. But just between you and me, Star is just an awful name. I think I'll call her Sweet Revenge."

A flash of anger sparked through Paula's veins. *How dare she?* Hot tears coursed down her cheeks as an idea grew in her mind. *It's a long shot, but what do I have to lose?* She crossed her fingers beneath the table. "Please, take good care of her. Her favorite food is chicken with liver, and she really loves having her tummy rubbed."

"Does she now?" With her free hand, Vanessa stroked the cat's white belly. "We're going to be good friends, now, aren't we?" Star yowled, clamping down on Vanessa's hand with all four sets of claws and the gun dropped to the table where it spun like a bottle in a chidren's game. "Ow, you little bi--."

Emerging from the bedroom, like an avenging angel, Cassie whacked Vanessa over the head with Paula's third place talent show trophy. Vanessa dropped to the floor like a bag of wet cement as Paula grabbed the gun, holding it as she might a full diaper. "Her name's Star, dammit."

Her chest heaving, Cassie raised the trophy above her head. "Maybe I should hit her again."

Paula crumpled against Cassie and grabbed her arm. "No! No, more. You might kill her. It's over. It's all over. Thanks to you, it's all over. She's out."

Wrapping Paula in her arms, Cassie brandished her phone. "You know what else she is? Busted, that's what. The sheriff heard every bit of her confession, and he'll be here any minute."

A siren sounded outside as Paula collapsed onto the bench. "I...I really thought I was going to die."

Cassie's bravado evaporated as her own tears cascaded down her cheeks. "Oh, Goldilocks, I was terrified. My mind wouldn't work beyond contacting the sheriff and the whole time I was afraid Vanessa would hear me and shoot you. If I did the wrong thing, you might have...You might have died. And I didn't know what the right thing was. I was useless. I let you down."

Paula clung to her. "No, never. You saved me. Without you..."

"Shh," Cassie said. "It's us. You and me. We saved each other."

CHAPTER EIGHTY-SEVEN

Paula leaned against the front door as Sheriff Hill led a wobbly Vanessa away in handcuffs. *I'm not giving her any of my accumulated wisdom. I hope she starts talking and never stops.* Paula said, "I know this is all going to hit me like a freight train later on, but for the moment, I'm just relieved."

Cassie draped a sweater around Paula's shoulders and wrapped her arms around her. "You're shivering, though, and probably in shock."

They watched as Sheriff Hill bundled Vanessa into one of the squad cars and closed the door behind her. "Eugene, take Ms. Allen on back to the station and lock her up. Go over her Miranda Rights again. With that goose egg on her noggin, she might not remember hearing them. Call Doc Stephens in to take a look at her, but don't question her 'til I get back."

Sauntering over to Paula and Cassie, the sheriff took a notebook from his shirt pocket. "Are you ladies up to giving your statements?"

Paula clutched at her head. "Do we have to right now? I think I might..."

The sheriff caught Paula as her knees buckled. "Whoa! Let's get you into a chair. You, too Ms. Cassie. You're looking a little poorly yourself."

Expelling a quivery breath, Paula straightened her shoulders. *I'm not going to be some simpering female.* "Let's stay outside, okay? I'm not quite ready to revisit the scene of the crime."

Sheriff Hill unfolded three lawn chairs, then waited for Paula and Cassie to be seated. "That suits me just fine. I'll take the outdoors over the indoors any time I can. Now, let's talk about what happened before Ms. Cassie got me on the phone."

Paula twisted her hands in her lap. "I thought she was Mark. Dr. Fields, that is. We were expecting him and like an idiot, when I heard a knock at the door, I just assumed... I didn't check before saying, 'come on in.'" She buried her face in her hands and sobbed. "I could've gotten Cassie and me both killed."

A familiar hand caressed her cheek. She looked up into a pair of tear-filled hazel eyes. *Mark!*

He pulled her into his arms. "I'm so sorry! I should have been here. What was I thinking sending you two off alone when we knew Vanessa hadn't been taken into custody yet?"

Cassie said, "You were thinking we are two grown women who are perfectly capable of taking care of ourselves. And as it turns out, we did just fine."

Melinda appeared at the edge of the campsite. Her eyes darted about, then came to rest on Cassie. "Oh! Cassie Campbell, promise me you'll never scare me like that again."

Dissolving into tears, Cassie ran into Melinda's embrace. Between sniffles, she said, "It's okay now. We're all okay."

The sheriff cleared his throat. Closing his notebook, he said, "I think I've got all I need for now. Ms. Paula. Ms. Cassie. We owe you two a big thank you. It looks like I'm leaving you in good company, so I'm gonna get back to the office and question Ms. Allen."

Paula pivoted in Mark's arms, then wiped her eyes with the back of her hand. "Wait! What about Jake?"

Settling his hat on his head, the sheriff said, "As far as I'm concerned, he's clear. There may be some loose ends to tie up, but he should be a free man soon."

Clasping her hands, Paula said, "Oh! That's wonderful. Thank you."

CHAPTER EIGHTY-EIGHT

Wrapped inside a warm blanket, Paula reclined on a lounge chair, basking in the rays of the afternoon sun. *Finally, the shivering's stopped.* Cassie and Melinda had returned to the main cabin, and Mark's hand rested on Paula's thigh, providing an anchor in the roiling sea of her thoughts.

"Mark?" Paula asked.

"What, sweetheart?"

"Could you maybe never leave my side again?"

His chuckle was a soft, comforting sound. "As much as I'd love to keep you within arm's length for the rest of my life, I'm not sure the hospital would go for that arrangement. Although maybe they'd make an exception for you. I mean, I could operate with one hand..."

Paula snorted. *The rest of his life!*

Mark knelt beside her, his gaze sweeping over her face, then lighting on her eyes. "How are you feeling?"

"Better. I'm not cold anymore. In fact, I could lose the blanket now if that's okay with you. I'm a little too warm."

He took her hand in his, then examined her fingernails. "Your color is much better. Your eyes are almost back to normal. I think we can dispense with the blanket."

With Mark's help, Paula adjusted the lounge chair into an upright position. Cupping his cheek, she said, "I love you."

Tears sprang to his eyes. "Even though I let you down today?"

She took his hand and squeezed. "You did nothing of the sort. No one could've imagined that Vanessa would come here. And, if anyone let me down, it was me. I promise I've learned my lesson, though—always see who's at the door before you invite them in."

Mark's phone buzzed. He kissed Paula's forehead and stood. "Hey, Melinda. What's up? Oh, right. I'll see what Paula thinks. Bye."

Paula furrowed her brow. "What Paula thinks about what?"

"Well, we have some visitors. They want to know if it'd be okay to come out here. But I don't want to do anything you aren't comfortable with. Especially after all you've been through."

"Now you've got my curiosity up. Who is it?"

Mark offered a wry smile. "My folks and my sister, Janie."

Paula said, "Oh." *How* do *I feel about that?*

"I'll call them back and say we'll do this another day."

With a shake of her head, Paula said, "No, don't do that. I'm ready. But how about we go to them?"

Mark squeezed her shoulder. "Good idea, but if it all gets to be too much for you, let me know."

"I'm a little nervous, but that's normal, right? First time meeting the parents and all..."

He took her hand and pulled her to him. "They're going to love you. Just like I do."

Paula raised an eyebrow and Mark blushed. *"Just* like you do?"

With a twinkle in his eyes, he said, "Well, you know what I mean. How could they not love you?"

CHAPTER EIGHTY-NINE

Hand in hand with Mark, Paula fought against a rising panic as they made their way to the main cabin. *Stop. It's Mark's parents. They raised this wonderful man. It'll be fine.* "Do I look okay?"

"You're beautiful. Just like always," Mark said.

She ran a hand over her chin. "I think the bruise is particularly attractive."

Planting a kiss on her knuckles, Mark said, "You wear it well."

The back door opened as she and Mark approached. An older woman emerged and closed the distance between them, her arms open wide.

"Paula? You poor dear. Come here."

And Paula obeyed.

Wrapped in the comfort of Mark's mother's arms, Paula's defenses crumbled. She sobbed for Arlene and for Jake. She even wept a little for Vanessa. As Paula unleashed her emotions, Mark's beautiful mother held her, patting her back in a comforting rhythm. When her tears subsided, Paula pulled away. Swiping at her tear-stained face, she said, "I promise, I'm normally not like this."

Mark's father, an older, slighter version of his son, navigated the steps on the arm of a younger woman. Reaching his wife's side, he said, "You aren't? Mark told us to expect a hysterical woman. We'd be sorely disappointed if you didn't fit that description."

Mark's mother, who bore the stains of Paula's crying jag all over her floral printed blouse, poked an elbow into her husband's side. "Oh, Gerald. Paula don't listen to this man. He's full of it. Always has been. You have every right to those tears. In your shoes, I'd have fainted dead away."

Paula rested her head on Mark's shoulder. "I came close."

Mark slid an arm around Paula's waist, pulling her to his side. "Let me introduce you properly. Mom, Dad, Janie, this is Paula. And Paula, the woman you just cried all over is my mom, Freida, and this is Janie, my youngest sister. And even though Mom already spilled the beans, this is my dad, Gerald."

"We have heard only wonderful things about you," Freida said.

Nodding toward the cabin, Mark said, "Melinda's motioning for us to come in. Let's get Paula inside. She doesn't need to be on her feet too much."

Janie looped her arm through Paula's and said, "I had this whole interrogation routine planned for our first meeting. I'll just have to tell my sisters that you passed with flying colors."

Paula's eyebrows shot up. "I did?"

A smile lit up Janie's face. "You didn't hesitate to cry on Mom's shoulder. Not even for a heartbeat. That told me everything I needed to know, well, that and the way you and Mark look at each other."

CHAPTER NINETY

As Paula entered the main cabin, she extracted her arm from Janie's and gaped at the number of people milling about. "What is this?"

Melinda, her eyes brimming with tears, embraced Paula. "You sound surprised, but folks needed to see for themselves that you and Cassie were all right."

Paula squeezed Melinda's hands. "Oh mercy! I—I don't know what to say."

Holding Paula at arm's length, Melinda said, "You don't have to say anything, but let's get you settled somewhere. How about the sofa where Cassie is? I think she's having a harder time processing her feelings about what happened this afternoon than she realizes."

Paula said, "She's not nearly as tough as she pretends to be. Oh, have you met Mark's sister, Janie?"

Melinda and Janie exchanged smiles. "Yes. Janie and her parents held down the fort with me while Mom and Mark practically paced holes in my rug. No one was allowed in the campground until we had an okay from the sheriff's office."

Janie said, "I've never seen my brother so agitated."

Surveying the room, Paula's eyes met Mark's and she melted. *It's a wonder that every woman in the room doesn't swoon from that look.*

Cassie stood, and tugged Paula down beside her. "You're looking much better than you did earlier."

Squeezing Cassie's arm, Paula lowered her voice to a whisper, and said, "I still can't quite believe what went down this afternoon."

Covering Paula's hand with her own, Cassie said, "Me either. But look at us—a couple of badass survivors."

Paula stifled a giggle. "That's us—Badass to the bone."

CHAPTER NINETY-ONE

Paula and Cassie held court for a while, reassuring folks that they had emerged from their ordeal just fine. *Even if we're still a little shaken,* Paula thought.

When Delbert and Sherry stopped by, Paula accepted their hugs, then groaned. "Oh, Delbert. We were supposed to sign papers on the resort!"

He pulled up a chair and took her hands in his. "There's no hurry. I'm just so relieved that you and Cassie are okay."

Looking around the room, Paula took a deep breath in, and exhaled. "But we really should do it. Now, with so many of our friends here."

Delbert frowned. "Are you sure you're up for that?"

"Check with Mark and see what he thinks, but I'd like to have it all made official. I mean, after what happened today…" She took a deep breath. "Well, I don't want anything left to chance."

* * *

With their friends and family members gathered around the dining room table, Paula and Melinda sat across from Delbert. The stack of papers between the women and the attorney appeared immense in relation to the transaction they were about to undertake.

Paula wiped her palms on her jeans. *Wish I'd paid better attention when Cal was doing all this kind of stuff.* She grimaced. "That's a whole lot of paperwork."

From behind Paula, Cassie said, "Didn't you know that Aggie lawyers get paid by the page?"

Delbert smirked. "Campbell, don't make me exclude you from these proceedings."

"Zipping up my lips now, Mr. Derryberry."

"Okay, ladies, are we ready to begin?" Delbert asked.

Paula and Melinda gripped each other's hands. "We are," they said, almost in unison.

Delbert looked around the room and cleared his throat. "I'm not used to having an audience for such proceedings, but I reckon this merger is worthy of one. I almost think we need a bit of ceremony."

He extracted two pens from a box on the table, handing one to each of the women, then addressed the room. "Folks, we are here today to create a new partnership between Melinda Murray Arnett, Calvin Arnett's first wife, and Paula Purdy Arnett, his beloved Goldilocks. Once our transaction is complete, Melinda will be the majority owner of the resort and Paula will be her minority partner. And, ladies, I do believe Cal Arnett is smiling down on us all. And he's so proud of you both."

Melinda squeezed Paula's hand and Paula returned the squeeze, fighting against the tears that glistened at the corners of her eyes.

"I feel like I'm saying, 'I do,'" Melinda said.

Paula considered the ramifications of the adventure they were about to embark on. "We kind of are."

Delbert nodded at the paperwork. "Shall we proceed, ladies?"

As the attorney went over each document, sliding one after the other in front of Paula, she nodded in all the right places, initialing here, and signing and dating there. Signing her name for what seemed like the fiftieth time, Paula looked up to realize they had come to the bottom of the stack. "Is that it?"

Delbert   raised   his   hands.   "That's   everything. Congratulations, ladies. The Happy Valley Motor Inn and Resort is now officially under the ownership of Arnett Squared, LLC."

"Everyone, hold still for a minute," Mark said. "I want to get a picture of this moment."

Zeke popped the cork on a bottle of champagne as Paula and Melinda shook hands, and Mark captured the precise moment the women reacted to the sound, forever memorializing their astonished faces.

CHAPTER NINETY-TWO

Paula accepted a glass of champaign from Zeke. She took a sip, then frowned. *Wait, maybe I'm not supposed to have this.* "Mark, am I allowed to drink?"

"I don't know. Are you?"

She elbowed him. "I'm taking that as permission."

With a grin, Mark said, "You may have that one glass. No more."

Nibbling on her third miniature bacon-laced quiche, she licked her lips. "At least I can have as many of these delightful little things as I want."

She contemplated grabbing a fourth appetizer when Mark grabbed her hand and tugged her into the kitchen. His eyes, filled with an obvious mixture of concern and desire, searched her face.

"What?" Paula asked. "Do I have crumbs on my mouth?"

He examined her with narrowed eyes. "Not any that I can see. Wait. Maybe one here." He kissed the corner of her mouth. "And another one there."

She giggled. "You should just kiss me and get it over with."

He chuckled and pulled her close. "I should, shouldn't I? I really don't want to let you go."

Paula rested her forehead against his chest. "I say we find someplace and make out."

"I say that's a great idea, but first I need to get the folks back to their place."

"Darn. But I guess that's a good enough excuse. Your parents are wonderful. And I really like Janie. Did you know that she'd planned to interrogate me?"

Mark kissed the top of her head. "Um, I might have encouraged it. She was going to play bad cop and I was going to be the good cop."

Looking up into his twinkling eyes, Paula said, "You should be ashamed of yourself!"

"I'm so ashamed. Maybe you should send me to bed early tonight. As punishment, you know."

"Hm. I'll take that into consideration. So, let me say goodbye to your family before you go." Paula led Mark back into the living room where his parents were in conversation with Martha and Zeke.

"There's our Paula," Martha said.

Paula kissed Martha's cheek. "I thought you and Zeke were headed to Houston for a juggling convention."

"We are, but the convention isn't until next weekend. We'll leave tomorrow morning. Zeke wants to stop and visit with some friends on the way. Freida and I were just exchanging phone numbers so we can all get together next time Zeke and I come through Happy Vale."

Paula perched on the arm of the couch. "What a great idea. Freida, I'd like to get your number, too. I'm going to have a little get-together for my girlfriends one night soon to christen my motorhome. I'd love for you to come."

"Sounds wonderful. Has Mark told you his good news yet?"

Paula wracked her brain. She squinted up at Mark. "Did you tell me something and I forgot it?"

Taking Paula's hand, Mark said, "I've been saving it. And I intend to save it for a little bit longer."

Freida covered her mouth. "Oops, sorry, dear. I didn't know it was a surprise. I guess it's time for us old folks to head to the house before we spill any more beans. Now, where's Janie?"

CHAPTER NINETY-THREE

Searching the room for Janie, Paula thought, *What kind of secret can Mark be keeping?* She rubbed her hands together. *He'll confess everything later under my carefully crafted questioning techniques.* "There she is, over by the door to the office, visiting with Melinda and Cassie. I'll get her for you."

As she approached the giggling trio, Paula's ears perked up at the mention of her name. "Okay, I'm right here, you know."

"Janie was just telling us about how her intention to play bad cop to Mark's good cop never got off the ground," Melinda said.

Paula's hand went to her bruised chin. "It's a good thing, too. I'm not sure I was up to handling a prank. So, tell me now, what was it you wanted to know."

Grinning, Janie said, "I was mainly going to ask what your intentions were in regard to my brother."

A pair of arms encircled Paula from behind. "Can I tell everyone what I *hope* Paula's intentions are?" Mark asked.

Paula resisted the urge to fan herself and cleared her throat. "Okay. Enough. Your folks are ready to go, so…"

Laughing, Mark kissed Paula. "You're off the hook for now, but we'll be talking about those intentions later. C'mon, Sis."

* * *

A wave of pain began to surge in Paula's head while she and Cassie waved goodbye to Mark and his family. By the time Delbert, Melvin and their wives were on the road, the wave had grown into a full-blown tsunami. "I think I'm going to go rest for a bit. Maybe I'll take one of the pain pills the doctor prescribed and put my feet up."

Cassie eyed her. "That's not a bad idea. Need me to come along?"

"No, I'll be okay. Besides, shouldn't you head back to Dallas?"

Cassie huffed. "I really ought to get on the road. It'll sure be nice when I'm through with culinary school and can make this my home won't it?"

Paula closed her eyes and smiled. "I'm looking forward to it more than you can even imagine."

"Give me a goodbye hug then. I'll go say my goodbyes to Melinda and Martha and be on my way."

"Dear friend, be safe."

"You, too. Lock your camper and don't yell 'come on in' ever again unless you're certain you know who's on the other side of the door."

Paula managed a salute. "I promise."

CHAPTER NINETY-FOUR

A bushy tail flickered across Paula's nose, and she awakened with a start to find a furry kitten bottom just inches from her face. "Um, Star, that's not your best side." She patted the mattress, and the cat abandoned her cozy spot on Paula's chest to curl into a ball beside her. "That's better, isn't it?" The cat responded with a hearty purr.

When her phone buzzed, she reached across Star to answer it.

"Melinda? Hi."

"Paula, before Cassie left, she mentioned you were going to take a nap, and I wouldn't have disturbed you, but there's someone here who wants to talk to you, and I think you'll want to talk to him."

"Can you give me a hint?"

Paula stroked Star's fur as Melinda spoke with someone in the background. "He says, 'there once was a lady from France.' Is that hint enough?"

"Oh! I'll be right there."

When Paula arrived at the office, Melinda said, "Jake's out in the kitchen. I thought y'all might have a little more privacy in there."

Paula stepped into the kitchen to find Jake talking to Ray while nursing a Dr. Pepper.

Jake stood and held out his hands. "You. I'd like to hug you if that's okay."

"Oh, Jake. Absolutely, but I'll be the one doing the hugging." Jake nodded and Paula held him close, letting him cry in much the same way Mark's mother had allowed her to cry, until all the tears had dried up and her shirt was soaked in several spots. *Full circle.*

When his sobs were reduced to hiccups, Jake pulled away with a shy grin, using his t-shirt to mop up any stray tears. "Real men don't cry like that."

"Maybe more of them should," Paula said.

Ray pulled out a chair for Paula. "From what Cassie's told us, it's me who should be hugging you and thanking you. It just blows my mind that Vanessa wanted to murder Arlene and frame me for it. I don't understand why. We had two dates in high school. Two. And I thought we parted amicably both times."

Paula slid onto the chair, tucking one foot under her bottom. "Vanessa had blown your relationship with her, brief as it was, completely out of proportion. She seems like someone who needs a lot of help. Let's hope she gets it."

Jake cleared his throat and clapped Ray on the back. "Um, buddy, do you mind if Paula and I visit by ourselves for a minute?"

"Of course not." Ray hugged Paula and slapped Jake on the back. "Let me know when you're ready to hit the road. My trailer's out front and I'll be ready to leave when you are. Paula, it was great hanging out with you again."

Jake waited until Ray left the room, then said, "I don't know where to start. I'm a little afraid that talking about it will make me bawl again. And, neither of us wants that."

They shared a smile. Paula lifted the hem of her t-shirt. "There are still a few dry spots on my blouse if you have any tears left, so go for it."

He tapped a nervous rhythm on his soft drink can. "Okay. You asked for it. Paula, no one has ever stood up for me like you did. You sent your friend, Delbert, to me. He's a helluva guy, isn't he? But even then, you kept fighting for answers. Have they told you yet why they decided to look at Vanessa as the prime suspect?"

Paula shook her head. *Dang, I should have asked. A good detective would have asked.*

"That note you kept as evidence--the one Arlene supposedly left on the front door? The deputy from Sabine County--oh, what's her name?"

"Gray. Deputy Gray."

"That's it. Anyway, after you pestered Sheriff Hill about the handwriting samples, he faxed a copy of the letter over to Sabine County and asked Deputy Gray to compare it to the business card with Arlene's writing on it. She just happened to recognize the writing on the note as Vanessa's."

"But, how? I don't get the connection."

"So, when they were questioning us about Arlene's kidnapping on Saturday night, Deputy Gray talked to Vanessa and the two of them hit it off when they realized they were both into running triathlons. The deputy is just getting started in competitions and Vanessa wrote out a list detailing her training schedule. They even exchanged contact information so they could hit a few events together."

"Wow."

"I know. And as soon as Deputy Gray saw the handwriting on the note, she had a pretty good idea where it came from."

Paula sat back in her chair and crossed her arms. "Maybe all those hours I've spent bingeing Criminal Minds haven't gone to waste, after all."

"Of course, even then, they were reluctant to let me go because of my past. But then you got Vanessa to confess to everything and Cassie had the presence of mind to get the sheriff on the line to hear it all, and the rest, as they say, is history.

Paula, you were so brave. Cassie, too. If either of you ever need anything. And I mean anything, I'm here for you."

Paula searched his eyes. *The sadness is still there, but it's lighter somehow.* She squeezed his arm. "I can't speak for Cassie, but I'm here for you."

He took a sip of his Dr. Pepper and seemed to search for his next words. "I know Delbert told you everything about my time with Fair to Middlin'. And about my stint in prison. I just want you to know that I didn't kidnap Amelia. But my stupidity and addiction killed her. I've paid for her death every day since, and I'll continue to pay for it for the remainder of my life."

Jake paused to swallow hard. He closed his eyes as if struggling with his next words. "I can never undo what happened that night. All I can do is try to make amends however I can. I'm clean and sober now. Haven't had a drink or any other mind-altering substance since Amelia's death. They could've sentenced me to a hundred years, and it wouldn't have been enough, though. And now you know my secret."

They sat in silence as Paula's heart broke for her friend. *I wish words were enough.* "You asked earlier what *my* secret was, and I told you truthfully that I don't have one. I still struggle with losing Cal. I still have breakdowns."

She choked back a sob bringing fresh tears to Jake's eyes. When Paula found her voice again, she said, "I joined a grief support group, and it helped knowing I wasn't the only one going through the pain. Even so, some days, it does feel like I'm just surviving. And on those days, that has to be good enough. I sometimes ask myself if Cal would want me to just tread water or if he'd want me to swim. I'm pretty sure he'd want me swimming. Huh. Maybe that's my secret, who knows? If Amelia loved you like you loved her, then, you have to keep swimming."

Jake took her hand. "I'm going to try. I really am. And, I have some good news. I think I told you I'd auditioned for a band. Their manager called me today and they want me back in

Nashville as soon as possible, so I'm heading north when I leave Happy Vale."

Paula said, "That's wonderful news.   I hope this opportunity is everything you've dreamed of."

Jake wiped away a tear. "Thank you, sweet lady. Would it be okay if we stayed in touch? I promise I won't bug you too often but reconnecting with you has meant so much. I don't want to lose this friendship, so how about we exchange numbers?"

Paula took his hand. "Of course. I mean, it would be kind of hard for us to be there for each other if we don't have those phone numbers. But first, how does the rest of that limerick go?"

CHAPTER NINETY-FIVE

Two weeks after their class reunion, Paula had grown comfortable in her life as a full-time camper. She bustled about the campsite arranging chairs while Star watched her every move. Paula said, "Now that Vanessa's safely behind bars, I think it's high time for a girls' night out party. Don't you? We have so much to celebrate."

Star sniffed the air and meowed.

"What girl? Oh mercy!" The acrid odor of burnt toast emanated from Paula's motorhome. She rushed inside to turn off the oven. Eyeing the clock above her stove with a frown, she mumbled, "My guests will be here any minute. Why didn't I let Cassie bring the hors d'oeuvres like she begged to?"

In a mad dash, she raised every window and propped open the doors. *This smell isn't going away any time soon. Ugh.*

"Knock knock."

Paula blew out a breath. Ready or not, here we go. "I'm coming."

Delilah Oaks stood on the top step holding a tray, a wry smile on her face. "I brought food..."

"Thank goodness, since I just burned my fancy appetizers."

Fanning her face, Delilah said, "Whew, girl, you sure did. How about we set up out here, at least until the place airs out."

"Good idea. Let me find something we can use as a tablecloth."

Paula grabbed an old quilt top and hurried to spread it across the table nearest her campsite then stood back to admire the age-muted squares of greens and blues that transformed the table into a work of art. *That'll do nicely.* "Thank goodness it's a pleasant evening."

With care, Delilah arranged a selection of canapes on her tray. "We've got a cold front moving in later tonight, so it'll be good to enjoy this weather while we can."

"Absolutely. What can I get you to drink? Wine? Coke? Beer? Tea?"

Delilah covered the appetizers with a napkin, placed her hands on her hips, took a deep breath in and blew it out. "Nothing just yet. Can we talk for a minute? Before everyone else shows up?"

Something in Delilah's tone sent off a minor warning bell in Paula's head. "Um, sure. Let's sit." She dusted off two of the new outdoor chairs she purchased the week after the reunion and pulled them close to the table.

Paula dropped into one of the chairs. "What's up?"

Taking her place in the other chair, Delilah said, "I'm not going to beat around the bush; that's not my style. How long have you known that McKenzie is pregnant?"

Paula's first impulse was to pretend ignorance, but she couldn't let herself off the hook. "Oh. Hm, let me think. I found out in July. Just before Martha's wedding."

Delilah covered her face with her hands and slumped back in her chair. "So, I *was* the last to know. I mean, Jeffries and McKenzie told everyone but me? Her mom and grandmother, and everyone else at the wedding and probably half the population of Happy Vale knew, but they couldn't tell *me*?"

The hurt in Delilah's voice pinged a hole through Paula's soul. "It wasn't like that. Honest. I only found out because Melinda discovered the pregnancy test results in McKenzie's bathroom trash can and was too distraught to deal with what it meant by herself. She needed an outlet. I was the outlet. Martha figured it out before anyone else did because, well, she's probably the sharpest one in the bunch, despite her age. The few others who knew, like Cassie, found out by accident. That girl's got a wicked tendency to eavesdrop..."

"Do you know how it feels to be left out of that kind of news? News that will change the lives of my son and our entire family? To be told almost as an afterthought?"

Paula closed her eyes and sighed.

"Paula? Are you okay?"

"Yes. Honestly, I do know how that feels. When Cal died, and I discovered he'd bought this resort without my knowledge...and that he'd been married before, well, it hurt like hell. I felt betrayed. I imagine you might be feeling that as well."

Delilah brushed an auburn curl off her face. "Oh Paula, I'm so sorry. But why couldn't they tell me? Did they think I couldn't handle the news? Or worse, that I'd be disappointed in Jeffries?"

Paula spread her hands. "Here's where you have an advantage over me and the situation I found myself in. All those questions I still have? You can ask Jeffries and McKenzie; I can't ask my late husband anything. My guess is that they were just trying to get all their ducks in a row before they came to you with their news. The problem with ducks is, they don't mind very well."

At that, Delilah snorted. "No. No, they don't."

The jovial chatter of multiple women approaching Paula's campsite brought their conversation to an end. "How about I get us something to drink now?"

"Sure. Red wine would be good."

"Got it. And, Delilah, you can talk to me anytime, and just in case you hadn't already considered this, you're going to be a wonderful grandmother."

The look on Delilah's face was like sunshine on a cloudy day. "Me. A grandmother. Now, there's something to look forward to."

CHAPTER NINETY-SIX

As a variety of hors d'oeuvres arranged on colorful platters filled up every inch of surface on the table, Paula relaxed. *Thank goodness no one listened to me when I said I'd take care of the food. There seems to be enough here to feed a small army.* She speared an intriguing appetizer from a tray and held it up for inspection. "Cassie, did you make these?"

"I did. Bacon wrapped dates. Tell me what you think."

Paula popped the tidbit into her mouth and sighed with pleasure. "Yum. Bacon makes everything better."

"No argument there," Cassie said.

Paula lingered over a glass of wine and surveyed the women gathered in small groups. She hid a smile as she noticed Mark's mother and sister sitting with dazed expressions as they visited with Shirley in the shade of an oak tree.

Delilah and Melinda stood a little apart from the group sipping wine and chatting in lowered voices as McKenzie looked from one to the other. When Delilah laughed in response to something Melinda said, Paula breathed out a sigh of relief. *They'll all get through this with flying colors. And we'll have a baby around here. A baby!*

Ellie, and her daughter, Lindsay, seemed enthralled by a tale Cassie was spinning. The sound of Lindsay's giggle rang out across the campsite.

If Martha could have been here tonight everything would be perfect. Maybe we'll make this a regular occurrence, and she'll be able to attend when she's here on a visit.

Paula snatched a bottle of wine from the table and approached Freida. "Refills, anyone? I'm glad you ladies are getting to know Shirley. Someday soon, we'll pay her nursery a visit, if you'd like."

"Definitely," Freida said. "Hidden Pines has a beautiful garden that residents are invited to help tend, and I have every intention of getting to know what grows best in this part of the country."

"Mom and Dad have always been into gardening. The garden at Pines was one of the reasons they decided to move here. That and the proximity to Mark," Janie said.

Shirley extended her glass for more wine. "You're welcome to visit any time."

Paula peered at Freida over her own glass. "I don't suppose you want to share Mark's news with me?"

Freida hesitated, and Janie wagged a finger at her. "Mom..."

"Oh, I can't. But he'd better tell you soon. I'm awful at keeping secrets."

"Can't blame me for trying, can you?" Paula asked. "I'd better go circulate." She squeezed Cassie's shoulder on the way by and winked at Ellie and Lindsay. "Don't believe everything Cassie tells you."

She sidled up beside Delilah. "How about a refill."

"Thank you, dear. You're just in time for some big news."

Paula's eyebrows shot up. "Oh?"

McKenzie nodded and Paula squealed.

"Want to let everyone know?" Paula asked.

McKenzie nodded again.

Paula said, "Hey... Everyone...Excuse me!... Just a second. I need more volume." She hurried to Cassie and whispered in her ear.

Cassie put her fingers to her lips and whistled. "Like that?"

"Just like that," Paula said, as everyone looked their way.

"Okay everyone, McKenzie has some news to share, so your attention for just a minute, please."

All eyes focused on McKenzie. She raised her left hand high, displaying the diamond that glittered there. "Jeffries and I are engaged!"

CHAPTER NINETY-SEVEN

Paula brought out a glass of iced tea for McKenzie and two new bottles of wine for the other guests. Once everyone had a drink in hand, Paula raised her glass. "Here's to the bride-to-be!"

"Have you set a date?" Ellie asked.

McKenzie ran a hand over her stomach. "Soon. It won't be anything fancy. Just family and close friends."

A hand on Paula's shoulder startled her. *Wait, I just saw Shirley over there, and now...Yep, she's at least part fairy.* As her heart rate returned to normal, Paula said, "I'm so glad you could make it tonight."

With a wink, Shirley waved a hand in the air. "I wouldn't have missed it for the world. And now, with this wonderful news, it's become an especially significant evening. I can't wait to get home and let the bees know. They'll be thrilled."

"I'm sure they will," Paula said, scanning the area for honeybees in case any had tagged along. She nodded at two unoccupied chairs. "Mind if we sit a while?"

Settling into a chair, Shirley swirled the wine in her glass. "Thank you for inviting me this evening. I confess that I don't socialize much. My family and the nursery take up most of my time."

Paula took a sip of wine and considered her next words while peering at Shirley over the rim of her glass. "I hope we can do this again. And you're always welcome here."

Shirley leaned back, soaking in the rays of the sun as it neared the horizon. "You've picked a lovely space to park your home."

"Thank you. I love how close I am to the lake. It's a novel experience after growing up in the dry, dusty plains around Dempsey."

Reaching into one of the pockets of her sweater, Shirley extracted a small cloth wrapped bundle and offered it to Paula. "I've brought some sage for you. Burn it inside and outside the camper to rid the immediate area of any negative vibes that Vanessa might have left lingering after her visit."

"Oh? I should burn sage, eh? I hope that works better than burning toast."

Shirley's musical laughter lilted on the evening air. "I should hope so, as well. And it will smell so much better."

Tapping a fingernail on her wine glass, Paula asked, "So, um, now that Vanessa is in jail awaiting sentencing for her attempts on Arlene's life, can you tell me what you read in her cards that afternoon?"

Shirley sat in silence with her eyes closed. Paula worried she had offended her. When Shirley spoke, it was almost a whisper. "I wish I had told you then, but how was I to know that the cards referred to actions Vanessa herself might have taken or was considering taking? I thought at the time that perhaps she was in danger of some act of retribution being enacted on her or on someone close to her. I'm generally much better at reading people, but she certainly pulled the wool over my eyes."

Paula waved that idea away. "Oh, please, don't be hard on yourself. She fooled all of us, even Arlene who'd known her since childhood. Without going into details about the whole reading, though, was there a particular card that concerned you?"

Shirley removed her phone from a different pocket and tapped on the photos file. She scrolled through the pictures and stopped, nodding. "Yes. I remember clearly. This card, the Five of Swords, came up in her reading. Victory through dishonesty is basically what it symbolizes. Coupled with the other cards that were laid on the table that day, the message was clear. Just not clear enough. If she had done permanent harm to you, I'd have felt responsible."

Paula shook her head. "But no. You warned me to be vigilant. And I was, or I tried to be. But I was also a little reckless."

"You're a trusting soul. That's a wonderful thing, luv, but I do hope from now on you'll lock your camper."

"No worries. I've had enough lectures on that topic to last me for the rest of my life. Oh, and on not just inviting someone in without knowing who's at the door."

Shirley said, "Sound advice. I do believe Cassie is attempting to get your attention."

Paula looked across the campsite to where Cassie was waving. "Yes?"

"Is your television working? There's something we need to watch tonight."

"Sure." She extended a hand to Shirley. "Let's go see what's so important. Ladies, shall we adjourn to my parlor?"

CHAPTER NINETY-EIGHT

The women crowded inside Paula's motorhome, taking seats wherever possible. The odor of burnt toast had somewhat faded into a ghost of culinary disasters past. *Maybe Shirley's sage will aid in my future cooking endeavors, too. It couldn't hurt.* As everyone found a place to sit, Paula turned on the television. "Cassie, what station?"

Cassie took over, tuning the TV to a local channel as a news anchor's report segued into an introduction of the station's newest sports commentator.

"...Speaking of new additions, KNGD is pleased to welcome Seth Boone to the nightly news lineup covering local, national, and international sporting events. Seth comes to us with a depth of knowledge from his days on the college and professional gridirons, and we feel honored to have him join us."

Paula and Cassie exchanged amused smirks as Seth appeared behind the news desk, looking dapper in a dark suit and red tie. "Thank you, Curt. It's good to be here."

"Now, why are we watching sports?" Freida asked.

Melinda chuckled, "Because that's Cassie's old high school boyfriend."

Freida eyed Melinda. "Oh. But isn't she...? I mean, aren't you two...?"

"Yes, she is and, yes, we are." Melinda laid a hand on Freida's arm. "And now she gets to be herself and we get to be together."

At the end of Seth's sportscast, he tapped his index finger to his forehead. "This is Seth Boone, tapping out."

The look on the anchorman's face spoke volumes as he took over from Seth with widened eyes. "Alrighty then. Next up, are you prepared for the cold front that's blowing in later tonight? Join meteorologist Crystal Fountain for her report on how to prepare for the frigid temps after these messages from our sponsors..."

Paula giggled. "Oh, Cassie, please contact Seth and tell him that's a ridiculous sign off."

Cassie held up a finger. "Oh, about that. Everyone, Seth sent me a text telling me there was a message for me in this broadcast." She scrolled through her phone. Here it is. 'Dear Cassie, When you see me tap my forehead tonight, that's all for you. I'm tapping out and moving on. I'm just so glad to know that it wasn't me all these years. It was you all along.'"

Janie guffawed. "He sounds like the kind of man I always end up with. All ego and no substance. At least he's pretty to look at."

"He certainly is," Freida said. "And, Janie, sounds like he's single."

Janie rolled her eyes. "Oh, Mom. That's really not the kind of man you want for me, now, is it?"

"You aren't getting any younger, dear..."

Cassie switched off the television. "Since that's out of the way, Paula, several of us have brought housewarming gifts for you. Want to open in here or outside?"

"Y'all weren't supposed to get me anything. I specifically said no gifts."

"Yeah, you specifically said no food, too, and aren't you glad we ignored that?" Melinda asked.

"Point taken. Let's go outside so we don't have to sit in one another's laps. I'm going to have another glass of wine. Anyone else?"

CHAPTER NINETY-NINE

Once all the guests except for Cassie and Janie returned to their homes, Paula fired up her brand-new propane fire pit. She settled back in her chair and took in the magnificence of the stars twinkling in the early autumn sky. With the fire warming her feet, Paula said, "This is a perfect gift, y'all. Especially with this cold front moving in tonight."

Cassie stretched her hands toward the fire. "On behalf of Melinda, McKenzie, and myself, you're welcome. You got several really cool things, didn't you?"

"I did. Janie, I am so grateful for the doorbell security system you and your parents gave me. I'll get Mark to hook it up next time he's here."

Janie finished her glass of wine. "It was his idea, you know. After all you went through, he thought that would be a better gift than something decorative; although, that sign Shirley made you is so cute."

From beside her chair, Paula hefted the colorful sign that read WELCOME TO PAULA'S PLACE, spelled out in a motif of tiny bees and flowers. Holding it up for the others to admire, she said, "Knowing Shirley, she talked the bees into posing for this."

Chuckling, Cassie stood and tossed her Dr. Pepper can into the new recycling container that Delilah had gifted Paula. "Hey, Janie, we probably need to get on the road if you're going to make that flight in the morning."

Paula frowned. "Oh, Janie, I forgot you were riding back to Dallas with Cassie tonight."

With a nod, Janie said, "Yes, I was trying to forget it, too. I really appreciate the ride, though. Since Cassie is going that way anyway, it made perfect sense and saved Mark a trip into the city."

Janie stood and stretched, her gaze wandering around the campground. "I just hate that I have to leave, though. I'm not ready to go back to the real world. Paula, I can understand why you decided to move here. I'm not close to retirement yet, but this area will be on my radar when I do. It's a special place."

Paula hugged her. "We sure think it is. I'm so glad we had this time to get to know each other. And you are always welcome here. Now that your folks are just down the road, I hope you'll be a frequent visitor."

"I will. Promise. And if my baby brother doesn't behave, just let me know. I'll keep him in line."

Paula snorted and hugged her a second time. "Yes. I've seen you interact with Mark. You're a real tough cookie."

"If you tell him this, I'll say you made it all up, but he really is a catch. Glad you're the one who caught him."

"Aw. Thank you."

"I need a goodbye hug, too, Goldilocks. Remember, you can come hang out with me in Dallas any time you want," Cassie said.

"You know how I detest driving in the city, but maybe I will. That is, if I can find someone to come with me. Like, maybe Melinda..."

"There's an idea. I like it."

"Drive carefully. You know the deer are as thick as cold oatmeal on nights like this." Paula hugged Cassie and sent her and Janie on their way, waving until they were out of sight.

CHAPTER ONE HUNDRED

After sending Cassie and Janie on their way, Paula sat for a moment, reveling in the silence of the night. She looked to the sky to find the star she thought of as Cal's star. Zeke always told her he was certain the star she had chosen was Venus, but she didn't care. "Thanks for watching over me, Cal."

A gust of wind blew through the camp, scattering the few items that remained from the party, and enticing the flames into a merry dance. She glanced at the sky again. "I could have done without that, though." Paula tidied up outside, securing all the chairs, and turning off the fire pit. *It really is a perfect gift*.

Star sat in prim patience on the bench inside the motorhome, an inquisitive look on her little face as Paula opened the door.

Running a hand over the kitten's silky fur, she said, "It's just the two of us tonight, girl. Mark starts back to work in Nacogdoches tomorrow. I know, I miss him, too. How about we clean up in here, then make a cup of hot chocolate, and read for a while?"

Star ducked into the bedroom and Paula called after her, "Sure, leave me to do all the work."

By the time Paula had everything straightened up and was settled in bed with an Ed McBain *87ᵗʰ Precinct* novel and a cup of Nestle's hot chocolate with marshmallows on the table beside her, the wind outside began to blow in earnest, whistling through the trees and rattling the motorhome. Star hunkered down beside her on the bed and Paula rested her hand on the cat's head. "It's okay, kitty. At least I'm pretty sure it's okay."

Her phone buzzed. "Hey, Melinda."

"Hey yourself. A couple of things. First, Deputy Eugene returned a piece of evidence he said you were fond of. I'd bring it out to you, but that wind is vicious."

Pressing a hand to her chest, Paula said, "Oh, thank you so much. If you could stick it under the computer, I'll pick it up in the morning."

"No problem. It's in an envelope with your name on it. Of course, you and Star could come stay in the cabin tonight to ride out the storm, and you could claim your envelope now. There's plenty of space, you know. You can have your choice of Mama's or McKenzie's room."

"Aw, thank you, but we'll be fine. I can't wussie out now."

Melinda chuckled. "Okay. Oh, better go. We just had a walk-in, but if you change your mind, you've got a key to the office."

"I sure do. 'Night."

Paula settled in to discover what heinous crimes detectives Steve Carella and Meyer Meyer were attempting to solve when she thought she heard a knock at the door. "Probably just the wind, but we'd better check." Star insisted on being held and Paula carried her to look out the window. Inky blackness obscured her vision. "Is someone there?"

"For now, but there's a good chance the next gust is going to blow me into another county."

Paula threw open the door. "Mark, get in here."

He struggled to close the door behind him and pulled her close. "You're sure bossy tonight."

"It's the real me coming out. What are you doing here? I thought you were in Nacogdoches until next Saturday."

He shivered and nodded at the Nestle's box on her counter. "It's cold out there, and I didn't think to wear a jacket. Got any more of that?"

She fetched a blanket from the bedroom and draped it around his shoulders. "Sit, and warm up. I'll make you some hot chocolate. Marshmallows?"

Mark looked indignant as he shivered.   "Of course. What's hot chocolate without marshmallows?"

A fresh gust of wind blew, and they exchanged wide eyed looks as the camper swayed in response.   "It's certainly not like weathering a storm in my brick home back in Dempsey," Paula said.

Mark accepted the cup and patted the bench beside him. "But here you have adventure. And me."

Paula snuggled close. "Mm. I like having you."

"Careful with that kind of talk."

Paula shivered in anticipation as Star jumped onto the bench, curling up between them where she began kneading the blanket in a slow, steady rhythm.

Rubbing a hand in lazy circles on Paula's back, Mark said, "I think you're going to like the secret my mom almost divulged the other afternoon."

Paula crossed her fingers beneath the covers. "Oh? Was there a secret? I'd forgotten."

His lopsided grin made her insides go all gooey. "Sure, you had. Mom said you've tried to work it into more than one conversation."

"Okay. Maybe I've thought about it once. Or twice. So, give it up."

He pulled her onto his lap, sending Star scrambling for safety. "I'm joining the staff of Hemphill General. They've got a satellite clinic here and one in Center, and I'll be rotating between the three locations. Paula, I'll be in Happy Vale every night. With you, I hope."

CHAPTER ONE HUNDRED-ONE

Paula feared her heart might beat loudly enough to drown out the battering winds of the storm. *Are we ready for this?* She fought back a gulp. "You will?"

Mark nuzzled her cheek. "Of course, there are details pending. I'll still be working some in Nacogdoches until we can get everything lined out. And, I haven't really thought about getting a house or anything."

Okay, I can deal with that. "You'll stay here until you do, of course. Or, for as long as you want."

"I knew you'd offer, and I really am tempted to do just that, but we're still getting to know each other."

"I don't know about you, but I've sure enjoyed our meet and greet sessions so far," Paula said. *There's that brazen hussy again. My newest friend.*

His laughter vibrated through her chest. "Oh, me too. But picture this—I'm going to rent Room One at the resort on a long-term basis. I've already arranged that with Melinda. No more freeloading for me."

Paula adopted a mock scowl. "A freeloader? No way. Melinda kept that room open for you because you treated her cancer even when she didn't have insurance. You could stay there for a million years, and she still wouldn't think it was enough to repay all you did for her. None of us would."

He pulled her closer. "I want to be a paying customer. And we'll each have our separate spaces until we're ready for more. Whatever *more* might entail. You can—"

At the word *more* Paula's throat constricted. "Wait. There's something I need to tell you. And then if you still want to, we can talk about being ready for more of, well, whatever this becomes."

He cocked his head. "I'm all ears. My childhood nickname was Dumbo, remember?"

She slapped a hand against his chest. "I'm being serious here."

Mark entwined his fingers with hers. "Okay, hon. What's got you so worried?"

Paula sat up straight and searched his eyes. *How do I broach this subject? Just say it. Pull the bandage off in one swift stroke.* The words tumbled out. "I can't have children. Cal and I tried. After three miscarriages in four years, I just didn't have the heart to continue down that path. I know I should have told you earlier, but it didn't seem right to put it in a text, and I didn't want to presume anything, and--"

"And, as I was saying, you can stay at my place some. I can stay here some. And we can choose to be alone sometimes. We're grownups."

"Mark, damn it, this is a big deal. Don't just skim over it like it's not important."

He pulled her close and nuzzled her cheek. "I'm sorry. It's just that I'm perfectly happy to be with you. If we decide to marry someday, and discover we really want to be parents, we'll adopt. My oldest nephew is adopted. Or maybe it's the second oldest one? I forget."

The motorhome trembled in the storm as she absorbed his words. *He's so matter of fact. Cal wouldn't even discuss adoption.* "You're serious?"

"About the nephews? Yeah. I can never remember if Tim's the adopted one or if it's Grant..."

Relaxing in his arms again, Paula said, "Silly man. I meant are you serious about adoption being an option?"

He tightened his hold on her. "I'd cross my heart, but you're covering it up at the moment."

Tears pooled in her eyes as she clung to him. "Thank you."

"There's nothing to thank me for. Now, what do you think about my suggested living arrangement?"

She rested her head on his shoulder. "I like it. It'll be wonderful having you close every night, but even so, I've found that I enjoy having my own space."

"Even when we might end up in the merry old land of Oz if the next blast of wind is anything like the last one?"

"Yep."

Mark cupped her chin, lifting it so they were eye to eye. "Nonetheless, I need to see those captivating eyes when you answer my next question. You're okay with all of this? I don't want you to feel crowded or rushed. I love you too much to put you in a corner."

Paula blinked at least a dozen times and touched her lips to his. "Yes, I'm more than okay with it. And, by the way, your use of the word nonetheless is a real turn on. One more time and I'm all yours."

"Nonetheless, in that case, may I sleep here tonight?"

She snuggled closer. "Mm. Moreover, you can do more than sleep."

Lifting Paula in his arms, Mark carried her to the bedroom. "Moreover? Now, you're talking."

THE END

ACKNOWLEDGEMENTS

I loved writing this book. It's probably got more of "me" in it than any of my previous novels. And in some ways that made it more difficult. Pre-editing, I'd glossed over parts that were critical to imparting the emotions of the scene. Thanks to my wonderful editor (and cover designer), Rachel Carrera, who reminded me that even in light-hearted books it's important to allow characters to deal with their fears and their pain when the story calls for it.

Many thanks to my terrific and thorough beta readers, Flo Diehl, Cynthia Hickerson, and Sandi von Pier who found so many little glitches in early drafts of the book--things that my old eyes never even noticed. Thank you all!

Everything I know about setting up a camper I learned from my brother, Kelly Hall, and my friend, Flo Diehl. If I got any of it wrong, don't blame them.

When I couldn't come up with a name for the Dempsey High School mascot, I did what any modern author does—turned to Facebook for suggestions. My friend, artist and minister, Sharyn Richey, came up with Diamondbacks and I fell in love with it instantly. The Dempsey Diamondbacks. Perfect.

376 REUNION AT THE HAPPY VALLEY MOTOR INN AND RESORT

Thanks to everyone who supports me in my writing endeavors:

David Noyes--my long-suffering husband and wise-cracking raconteur

My children, Jason and Ashley, and grandchildren, Dominique, Garrett, McKayla, Jackson, and Harper, because they love me and don't try to shut me up when I'm talking.

My motorcycle "gang": Janice, Nancy, Flo, Nicky, Tammy, Ann, and Mary. We might not ride much anymore, but we're still standing.

My best friends since junior high: Lou Ann, Dana, Cindy, BraVada, and Kathy

Love you all.

And last, but not least, you, dear readers, who have been so good to me. I never dreamed there would be a sequel to *Mayhem at the Happy Valley Motor Inn and Resort*, and now there are two (with a third one rolling around in my head)! This never would have happened without your encouragement and support. I hope you enjoy *Reunion at the Happy Valley Motor Inn and Resort* as much as I enjoyed writing it.

ABOUT THE AUTHOR

Leslie Noyes grew up in the panhandle of Texas many, many years ago. She married her high school sweetheart, and they now reside near Tallahassee, Florida, with their cat, Gracie. They have two terrific children and five way above average grandchildren. When she's not writing, Leslie is either reading or trying to figure out the meaning of life. She's pretty sure it has something to do with wine, but more trials are necessary before she can reach a conclusion.

You can visit her blog, Praying for Eyebrowz at www.nananoyz5forme.com and follow her on Facebook at **Leslie Hall, Author** and on Twitter **@NoyesNananoyz**.

Made in the USA
Middletown, DE
24 January 2023

23055015R00215